AUTO NO MO US

Origins:
Mara's Memories

Christopher L. Truxaw

AUTO NO MO US

Part Three

Origins:

Mara's Memories

August 2019—April 2039

Christopher L. Truxaw

Self-published by the Author.
Christopher L. Truxaw
Santa Ana, California
www.autonomousbooks.com

ISBN: 979-8-9922584-3-1 (Paperback)

PDF generated:
Saturday, May 9, 2026 (minor edits)

Table of Contents

Mara's Memories

As found in the family safe in late May of 2056.

MY RECOLLECTIONS

April 05, 2037, WHY?

I don't expect to lose my memories, but Perry didn't expect to either, and recently facing death myself makes me realize that life and memories can be fragile. I don't want to count on always having my vivid photographic memories or even being around to recall them. Perry would have liked it if I made an autobiographical AM Game story world. Maybe I should do that, wouldn't be too hard, and it's supposed to be secure, but is it really? Better to keep it simple and old-fashioned. No electronic copy. Paper is more secure from hacking and electronic obsolescence, and I can keep the pages in the safe.

It would be safest if I used a pen to avoid putting anything in a computer, but that is not going to work. No one would be able to read my handwriting, even me. That would be a sure way to lose my memories. I'll just print pages as I go and immediately delete and expunge the files.

What should I write about? I can describe things from images in my memory. I can cut and paste bits from my phones or other devices to save time. We'll see. I guess no videos. Just things that I can put on paper.

Maybe these notes are just for me in case my memory slips, or maybe I'll share them with Balaji someday, or put them somewhere he can find them when I'm gone. Depends on how much I end up saying. Some of my memories I probably don't want him to know about.

Where to start? My childhood? Stories about my parents? The day that Perry and I met? That might be good. I'll come back later today or tomorrow to get started.

Tuesday, August 13, 2019, Midmorning, Hiking

I didn't have a watch with me then, so I'm not sure of the time. I was taking a walk to clear my mind and make some decisions. Like other young people in their early twenties, I was facing adulthood with choices about who I wanted to be. Okay, my situation was a bit different from most people my age. My parents had handed me a career path, if I wanted it, but I wasn't sure I wanted it. Recent events had revealed secrets that challenged my beliefs about my parents and myself and forced me to make some big decisions.

My mom seemed to always have a plan for everything. I frequently disappointed her by not accepting her plans or making and sticking with my own. Repeatedly disappointing her stressed me out, but I kept doing it anyway. Each time, my dad would convince her to let me try a new plan, saying eventually I would find my path. I think he may have felt a kinship with me in that he disappointed her sometimes too.

Many different paths were interesting, and I wished I could follow more than one. I had changed majors in college a few times and tried out a few different kinds of internships that my parents had arranged. I always did well. Competence was not the problem. I was the smartest person I knew. I didn't have a lot of friends since I couldn't tolerate dumb people, and most people were pretty dumb by comparison. My parents were both pretty sharp, but not as smart as me. It was just that I hadn't found my calling.

Now events were forcing me towards a role that I knew I could do but I didn't want. I had a hard choice to make: Walk the path my parents had shoved in my face or just walk away. My dad wouldn't intervene this time and give me other options. I would have to decide for myself.

On this hike it may have looked like I was walking away, but I had a plan that included returning. During this walk, at least, I wanted to be like my mom and stay on a plan. I had carefully chosen a remote route through the high mountain country. I knew it was risky, but I had to do this alone.

If I didn't survive, people might not ever find me and that would be an easy way of deciding not to take the path my parents had forced on me. But after weeks on the trail, it looked like I was probably going to survive and would have to say yes or no to the new role when I got back to civilization in a couple weeks. I still didn't know which I would choose, or if I might still just have an accident to get away from the decision. I was trying to reach calmness and find my center on this trek, but I was still anxious most of the time.

Planning minimized surprises and preparation allowed for dealing with those that arose. So far, I had survived and stayed on a schedule. Even with planning and preparation, some things, like animals, other people, and the weather, were not completely predictable. I had been lucky so far in my close encounters with wildlife and had almost completely avoided contact with other people. As for the weather, I had prepared well enough. After the last few uncomfortable days with rain, I was enjoying the warm sun this morning. I started out early today, walking fast and building up a sweat. I decided to stop and cool off by splashing in a cold stream.

I was holding my breath, crouched and bent over in the water, looking down at sunlight making patterns on the stones and my sandaled feet. I wondered what would happen if I just stayed underwater. The CO_2 building up in my lungs and my limited tolerance for cold both insisted it was time to stand up. I gave in and almost leaped up into the air and sunshine, took a deep breath, and screamed. The waist deep icy water splashed around me.

I shook my head and arms and shivered all over. I dunked under water once more and rubbed more of the trail dust off my face and arms and out of my short dark hair both on top and down below before rising again and stepping towards the stream bank. I briskly rubbed my brown arms and squeezed the icy water off the front of my tee-shirt and down my belly. "I have abs," I smiled to myself as I wiped down my firm belly. "That's new." With the edge of my hand, I squeegeed water off my clinging panties and brushed it off my legs, noticing that the scrapes on my knees were now almost completely healed. I stepped carefully on the rocky and slippery stream bottom until I reached the shallows near the shore where the water barely covered my sandaled feet.

"Hey, you are looking strong Mara… Strong." I complimented myself out loud and thought, "Maybe the name fits." After admiring the firm muscles and lack of flab on my arms and legs, I reached over to the shore and grabbed a small towel hanging on a large root near the water's edge. I rubbed the towel first on top of my head and worked down. I had cut my hair short just before the hike. It was still short and easy to take care of. After wiping dry each area, I inspected the towel to see how much dirt it picked up from my skin. When it looked dirty, I dunked it in the stream to rinse, and lifting it up out of the water, it was very heavy, absorbing and holding a lot of water. Stretching it one way and then the other, it released a heavy stream of water and then snapping it twice it was cleaner and totally dry and ready to wipe down another part of me. Nice.

I stepped one foot out of the shallow rocky water and tested my new flexibility by placing my waterproof-sandaled foot shoulder-high on the big root to finish wiping off that leg. It would only take a couple minutes here in the sun to finish drying before getting dressed and starting again on the hike. Still on plan. I looked at my watch. Actually, slightly ahead of schedule.

I paused and looked at my outer layers of clothes draped over my small pack. The clothes were dusty and dirty, but not too bad for the time I had been on the trail. I adjusted and tightened them as I got thinner. Even with the adjustments they now fit loosely. Before the hike I had calculated I might lose up to 30 pounds on the whole trek, and I was pretty sure I had lost more than that already. But I was feeling stronger than ever. How could I take advantage of my new fitness? Would it matter for my choice about the job? Probably not.

I was pleased with how well the clothing layers had worked. They were extremely lightweight but gave great protection from sun and bugs and heat during the day and also kept me warm and dry enough during rains or colder nights. Some nights when it didn't rain, I didn't bother with my micro-tent but stretched out on a patch of ground and watched the stars until I fell asleep. I was glad I had such good gear. With money and connections many things are possible.

I planned to reach the next supply drop later today at a trailhead a few miles away. There would be some new clothes and other supplies. After the invigorating rinse in the stream, I could more than make up for the time of the stop. It would be nice to actually get fresh clothes again. Thinking about clean clothes led me to imagine a hot shower. How long has that been? Seven weeks? Even after rinsing off now, I must still smell like shit, but I couldn't really tell. It didn't really matter. I was keeping distance from others on the trail. Hot showers and all the other niceties of civilization would be available in two more weeks. That was something to look forward to if I made it back. But going back would mean facing the choice. Take a job I don't want or live with final failure to satisfy my mom.

I brought to mind the images of trail maps I had memorized. This remote trail connected to a bigger trail near the trailhead and according to the map there was a campground three miles down a dirt road from there. The map seemed to show that the campground had showers. If I moved fast enough, I could go there, take a shower, and get back on the trail. I did mental calculations allowing for six extra relatively flat miles of hiking to and from the campground, and time for a shower and concluded, "I could make it. I'll just need to skip some of my meditation time today."

But then I thought about complications. I would almost definitely run into people at the campground and one of the main points of my solo hike was to avoid other people. I wondered if I could sneak into the campground for the shower without running into others.

My ten-week solitary trek of meditation and personal discovery was supposed to help me find clarity about who I wanted to be and choose a path for the next steps in my life. In my planning I had read various writings about different traditions for coming of age, self-discovery, and vision quests. I combined elements from various things I read and concluded that a 70-day solo hike with daily periods of meditation should help me find my center without using the hallucinogens some recommended. Fifty-six days in, I didn't feel like I had any great insights so far. Maybe I should have gone for the mushrooms? But at least I had lost weight.

Maybe it would be okay to go off plan this once and find that shower.

No. I needed to stay on plan. There were too many risks if I went off plan.

I realized there was also the issue of money. If the shower was hot, it would probably not be free. If it was cold what would be the point. I wasn't carrying any money, phone, or credit cards. But my gear was worth something. After I picked up my new supplies, I could try to trade some of the old gear for a shower.

No. That would definitely mean interacting with people.

I brought to mind the image of packing my five daypacks and one duffle bag before this trip. One daypack for every two weeks. Today's daypack had warmer clothes, enclosed boots, replacements for other gear and a new supply of supplements and food. The duffle bag at the end of the trail held necessities for returning to civilization. Phones, money, ID, keys, regular clothes, and cosmetics.

I took the first bag with me when I started the hike and arranged with a supply drop service to have the others placed in locked bear bins at trailheads along the hike. At each stop I unlocked the combination lock, took out the new pack, went out of sight to change clothes, put the old pack in, relocked it, and continued on my hike.

The service was supposed to pick up the old gear a couple days later and I could leave a note asking them to include extra items at the next drop-off, but I hadn't done so. They would hold the old stuff for me until I picked it up or told them where to ship it after the hike. I could let them dispose of it for me, but I really should get back some of the proprietary items I had borrowed from the company.

In retrospect I probably could have kept using the same clothes and gear longer instead of changing them out at every supply drop and I probably should have included a little more food. My clothes were holding up well, even if they might be getting a little ripe and loose. The new clothes today might still be loose but would fit me better and provide more protection from the cold when I camp at higher elevations during the last part of my hike.

The idea of fresh clothes strengthened the argument for getting a shower today. Clean clothes would feel a lot better if I wasn't so dirty. Each time I put on new clothes over dirty skin it felt like they were immediately soiled. It would be so nice to be clean in clean clothes.

No. I didn't want to risk going off plan and spoiling the whole point of the trip. I thought, "Mom, are you watching me? I'm following a plan to pick a plan. Meta plan. Aren't you proud? You didn't think I could ever stick to a plan."

I could almost hear her say, "We'll see."

After considering a variety of different aboriginal coming-of-age traditions, my personal philosophy on this trip was minimalism. I wanted to be light and efficient while immersing myself in the natural world. I figured I had just done an example of efficiency by rinsing myself and my underwear at the same time. Plus I was literally immersing myself in nature. I could have rinsed and wrung my t-shirt and undershorts separately, and that might have gotten them cleaner, but I'd be getting new ones later today and I preferred not going completely naked near a trail, even one that was seldom traveled.

I wanted to be careful. Stay away from other people. This whole trek was supposed to face dangers and natural challenges, but no sense in making it more dangerous than it has to be by adding extra human contacts. That risk was low because I chose trails that were lightly traveled, but still, it was possible some people could come this way, especially today as I got closer to a trailhead.

On cue with that thought, a light-skinned tall young man in his twenties with a few days' growth of beard, a wide-brimmed hat, partly tinted glasses, and an extremely bulky backpack appeared on the trail twenty yards above the stream. Extremely bulky was an understatement. The pack was so big. It was almost like he was carrying a washing machine on his back. I stayed motionless, my right leg still raised with my sandaled foot high on the root, holding my tiny towel stretched between two hands against my thigh. I hoped I wasn't making a show with my wet panties clinging to my crotch. But he didn't seem to look in my direction. As I stayed motionless, I smiled when I thought to myself that his vision might be like a tyrannosaur and based on movement like in that movie I used to watch with my dad. As he lumbered along with that massive weight behind him, his hands were working with some kind of laptop or computer tablet attached close in front of him, giving his hands and forearms a bit of a short-armed tyrannosaur pose.

Strapped to the top, back, and sides of his pack were what looked like solar panels, which emphasized the big-box appearance of the pack, and some kind of antennas that looked oddly familiar were extending out of the top. He continued stepping slowly and carefully uphill on the trail, concentrating on the screen in front of him without looking down at me. He went in and out of view as the trail passed behind trees and large rocks. I followed him with my eyes, while staying otherwise still. He seemed to be hiking alone. I was relieved when he passed and still didn't seem to look my way, but just before he went out of sight behind the last large rock where the path turned away from the stream, he smiled and called out without taking his eyes off the tablet in front of him, "Didn't see anything. Have a nice day!"

I stared towards the spot he went out of view for almost a minute, expecting, maybe hoping, for him to reappear. I had been trying to avoid others on my trek, but there was something about him that caught my interest. For one thing, I was curious what he was doing backpacking with all that equipment. His pack must weigh over 100 pounds. I replayed in my head the image of him walking by. He walked slowly, but he seemed strong enough to handle the weight of that massive pack. He seemed pretty fit. His hands were positioned in that tiny-arm tyrannosaur pose, but even so, with rolled up sleeves on his shirt his arms looked like they had some decent muscles. He wore the kind of hiking pants that have zip-off leggings so they can turn into shorts, but his were oddly extremely baggy. I had only seen his profile as he walked along staring down at his tablet through those big glasses, but something about his looks and especially his smile at the end made me smile. I replayed the image in my mind and froze it again concentrating on that profile of a smile.

Then again, I had been purposefully trying to avoid others. "Good thing he didn't stop. This is a solitary journey of self-discovery," I reminded myself. And "You have to be careful about men on the trail. Most are people are good, but some are not. Be safe." My accommodations towards security included a small can of military grade pepper spray strong enough to disable a bear, a light-weight compact hunting knife, and a small fob hanging on the side of my pack that could give a high-decibel shrill alarm and activate a satellite-based emergency beacon, but primarily I relied on staying away from people. I had deliberately chosen a circuitous route that avoided most well-traveled trails. If I got in trouble and turned on the emergency beacon it might be hours before assistance arrived, assuming it worked at all. There probably wouldn't be anyone else close enough to hear the shrill alarm if I used it.

In my photographic memory I looked again at that smile.

I remembered what I was doing, lowered my sandaled foot to the ground, and wiped off the last few drops of water with the little towel. My t-shirt and shorts were now dry enough. I dipped the towel in the stream to rinse it, then twisted and stretched and snapped it twice and it was dry now as well. These advanced fabrics continued to perform as promised. This dual-mode hydrophilic-hydrophobic towel from the company's advanced materials lab was especially nice. I folded it and put it into a small pocket for it in my pack, next to the reusable sanitary pads that relied on similar fabric. I hadn't needed to test them yet. My period seemed to be on hold while I was hiking so much.

As I put on my pants, shirt, and hat, and picked up my small pack I thought about my plans for today and for my life. If I didn't make any other stops, I would get to the supply point in a couple of hours, or 75 minutes if I really hustled, and then to a good camp spot a couple of hours beyond that. I would have plenty of time for meditation and gathering food tonight. I didn't have a watch, but I was good at estimating time.

Then again, I could hike down to the camp with showers and still get to my next planned stop but give up most of my meditation time. I could even end this whole hike if I wanted to and head back to civilization today. Just press one button on the fob. It would be nice to end this.

I didn't have a phone or money or ID with me, so getting back to civilization before finishing the whole planned trip would mean using the emergency satellite fob to call for rescue team. I really didn't want to do that. It would be humiliating. Then everyone would know where I had been these weeks and that I had failed at one more thing. Not that anyone would really care.

But I had made it this far and could finish. I had a plan, and I needed to follow the plan. If I wanted to end it, there would still be some options along the trail ahead where no one would find me.

Every day on this hike I had known where I would be, according to plan, and I knew where I would be today and the next two weeks. I also knew what I would be doing the next few years in my life and career if I stayed on the latest plan my parents had dumped on me.

But some things had changed, and I needed to discover who I really was and be true to that self rather than to a plan my parents, Sandra and Carlos, had set for me. That was the main reason I was on this long, well-planned hiking trek. To consider whether to make some serious changes in my life path. If I was going to do it right and make the right long-term choices, I should stick to my hiking and meditating plan.

Then again, Rex, as I mentally referred to the Tyrannosaur man, was hiking the other way. I knew nothing about him other than what I saw in those 27 seconds or so as he passed by, but I was intrigued to know more. At the slow pace he was going I could catch up with him in a few minutes.

Then again, even though he was weighed down with the giant pack, he was tall and with his long stride he might be able to go faster than it looked. I was just over 5 feet tall, and he looked to be well over 6 foot. And there were a number of places he could go off this rough trail in the direction he was going. He could be on a different path by now where I couldn't find him. I thought about the possibilities. Even if I caught up with him, it would be a useless waste of time and against the plan.

I was used to hiking fast when I wanted to, and I was traveling very light, and he didn't look like he was an experienced hiker. He would probably be slow. He only had a few minutes head start so I felt sure I could catch him and ask what he's doing with that giant pack and probably still have plenty of time to get back to the supply drop and my next camp today. And the supplies should still be waiting for me tomorrow for that matter.

Then again, on this hike, I had a plan. I surprised myself for even considering going off plan. Hesitating here too much was risking putting myself behind today's schedule. I had probably already wasted 10 minutes thinking about this. Along with the time in the stream that was 25 minutes delay. I had almost used up the extra time I got from hiking fast earlier today.

I was totally dry and fully dressed now. I should get moving and stay on plan. I scrambled up the bank to take the trail to the left downstream towards the supply drop.

As I stepped onto the trail, I paused for a couple seconds looking straight ahead down the trail; I lifted my left foot to take the first step, then before putting it down I pivoted to the right, turning around, and planting that sandaled foot on the path to follow the Tyrannosaur man.

"Sorry Mom. Another change of plans. I'm not sure why I'm doing this. I hope I don't regret this…" I sniffed at my underarm and shrugged as I started walking quickly to catch him. "Watch out, Mr. T. Rex."

About 5 minutes later—about 15 minutes since our first encounter—I rounded a bend in the trail and saw him posed next to the stream. His massive pack was balanced on a log. He was out of his baggy pants and shirt, and soaking wet in his t-shirt and boxers, his bare right foot high up on a log, holding a large beach towel motionless above his raised wet thigh, apparently trying to mimic my pose from earlier. The stream didn't look deep here, but there was an empty pan on the ground near him. He had obviously just doused himself with water to make this wet pose. He stayed motionless as I walked past. I was trying not to be obvious as I glanced down at him out of the corner of my eye laughing. I continued with my head straight ahead until I reached a point where the trail went up over a little rise and then just as I went out of his view, I turned my head and called out, "Oops. I think I did see something. Have a nice day."

"Hey there! Wait! Hello!" he called out, but I continued out of his sight. "Oh shoot. Wait." I could hear him calling to me and scrambling to get back into his clothes.

I continued down the trail but walked extra-extra slowly to allow him to catch up. When he did catch up, he was still wet, but more-or-less back in his clothes, his huge backpack swaying and lurching since he had not strapped into it properly. He was huffing and straining a bit. He probably thought he had done a great job of moving fast to catch me, but I had been counting to ten between steps until I heard him getting close.

"Hey! Hey! Wait up a sec! Do you mind if I tag along with you for a minute? What's your name?" he said between gasps for breath as he started to catch up.

I hesitated a second and then decided to answer. "Uh. Mara. I'm Mara."

"Pleased to meet you, Mara. I'm Perry."

"Not Rex?"

"No. Are you expecting someone named Rex?"

"Never mind. It's not important."

We walked along for a minute slowly with me in the lead, then I stopped, stepped to the side, and motioned for him to pass. I had to step farther off the trail as he passed in order to avoid being hit by the massive pack. I wanted to look closer at what he was carrying.

"I can't believe you are carrying so much stuff. That is a really big pack. What do you have in there?"

"Oh. It's not so bad. It's lighter than it looks," he replied as he reached back with both hands and strained to lift it to shift the weight on his shoulders and on his waist strap, adjusting and tightening the straps as he continued to walk along. "96.4 pounds with empty water bottles, I think. So probably about 100 maybe 110 pounds right now. And pretty well-balanced. Just essentials: food, clothes, tent, stove, pots and pans, fuel, some books, computer, batteries, this and that, communications gear. The batteries are probably the heaviest part. But only essential stuff."

"I see." I noted that his pack was probably heavier than I was now after losing weight on my hike.

"Are you camped near here? You must be on a day hike, what, with that itsy-bitsy pack."

"No. I go light. Minimalism and all that."

"Okay. Yeah. I see. Overnight Minimalism, huh? Today is probably a good day for taking a chance on an overnight trip without much gear. Should be clear, not like the rain the last week. I waited a couple days for clearer weather before I started hiking this morning. I've got gear for bad weather, sure. Be prepared, they say. But why make it harder than it has to be." He paused, then continued, "The only trailhead I know of near here is at Crescent Rocks. Did you start from there this morning? I did. I didn't see you there. I spent a couple days at the campground near there waiting for the better weather."

"Actually, I've been on the trail for 56 days now. Eight weeks. I stopped for supplies four weeks ago, so I guess my pack is a little lighter than sometimes."

"O-kay…Really? That's hard to believe. Eight weeks? With gear I could fit in my pockets? If that's true you should have a film crew following you. That would be a story worth sharing. Where are the rest of your people?"

"Oh. My people? Just my brother… uh, Chuck… the Navy Seal. He's scouting out some campsites ahead. He'll be back any minute now. But no film crew. Unless, I suppose you might have one in that pack of yours."

"You know, I might. I'll have to check. But really. You need tell your story. How is it possible to hike so light? I guess I've heard of people who do stuff like that, but it's always seemed impossible to me. And when I imagine them, I picture ultramarathon runners or big super-macho rock climber guys. Like maybe your brother."

"You don't think I'm an ultra-marathon runner, or a rock climber, or a Navy Seal?"

"No offense. No offense. You certainly could be. You look pretty buff, tiny but powerful. But, still, how do you go so light? I've brought a few extra things, maybe." He reached back and patted the solar panel on the side of his pack. "But just my essential backpacking gear would fill your pack ten times over. And I'm only planning to be out here for a few days. And, you know, I thought I had good lightweight gear. The backpacking supply places sell some really nice stuff, if you are willing to pay. I couldn't afford the best stuff, but I got some things on sale and made some similar things myself. It's kind of a hobby of mine to make things. So, I guess your brother must be carrying the bigger load."

"No. I have to say he's going even lighter than me. He travels like a ghost. Me, I try to practice minimalism. I mean my brother and I; we try to… I try not to keep anything I don't really need. Things only weigh you down if you carry them with you. There are things that most people think you need, but you don't need to bring. Like food."

"Uh. Uh? What? You think you don't need food?? That's a different kind of minimalism. That really challenges some of my basic assumptions."

"I brought some, but I didn't need to bring much because I can find most of my food in the forest."

"I'm surprised you can find any food out here after all the fires and droughts in recent years."

"In some ways it's better as things grow back. The snow was good this year, and we had some rain recently. A lot is growing out here if you know where to look."

"But your pack is so tiny. How did you survive in the rain?"

"Sometimes it's a little uncomfortable. You learn to deal with that. But I've got good gear. The stuff I brought is compact and light."

"I'd still need 20 times the size of your pack. Even the best stuff I saw in the catalogs would be a lot bulkier than your pack. And that wasn't cheap."

"Well maybe. Minimalism means simplicity, economy of space, avoiding clutter, not always less money."

"Minimalism? Hmmm. Moneyed minimalism."

I could imagine him thinking that only rich people with no worries about getting what they need are willing to say that material things don't matter. But he didn't say that. Instead, he said, "I guess I'm taking more of a maximalism approach. Min and Max. So that makes the two of us like Minnie and Max-well, I guess."

"Uh…Yeah. So Max, tell me again, what ARE you doing out here with all that gear?"

"It's Perry. Oh. Okay. Max, if you like. Or Rex, whoever he is. So, Mini-Mara, maybe we take turns. You tell me a little about yourself and how you are surviving with so little, and I tell you a little about what I'm doing."

We continued walking and talking for over a mile, each resisting giving specifics about certain things: He was sketchy about his extra electronics gear and his pending job offer, and I tried not to say much about my space or military grade gear or my financial situation.

As we side-stepped some topics, it seemed to me that we had a number of things in common. Both of us said our main reasons for our hikes were to get away from other people to make some decisions about our futures. I was on a personal minimalist quest, seeking solitude, meditation, and freedom from distractions to find my center and to listen to my inner voice to help me decide on my career path. He was trying to stay intensely busy and distracted for a few days working on some hard problems to let his subconscious help him make up his mind about a job offer. Both of us were facing a major career choice, although neither of us would share specifics.

I did share that I was dealing with the recent deaths of my parents. I skipped or changed some details. For purposes of telling the story to a stranger, it was simple: "They died of the flu."

"Wow. That's terrible. So, you are an orphan now. That must be terrible for you, and your brother."

"Actually, I guess I'm a double orphan. I was adopted when I was a baby after my birth parents died."

"That's incredibly tragic. I'm so sorry."

"I know. Isn't it? Such a pathetic case."

He didn't respond, so I continued, "I was a baby. I don't remember them."

I had recently learned things about them that my adopted parents had never told me. But I didn't want to share the complications of that story with this stranger. Keep it simple.

"I'm really sorry."

"We all have stories, I guess," I said.

"We both have sad stories, but your pathetic story beats mine."

Perry shared that he lost his parents five years ago in a car crash. A distracted driver crossed over the centerline on a two-lane highway and his mom swerved and wrapped their car around a power pole. They were driving home after dropping him off for the start of his sophomore year at Stanford. He said, "At least it was quick for them."

I thought to myself, "He's lying. I don't remember seeing him at Stanford. Five years ago, that was 2014. I was starting my second year then too. If we were in the same class, I would have seen him. I have a great memory for faces." But I just said, "Well, this is such an uplifting conversation. I'm so glad we got a chance to talk."

I considered asking him more about what classes he took and places he hung out to catch him in his lie, but instead just let him keep talking.

He shared that losing his parents was really hard for him, especially at first. He said he wished he could help me somehow during this early part of my grieving.

"Do you have any suggestions about how to cope?"

"It's trite, but time helps. And maybe I'm not a good example. I kind of avoided dealing with it by keeping busy. For a few months there was so much paperwork for their estates and after that I was behind and had to really concentrate on classes. I haven't really slowed down since then."

"You had to deal with their estate?" I asked. "Did they leave you a trust or something to live on?"

"No trust. They barely had a will. But I ended up with a little money. Enough to get through college."

"Enough to get through Stanford sounds like a lot."

"Not really. I had to leave Stanford."

"Oh?"

"I stopped out that term to deal with their deaths and didn't go back. I transferred to UCI. It was still expensive but not near as much."

I thought to myself, "Okay. Maybe I could have missed him my freshman year. I was 16 and living off campus in Palo Alto that year and didn't socialize much. I guess it's possible."

He explained that he switched to UCI to save money and to be closer to home in Santa Ana. His mom had some life insurance through the hospital where she worked as a nurse. They had no real savings or equity in their house. His dad had a machine shop, but he was leasing the shop and most of his machines. The mom's life insurance was enough to get him through undergrad at UCI, and it helped his older sister, and her husband buy a house somewhere in the Midwest.

He hardly spoke with his sister since then. He thought she held it against him that their parents died on the drive back from taking him to college. He concentrated on studies after that and did almost twice the normal unit load, continuing straight into grad school at UCI. He also used his share of the inheritance to keep paying the rent on his dad's small machine shop, and he lived in the back room. His dad had let him help in the shop since he was a kid, and he learned a lot about the machines. The shop was closed since his parents died; but he did some small jobs as favors for people who used to come to his dad, and he used the machines to work on his own inventions.

I told him that my parents had left me okay financially, but I really missed them. I didn't mention that I didn't have a lot of other close friends.

I mentioned how I had completed most of the requirements for a number of different majors: engineering, computer science, business, which were all things my mom knew a lot about, but got my bachelor's in philosophy and psychology, which my mom was not especially happy about. I especially liked some eastern and indigenous philosophies. I finished college at nineteen and did some internships since then but hadn't settled on what I wanted to be. My mom wanted me to get involved with the family business and I might still do that, but it would be hard without her. My dad was a quiet guy. He never said much but was supportive of whatever I chose to do.

"Family business? What kind of business?"

"Well, they both had jobs for a long time at the same company. It felt like a family business."

He mentioned that he had degrees in computing, information science, and data analysis and had studied quite a bit of engineering and he really liked tinkering and inventing things. He said he had a knack for visualizing how parts of things move together in three dimensions and for electronics and computer hardware. He could continue doing post-doc research at the university or get a job in industry or government. He needed to decide soon about one particular government job offer.

Both of us had photographic memories, but in different ways. I explained that I could replay in my mind just about anything I had seen and paid attention to. When I played back my visual memories, I could watch them as they had occurred or change them, second-guessing my actions. He said he had to focus on memorizing things in order to make mental snapshots. But when he focused, his memory was very accurate.

We both had strong opinions about social justice and income inequalities, but with very different ideas about how to solve them. He tended towards bleeding-heart liberal, and I liked socially and fiscally conservative libertarian policies. Both of us held the ideals of personal liberty and freedom from oppression, to allow everyone to reach their potential, but with different ideas about what that means and how to get there. Both of us were concerned how diseases were becoming resistant to antibiotics and how epidemics were likely to be more frequent. His mom had seen a lot in her job as a nurse, and I had the experience of losing my parents. We both agreed that someday a nasty global pandemic was bound to happen when a contagious bug becomes resistant to treatment.

"One option I'm thinking of, is maybe I could still go to med school to work on that," I shared.

We both thought that the healthcare insurance situation was not ideal. We had different ideas about how to fix it. I thought Obamacare was the wrong approach; I said how I believed in free markets and lots of competition, possibly with some subsidies; He wanted a national plan like Canada or England.

"Some call it 'Medicare for all.'"

"It would cost too much," I said.

"It would be much less expensive overall. No country spends near what we do. Do the math," he replied.

"I've done the math, but let's set that aside for now. I don't think we're going to agree on this."

We disagreed on many things, but we both said, in principle, if enough reliable data proved us wrong, we would change our positions on just about anything. We had some disagreements about what constituted reliable data.

He shared his wish that self-driving cars would soon be perfected and become universal. His parents would probably still be alive if a human driver eating and texting hadn't caused the accident that killed them.

"Did they catch the guy?"

"No. There were no witnesses, but why else would they drive off the road?"

He admitted his mom sometimes used her own phone when she drove. He was considering looking for a job with a company doing self-driving cars, if he didn't take his current job offer.

Both of us also agreed that automation seemed to keep taking away jobs so automation, like self-driving cars, on its own would not be a panacea.

"In a couple years there won't be any more long-haul truck drivers," he said.

"Maybe a few years longer than that, but yeah, probably eventually. And watch out; 3D printing may eliminate the need for machine shops."

He resisted, "Nothing will ever take the place of a skilled machinist. Sure, I would like to have access to a good 3D printer for some things. But still nothing can replace a good machinist."

We agreed that something would have to be done to create new jobs for people who lost them to automation.

"You know Nixon wanted to give everyone a guaranteed minimum income, but it never got passed. Can you imagine if it had?" Perry commented.

"Who is Nixon?"

Perry looked at me puzzled.

"No. Just kidding," I responded. "I didn't complete a history major, but I've heard of Nixon. I didn't know he suggested a minimum income.

Yeah, taxes would probably be so high that the minimum income would also be the maximum income."

"Min meets Max once again."

We had some wildly different opinions about politics, but we could generally agree on some areas where data and science supported certain facts. We both had problems with the current administration, although I was okay with some of the policies.

"He's an entertainer. Ignore the words and look at the actions," I said.

"The words and the actions are both pretty awful," he said.

We agreed that the climate was changing, and people were impacting it but not on the right ways to address it.

We also agreed that the interconnected world of the internet age was definitely not all positive. Negativity and spreading of lies or at least inaccurate information was making things very dark.

As I pushed him to share more about what he was carrying in his massive pack, he admitted that he was testing out some of his inventions on this hike. He said he had built compact backpacking versions of a chair, table, stove, espresso machine, and mini fridge, among other things. His computer tablet, attached in front of him, had GPS plus some extra visualization software he was working on that helped show him the hiking path.

On my part, I mentioned I was also doing some testing. I was testing myself: my own self-reliance and autonomy. Oh. And my brother's. Also, some of my gear was kind of new so I said it was kind of a test of the gear as well. I wanted to rely mostly on myself. I didn't bring any electronics or GPS gadgets other than that emergency security fob, which I made a point of mentioning more than once, as well as the bear spray.

We had been talking and walking a while and he said, "Do we need to go look for your brother? Maybe something happened to him."

"I think he can take care of himself. He's probably watching us. Like I said, he's like a ghost."

"Rex, is his name?"

"Yeah, Rex. Uh… No. Wait. I mean Chuck. I said Chuck. Chuck."

"Are you sure?"

"I'm not going to worry about Chuck, or Rex."

Finally, I admitted that this was supposed to be a solitary journey of self-discovery for me. I was off plan today since I really shouldn't be talking to him.

He said "I'm honored you made an exception for me even if it was just for these couple of hours. Before you go on your own again, can I have your number? You do have a phone back home, somewhere?"

I said, "I'll think about it."

We continued to walk and talk. He got me to say more about the route I had been taking and things I had seen and challenges I had run into along the way. He seemed fascinated by how I had managed with so little. I described scenes and details from memory like I was watching them live, which I was able to do. I didn't bother to add a brother into the scenes I described. I only mentioned one of the re-supply drops.

Perry said he wanted to memorize everything I said about my trip. As he pushed to learn more about my ability to travel so light, I mentioned again that I was able to save space and weight by memorizing books and videos about wilderness survival and how to identify and prepare edible plants. I admitted I was lucky that I didn't make any fatal mistakes in the first few days as I put that memorized book-learning into practice. I talked in detail about specific areas where I gathered berries and roots and fungus and how I was able to separate the poisonous from the edible.

I also mentioned I didn't need to bring any maps other than in my head. I had memorized my planned path and good camping and food gathering locations along the way based on books and satellite imagery I had seen ahead of time. I only had to make minor changes from the plan when I saw things in person. The topo maps and satellite photos I memorized had limited resolution so what I thought would be a flat spot to camp sometimes turned out to be too steep.

Eventually I conceded that the gear I brought included some materials that were kind of experimental; I had used some of my parents' connections in the high-tech company where they had worked to get access to some gear that was not available to the public yet.

"Are a lot of high-tech firms into camping supplies?"

"You'd be surprised. There are more than you would think. Adventurers are willing to spend a lot on better, lighter gear. Companies will make things if someone will pay. And of course, there are military and space applications."

"Oh, so your parents worked for that kind of company. Well, I guess I shouldn't speak. I might be working for one of those or the government pretty soon myself."

He avoided answering my questions about the job he was considering, but I got the idea it might involve doing something he was not allowed to talk about. He did mention that it might use his data analysis skills from his university research. When I asked what his research was about, he said it was a little hard to explain: a kind of data analysis based on looking for emergent collective hive intelligence patterns, like how an ant colony or a hive of bees taken as a whole does things that seem intelligent even though each bee or ant on its own is not very smart. Kind of like figuring out what an ant hill is thinking by looking at what all the ants are doing and distinguishing the ants from different colonies based on their behaviors.

Around the middle of the day, we decided to take a break. I said there was a small lake, or a large pool in a stream, above the trail that we could climb to. I made no more effort to pretend I was expecting my brother. I had not stopped at this lake on my previous pass, but I knew where it was from the maps I had memorized.

As we scrambled off trail up to the lake, I helped push Perry's pack from below a few times as he climbed over boulders. Perry led the way and seemed to know how to find a good path despite there being no marked trail. He frequently referred to his computer.

8/13/2019, Late Morning, Coffee Break

After the climb Perry and I were resting, sharing a rocky clearing near a deep pool in a stream a couple hundred yards above and out of sight of the trail. I was squatting down sorting a variety of edible greens and roots I had collected nearby, spreading them out on a rock as Perry was digging through his enormous pack looking for something. His solar panels were off the pack and spread on the ground facing the sun.

As he dug in his pack he said, "I know. I know. You don't have to tell me. It would be easier to find things if I packed lighter, Ms. Minimalism. Minimal-ah. Mini-Mara."

He pulled out two narrow bundles of strips of metal, about two feet long. Each bundle was about an inch or 1 ½ inches wide. He pulled on one and twisted and it extended into a very compact lattice work chair which he offered to me to sit on. I did so, gingerly at first, and then relaxed as I discovered that it supported my weight just fine.

"Very cool the way that works. Where'd you find that?"

"Made it myself."

The next one opened in a similar way, and he sat on it.

"This one is actually supposed to be a table, but it's strong enough to use as a stool."

I replied, "I'll concede, if you packed for minimalism, you might not have furniture and a full kitchen including a refrigerator. I don't know how I've managed to get by these last few weeks without those. By the way I still want to see that espresso machine you mentioned."

I had considered bringing something to make good coffee myself, but decided it was not strictly necessary, so I left it behind. It had been eight weeks now since I had a cup of coffee. I missed the caffeine jolt the first couple of weeks but actually felt better now without it.

"Sure. Espresso coming up in a minute." He continued taking items out of his pack and arranging them on the ground in front of his chair. I recognized some of them as similar to gear I had researched before my trip, but others were a mystery.

I figured he was an inexperienced backpacker who wanted to bring all the comforts of home. Even while staying out of sight of other hikers, I had seen some passing on the trail who overpacked, but Perry beat them all. His load was extreme, and the computer, solar panels and antennas were a bit different from anything I had seen elsewhere on my hike. I still doubted his stories about inventing most of the gear he claimed to be carrying, but I was curious what kinds of comforts from home he had brought.

I had also been inexperienced as a hiker when I started, but I did my homework ahead of time. I thought I had researched everything on the market when I was choosing what to bring and Perry's items were different enough that I started to think maybe he really did make some of this stuff himself. The way the chairs twisted and unfolded was definitely something I hadn't seen before.

If Perry had the heaviest load on the trail, I had the lightest. I observed others on the trail who packed very light, including some ultradistance mountain runners doing 1-day extreme hikes and day-hikers close to trailheads, but my load was lighter than all of them.

Perry reached behind him and tilted the solar panels to get more direct sun.

"The battery charge should be good enough now."

His eyes brightened as he returned to digging in his pack and found something.

"If Max packed like Min, I also wouldn't have this!"

He pulled a medium-sized glass bottle of tequila out of his pack.

"But then again, some things are essential."

"What the F?! Okay. Yeah. The epitome of essential!" I said and we both laughed.

"And was someone asking for espresso?"

He pulled a medium sized bag from his pack marked COFFEE and took out a small cylindrical metal object.

"Would you like yours with or without tequila? And I've got some milk in the fridge; I can froth some to make a cappuccino or latte if you'd like."

"No thanks. You go ahead."

I watched skeptically as he moved quickly. He took off small metal cup-shaped covers off the top and bottom of the cylinder. He flipped open a small chamber on one end, scooped in some ground coffee then closed it set it on one of the cups.

"Oh. I've also got a grinder if you want fresh ground, but I ground this today, so it is still pretty fresh."

I waved my hand to say it was okay.

"You put ground coffee in here and seal it, plug the power wire from the solar panels or battery in here. Pour a couple ounces of cold water through here. As it's heated that closes a valve to pressurize it until it is released through the grounds into the cup below. Pretty simple. I usually do one dose for a single shot, but you can run more water through it if you want an Americano or something."

He poured water from a metal water bottle into an opening on the top. It started to steam up and a valve abruptly sealed, stopping the steam. Then a few seconds later with a foosh sound it released a steaming shot of espresso into the bottom cup. It smelled good.

"You can also use it to make boiling water for cooking or tea without the steam pressure if you remove the coffee capsule. There were plenty of coffee devices available for camping that weren't outrageously expensive, but most of them were more of an aero press where you need to add hot water and pump it to get pressure. I built this one myself because none of the others worked quite the way I wanted. I wanted the right steam pressure, and I knew I would have electric power. It's pretty efficient since it only heats up when water is poured in."

He held the cup for me to smell. I sniffed and nodded approval, but when I didn't take the cup, he asked, "More water? Or Cappuccino?"

"Actually, I usually don't have coffee this time of day. In fact, I've been getting by without coffee on this trip. It might not be good to start again. You go ahead and have that."

He held the cup close enough for me to smell the coffee again. I sniffed and smiled and then my expression changed to one of concern.

"And why did you bring a big glass bottle of tequila? That's just crazy?! Were you expecting a big party? Or are you some kind of alcoholic?"

"Long story about that… Well maybe not so long."

"Go on."

"This was my dad's favorite tequila. It's not the fanciest, but it's what he liked. His birthday is tomorrow. He liked many things from Mexico, especially my mom and this tequila. And the anniversary of their deaths is next week. I wanted to toast their memory."

He held up the bottle to see refracted sunlight through the glass and liquid.

"I like this bottle. Of course, I didn't need this much for a toast, but I couldn't put it in a plastic flask. That would be just wrong."

He reminisced about his parents, "My dad was a great machinist. He could make anything. I learned a lot from him. My mom was a nurse. She was a saint, but with an attitude. Nobody would ignore Abbie Lee, RN, when she had something to say. I miss both of them."

I hesitated and then took the cup with the espresso, and said, "Okay, maybe I'll have a taste of this with some of that tequila. For your dad. And your mom."

"That's the spirit!" Perry responded. Perry handed me the tequila bottle. "Sure no cappuccino? I make it good."

"No. This will be fine."

"Okay then, I will join you on that."

He dumped the old grounds in a can marked "Compostable" and added new. His hands moved quickly through the steps almost without looking until another shot of espresso was being released into another cup with a FOOSH sound.

"You've done this before," I said.

"Yeah. I built this a week ago. So yeah a few times."

I poured a generous shot of tequila into his cup as he held it out to me and then also into mine.

"Cheers! Or Salud! Or Happy Trails! I don't know what is appropriate in this situation," Perry said as he raised his cup and took a sip.

"Happy Trails is as good as any," I answered as I also took a sip. "And Happy Birthday to your dad!"

"May he watch over me and help me make good choices. And you too, Mom. I miss your advice."

He raised his cup and looked skyward.

8/13/2019, Early Afternoon, WTF

Sometime later that day, we were still at the lake or pool in the stream, and various other items from Perry's pack were arranged around us. The tequila bottle was half empty. A small cube of a refrigerator was making a low hum connected by wire to a battery pack. A black plastic bag of a sun shower bulging with water was lying nearby on the rock warming in the sunlight. A shower stall was set off to the side of the clearing. It was made of a telescoping pole with a folding base and a hook at the top for hanging the shower bag. A square curtain rod was draped with a tent rainfly as a shower curtain on two sides of the shower for a semblance of privacy. A pan on the small stove was ready to cook something. A tarp was spread out on a flat area with a tent and sleeping bag still in their sacks.

We both downed one more tequila shot, and I asked, "You know. I've been meaning to ask. The way you were posing by the stream when I passed. Very cute by the way. The second time we met. You were posing like I was the first time."

"Really?"

"I mean you pulled off a wet pose pretty well. You looked good."

"Uh, thanks, I would say you did too, but I said before I didn't see anything. But what about that?"

"Yeah. I was wondering, how did you time that out? Were you just waiting there like that until I came along? How did you even know I would go that way on the trail? The way the trail twisted and turned I didn't think you could see me coming."

"Just a happy coincidence, don't you think?"

"Probably not."

"It was a 50-50 chance you were going that way."

"Maybe."

"Do you believe in fate and destiny?"

"I do, but what we do has a big impact on our fate."

"Okay. Okay. Okay. Yeah." He paused and thought then came to a decision and continued, "I won't hide anything from you. Let me show you something."

"Uh oh."

"Nothing like that. On the computer."

"Uh oh?"

He fumbled a bit and dropped his computer tablet as he removed it from the custom hinged clasp attached to one of the straps of his backpack. He caught it before it hit the ground.

"Maybe too much tequila," he said. He touched the screen a few times and moved with his stool/table next to me.

"Don't tell anyone, but this isn't just GPS software I was testing," he confided.

The tablet showed a satellite view of a high mountainous area with a trail following a stream. I recognized it as a satellite view of the general area where we were hiking much like with any mapping software.

"It looks like GPS and mapping software," I said.

"Sort of. And a little more. This is a playback from earlier," he replied. The image zoomed down in on a young man in a wide-brimmed hat carrying an extra-large backpack with solar panels and antennas. He was walking on a trail looking at a tablet attached in front of him.

"Recognize anybody?" he asked.

Then the image panned out to show more of the trail ahead, including a small young woman with short dark hair in a tight-fitting t-shirt and not much more splashing and dunking underwater in a stream about a hundred yards further down the trail. The time stamp was from earlier that day.

"WTF! Are you shitting me! Really??! You have a drone? I hate drones. I thought they were illegal in this wilderness."

"Not a drone exactly. I was just testing my system for visualizing the trail where I was going, and you happened to be there. I didn't memorize all the maps ahead of time like you did. I didn't mean to spy on you, but then again, you were right out there in open view of any ZN23 satellite that might be passing over, so you really can't have an expectation of privacy."

I was surprised. Not happy. But before I could reply he continued, "So… the truth is, I did use this to kind of watch and see you were coming my way before I posed by the stream. Sorry about that."

"Spying? With a satellite? That's bullshit."

"Sorry."

"The ZN23 satellites are not available for just anyone to use. They aren't even officially online yet. More likely you've got a drone in that pack or somewhere near here."

I knew that the first few clusters of satellites were functional and being tested before going fully online later this year. The emergency beacon fob I was carrying was a prototype that used those satellites. I didn't want to believe that some random guy was able to hack the satellites.

"Okay. Sounds like you've heard about those satellites," he said.

"Sure. They were in the news. I've read about them. I don't forget anything I see or read. I haven't seen anything in the press about cameras on those satellites. They are supposed to bring high speed internet to a lot of remote places starting next year."

"Yeah. Internet. They might do that too."

I knew about the cameras, even though that was not public information, and maybe word had gotten out about them. But there was no way someone could get unauthorized use of the satellites.

"I still think you've got a drone here somewhere," I said.

"Just a sec," said Perry. He checked his computer tablet. "Yeah. Another cluster of the satellites should be in range now. Let me show you what my 'drone' can do."

He touched the tablet screen in a few places and the picture changed to show a couple sitting by a lake looking at a computer screen. Perry looked up and waved and the young man in the picture did the same. It was a real-time picture of them. I looked up in the clear sky straining to see it but didn't see the drone. The picture changed to a different angle view of the same scene, then panned out and out and out to show a hundred square mile section of the mountains. It then shifted and zoomed back in to show cars moving in line at a coffee shop in small town a hundred miles away.

"Would you like me to order you a coffee? If I'm using a drone for this, it's really high and really fast. Maybe my drone can deliver it."

"Who are you? How did you do that? I didn't think any satellite cameras could do that."

"The pictures are better than I expected. I wasn't sure how good the pictures would be or if I could even get it to work. I told you I'm just a guy who is good with technology and tinkering. I'm sort of using a free introductory offer with the new satellites."

"I don't think so. They don't do that."

"Sure, they do."

I glared at him in silence, and he continued, "Okay, so maybe I've found ways to use some satellites when they are not busy."

"Use them? So, you are some kind of cyber-criminal satellite hacker?"

"No. No. Not really. Okay. Whatever. It doesn't matter. Those satellites are really cool the way they coordinate and operate together independently without being controlled all the time from the ground. The way they operate together is kind of related to the hive-intelligence research that I do. The university got funding for my research from the company that makes those satellites. They shared some samples their hardware and information about their code with us and that gave me some ideas."

"So that is a ZZphase antenna in your pack? I thought I recognized it. You are funded by Zzynarji? That's crazy. That's where my parents worked."

"Really? Yeah. My research was funded by them or their foundation or something. My advisor knows. I guess in a roundabout way I was working for the same company as your parents. But that grant is running out soon. It might get renewed, but even so, the university doesn't pay like a real job. Anyway, the techniques they used on those satellites are cool, but not as smart as they should be. I was testing out a wild idea to make the hive of satellites think I'm one of them, so they would cooperate with me too. I didn't think it would work without a lot of tweaking the code. And I thought I would need to get up over 11,000 feet to access it with my low power equipment. I figured I would spend a week changing my code and tweaking the antennas to have a chance of getting it to work, and even then, it wasn't likely. It was supposed to be an all-engrossing, nearly impossible task. I turned it on this morning while I was walking, because a cluster of satellites was passing overhead, and it started working at lower elevations than I expected. I just turned it on while I was walking, and it worked! And then I stumbled on you."

I was shaking my head and looking repeatedly down at the ground, then up at the sky, then at Perry. I didn't have words.

He continued, "There are dozens of those new ZN23s in each cluster, and each has multiple cameras; they're not very busy yet. Because of the way they collaborate as a hive they don't report back to headquarters about everything they do for each other. And I figured it's safer to tap into them when they're out here over the wilderness. That's part of why I'm out here to test out my equipment. Elevation and remoteness, you know."

I didn't respond. I was bringing up a mental image of the source code for the satellites, trying to find flaws. I had worked on it a year ago when I was trying out one of my jobs at my parents' company. I was trying to find the vulnerability Perry used.

"But like I said before, I'm mainly out here to clear my head by working through what I thought was a really hard problem and make some choices about my future. This problem turned out to be a lot easier than I expected, so, so much for that idea. I still need to decide. I've got that job offer that I'm not sure I want to take. The pay would be better than university research, but less than a private firm and I'm not sure I want to work for the government. I could apply more places and probably make a lot more working for a startup or something. Like maybe a self-driving car company."

Perry paused and waited for a response. The expressions on my face probably showed I was going through a number of conflicting thoughts, but I didn't speak. I would get back to reviewing the code later. I was now thinking about the internal executive pitch for those satellites I sat in with my mom a couple years before.

"A growing constellation of orbital units soon providing continuous coverage over more than 75% of the Earth's surface. Each bird with six ultra-high-resolution cameras that can operate independently or in tandem for even higher resolution, and a comm array supporting over 1000 separate data links that can be flexibly combined for ultra-high bandwidth and resistance to jamming."

At the time I didn't think I would ever be the subject of such spying. Now it especially concerned me that their security was so weak that some random guy was able control them without permission. I realized I may need to make some changes at Zzynarji if I stayed involved in my parents' company. I would have to think about that. When I finished this hiking sabbatical, I would make those kinds of decisions. If I finished this hike and went back to civilization.

I had been leaning towards walking away from the company and my position as director of the family foundation if I returned from the hike. I could live off my family trusts and do something completely different. Let other people run things. Lighten your load. Don't keep anything you don't really need, except maybe a few billion dollars. Maybe I would still do that, but I needed to make some changes first at Zzynarji.

Then a scary thought entered my tequila-addled head. What are the chances some random guy would happen to be hiking in this remote area hacking into Zzynarji satellites right where the heir to the Zzynarji fortune was on her secret vision quest hike? No one was supposed to know where I was. I had been careful about how I made all my arrangements. The other directors of the foundation just knew I was going to be "away" for two or three months at a secret private retreat. I was equally opaque with my brother and my few friends. I thought I covered my tracks really well. The clues I left made people think I would be floating in a sensory deprivation tank somewhere. But someone at Zzynarji may have noticed that I collected samples from their materials lab and survival gear prototypes and figured out I was going somewhere remote. I thought my arrangements for the supply drops along the trail were all anonymous, but if someone could hack the security of the satellites maybe my precautions were not sufficient.

But then again, if someone sent this guy to follow me, it seemed like they picked a really unlikely choice. And what would be the point anyway? What would they be hoping he would do? I thought maybe it would all make more sense if I hadn't had so much tequila. I was not used to drinking. I looked at him watching me and patiently waiting for me to respond and decided it didn't matter why he was out here. I liked his liberal ass whoever he was.

After waiting for me to respond, and noticing my consternation, finally Perry added, "I'm sorry I spied on you. If you had been hiking the other way, it wouldn't have mattered. We would just have continued on our separate paths and never talked. In a parallel universe where you were hiking the other way, we would never have spent these hours together. Fate brought us together on this trail, one way or another."

"Uh. Yeah. Fate." I said slowly, looking at the ground, but then I continued, "What we do has a big impact on our fate." I looked up towards the sky once more and then back at Perry.

"I was actually supposed to be in that other parallel universe going the other way down the trail to my next supply drop, but I turned around and followed you because I wanted to find out what you were doing with all that gear."

Perry smiled, "Well I guess now you know. So, you've been backtracking on your hike for the last few hours while we've been talking?"

"Yeah. Pretty much. I'm gonna need to turn around again at some point if I'm going to get back on my plan," I sighed. "I was supposed to pick up supplies at the Crescent Rocks Meadow trailhead today." I stood up and was a little light-headed and sat back down. "I probably won't try to get there today."

"Well, if you run short on anything before you get back there, I've probably got extras I can spare." He gestured towards his pack.

I decided I would spend some time getting to know this guy better.

Tuesday, 8/27/2019, End of Hike

Two weeks later I arrived at the pre-planned end point of my hike. I almost ran down the last two miles of a busy almost-flat, mostly exposed, dusty stretch of trail. For the last week I had been covering twice the distance per day as my original plan. More hours of faster hiking each day. Less sleep and a lot less time for stillness and meditation to catch up from the week I spent with Perry. Now I was caught up or maybe a couple hours ahead of the planned end of my hike. I was going so quickly on this part of the trail I almost stepped on a six-foot rattlesnake in sunny spot right in the middle of the dirt trail.

"That would be a bad way to wrap up this hike," I thought to myself after I dodged off the dirt trail to get away from it. While I watched the snake slowly move away on the other side of the trail, I thought about the last two weeks.

Perry and I had spent almost a week together exploring features of the area where we had met and learning more about each other before I resumed my planned path at double speed. He listened to my detailed, mostly true descriptions of the first fifty-four days of my hike. He experimented a little more with his satellite link, and I gave him suggestions for places to watch. I picked up my supply package at Crescent Rocks the day after we met, but we mostly enjoyed the supplies that Perry had brought and mixed in some fresh roots, fungus, berries and other things that I collected. I still hadn't explained to him exactly who I was. He knew I came from a family with money, but he didn't know I was worth billions.

When we parted ways on the trail, he went back to his car, and I resumed my hike. Neither of us had decided yet on what we would do about our career decisions. We made plans only one week ahead. He promised that he would meet me at the end of my trail. I hoped he was serious. But I would be fine either way. I would make sure I made it there, so at least that was a decision on my part.

During that final week, I hiked alone after Perry went back home. Even though the weeklong delay put me off my plan, during my final extra busy week I did arrive at an answer to the question that prompted my hike. Even when you are on a set path there will be surprises and opportunities to take detours. So, if you don't have an obvious reason to change your path, keep going and see what happens.

I thought it would be nice if our paths would continue to overlap. I'd be fine if they didn't, but it would be nice if they did. I resolved to tell him he should take the job with the government agency even if it meant moving to the other side of the country. He said it had opportunities for his research he couldn't get anywhere else.

I might make some major course changes later, but to start I would take on the roles my parents had left for me. I would tell Perry I was staying with a job working with the Zzynarji Foundation, but that really meant that I would continue working as chairman of the Foundation and managing both of my family trusts. The Zynn Family Trust was set up by my adopted parents, and the Strong Family Trust was set up by my birth parents. Between the two trusts and the foundation I controlled the whole Zzynarji company. I would get more involved in the company and fix things like lax security on the satellite network.

Technically I had few assets of my own, which I noted was good from a minimalism viewpoint, but through both trusts I controlled 160 billion dollars of assets, give or take a few tens of billions.

After watching the snake disappear into some bushes, I continued forward and soon went back under a shady canopy of tall pines and cedars and crossed a couple of little bridges over trickling stream beds until I reached the trailhead at the end of a paved road. I was a little disappointed that Perry wasn't there, but I was early. I had said he could meet me either at the trailhead or at the lodge.

I found a set of bear boxes near the trail head. One had a familiar lock. I unlocked it like all the others with the pre-arranged passcode. Inside was a duffle bag. It included fresh new clothes in a range of sizes to allow for uncertainty about my weight loss. There were three pairs of shoes to match the outfits, two phones, a credit card, and some cash, including a couple of rolls of quarters. There was a personals bag with soaps, deodorants, cosmetics, shaver, hair dryer, and such.

I left my old pack in the bear box along with the sets of clothing that were way too big and locked it again. I put the strap of the duffle bag over my shoulder and walked quickly a few miles down a paved road that more or less paralleled a river. I became increasingly aware of my body odor and the layers of dirt on my clothes and skin as I passed other people stopped at viewpoints along the road. I was a different hue of brown than ten weeks ago before the hike.

I passed a couple of campgrounds and reached a small rustic lodge. I didn't see Perry at the lodge. I was fine with that. We had our own lives, and I was fine if that he decided not to meet me after all. I found the building with the laundry and showers. I used my quarters in a coin-operated shower. I repeated the shower over and over until the quarters ran out. I had some good shampoo, soaps, and lotions in my new supplies, and I used some of them up. I still felt dirty but figured it would have to do until I could get home or to a good hotel or spa. I wondered if Perry had decided to take the new job in DC. I could look him up later to find out.

After getting dressed, I walked a short distance to the lodge building and found the little snack bar restaurant. Still no Perry. I thought, "Oh Well. That is probably good. Easier to get back to my life." I bought myself a cheeseburger, fries, a bowl of chili, a few chocolate chip cookies and a large, sweetened iced tea.

As I ate, I remembered that I had not yet turned on my phones. I turned on my primary phone and looked at the messages from my assistants and my brother wondering where I was and if I was okay. I had promised my staff and brother that I would be back from my retreat in ten weeks, which meant today. I started to write a message to ask for a helicopter to pick me up near here, but before I sent it, I turned on the other phone. It was the one I used to make arrangements for the hike and had the number I gave Perry. I checked the app I told Perry to use to message me. It had hundreds of messages starting an hour after we went different directions on the trail a week ago. I would read all those later. I skipped ahead to last few messages.

Perry:

> *on my way, let me know when you get there*
> *Are you there yet? I'm getting close, I think*
> *I miss you and I'll be there soon.*
> *had to pull over to text*
> *this road is scary steep and winding*
> *looks like a desert around here*
> *hope this is the right road*
> *be there in about 15 minutes*
> *okay It's more than 15 minutes*
> *there was construction on the road*

and no signal for a while
see you soon

wish there was public transit to places like this
I hate driving but it's worth it to see you

just passed a tourist stop
a cave or something
the road follows a river now
think I'm almost there

in a campground now
asking where the lodge is
see you soon

<u>Mara:</u>

I'm at a food place in the lodge.
See you soon.

So, he was coming. My stomach felt weird. I wasn't sure if I was excited or nervous, or if I had been eating this greasy food too fast, but I kept looking around for him. A few minutes later I returned the tray to the counter and walked back to my table on the deck outside. Sitting down I saw Perry walk up to the food counter under the "ORDER HERE" sign. His beard was neatly trimmed. He wasn't wearing his glasses. He looked around and saw me sitting outside. I stood up as he hurried to me, and we hugged.

"Hey, you clean up well." He held me at arm's length to look into my eyes.

"Yeah. Thanks. You do too. No glasses today?"

"Contacts. I didn't take them on the hike. Not clean enough. You've got to take care of your eyes."

"Even with the full bathroom you brought with you in that pack of yours? I almost didn't recognize you without your glasses."

"Is that a good thing or a bad thing?"

"I can get used to this look."

"Okay. Sorry it took me longer than I thought to get here. I wanted to be at the trailhead when you got there. The road here was twisty and scary. I had to drive slowly."

"No problem. I guess I got here a little earlier than planned. I had time to take a shower and change."

"Yes. I see. Nice. You look very nice in city clothes. How did the shower here compare to the one on the hike?"

"Still trying to get compliments for all the comforts of home you carried in? Your solar heated shower was really, really nice after eight weeks on the trail. That first shower by the tiny lake was amazing even if it only lasted a minute. Being able to take a quick warm shower every day during that week I almost started feeling clean. Almost. But after this past week of non-stop hiking, I really needed a long shower. I showered for about an hour here and it still feels like I've got dirt that won't ever come out. I think I may need a few more hours of showers and maybe some long soaks in a tub or a trip to a spa."

"You look nice and clean to me. Very nice."

"Thanks. You look nice too," I said.

"So, what's good to eat here? How are the roots and grubs?"

I let him order me another burger.

As we both ate burgers he said, "I called on the way, and the lodge has a room available tonight."

I quickly answered, "We could do that."

"That's good since I already paid."

I looked around at the old lodge facility with not-quite-level floors and paint that was a couple decades or more past its prime. The snack bar was not exactly fine dining either, although I was relishing my second cheeseburger.

I was used to sleeping on rocks or dirt and pine needles so it would be a change from what I had been experiencing most of the last ten weeks, if not quite what I was used to in my prior life. I turned off my primary phone without sending any message.

Put that off until tomorrow. For today I'm still Mara. Tomorrow I can decide between a few hours' drive with Perry or arrange someone to drive Perry's car back for him while we take a quick helicopter flight.

For now, a room at the lodge and a few hours with Perry sounded great. Others could wait a day or two for me to resume my old life. Probably no one would declare me missing for a couple more days. For today, I could leave the other phone off.

Thursday, 12/05/2019, 7 PM?, Breaking Up?

Three months later I answered a call from Perry. He was at his studio apartment in an urban neighborhood near DC and I was staying at a family/foundation home on the beach in Santa Barbara. He had been calling me once or twice each day. Maybe more, but I turned off my 'Perry' phone for a good part of each day.

Each time we talked he would tell me about his day and ask about mine. He talked about the research he was doing and a little about the people he worked with, although he was circumspect about how much he said. After only a few weeks on the job he was getting excited about the extent of the data they let him analyze and the patterns he was starting to find in them. Despite his hedged comments, I imagined that his bosses wanted him to find terrorists and state actors working on plots and threats, and he felt like he was getting closer to giving them what they wanted. But he was most excited about how his models found various levels of emergent hive intelligence in the data.

I shared some anecdotes about what I was doing each day. He knew I was really well-off and had a job in a charity foundation that involved asking people for money and helping decide how to give away money, but somehow I had still kept my full identify from him. He still knew me as Mara Strong. He didn't realize I worked at my own family's foundation, or that I was not just a worker, but executive director. When he mentioned he couldn't find anything about me on the internet when he googled Mara Strong, I told him I tried to keep a low profile and didn't share anything on social media. He seemed to let it go at that. I wondered what other data his job gave him access to what if anything it said about Mara Strong.

I didn't tell Perry about the shakeup at Zzynarji that I had done after my hike. I wanted to make sure that mistakes like the satellite hacking vulnerability never happened again. I talked with all of the top executives and fired or demoted most of them. I gave more power to one of them. Carl Heinz was younger than most of the executives and he seemed to understand what I was trying to do to fix quality control. He had not been directly responsible for the areas that had slipped up, but he pointed out the lapses by other executives. I put him in charge, reporting only to me. I checked with him daily, usually by phone, but sometimes in person.

During the first few weeks after the hike, before Perry started his job, Perry and I met frequently in person, mostly at restaurants and other public venues that Perry chose. Even though I had a different look than before my hike I avoided going with him to restaurants and other public places I had visited before, since I didn't want to be recognized by people who knew me. Luckily most of Perry's restaurant and entertainment venue choices were different from places I had been. He still had a poor college student's sensibility.

He always tried to pick up the tab, but I insisted we take turns paying the bill. Once I let him visit one of my homes, a beach house on the bluffs in Corona del Mar. At the time I implied I was there to get it ready for a fundraising event for the foundation, but he probably noticed that I was familiar with the place. I don't think he saw my clothes in the bedroom closet.

When I was with him, I tried hard to avoid contacts with people who knew me. I was nervous about him finding out who I really was and how much I had, thinking that might change what he thought about me. I liked talking with him, but I wasn't sure where this relationship was going, so I was not totally honest with him. After a few weeks I was tiring of the charade and thinking it might be best to end it. He was from a different world than I was.

On his part he had seemed thoroughly impressed by what I told him about my lifestyle; the stories I told about the places I went and the people I met in my job. But he said he was most impressed by how easily we talked with each other. I liked that too. But I wasn't certain if I really liked him like a boyfriend. He frequently claimed he really liked me, but I wasn't sure I believed him.

In our daily conversations, while I didn't talk about changes at Zzynarji, I did talk about the Zynn Foundation. I shared some of the choices the foundation had to make about which charitable activities to support, and he gave me his opinions. When I agreed with his suggestions, which was more often than I expected, he was impressed by how quickly I persuaded the foundation to follow that advice. He didn't realize I usually was just able to tell them what to do.

When I turned on the 'Perry' phone that evening it rang within 10 minutes. It was about 10 PM in the east and 7 PM for me in the west. He must be just getting home from a typical day at the agency, probably eating some takeout Thai or Indian food he had picked up on the way home. I was getting ready to leave for an evening benefit at the home of someone really famous.

"Hi Mara. How was your day?"

"Hi Perry. You really shouldn't call so often. What did you say?"

"How was your day? You seem to be distracted. Not so eager to do that benefit party tonight? What's up?"

"I don't know. I just feel tired."

"Maybe you should skip it. Let someone else do the schmoozing. Get away from that stuff for a few days and come here and visit me. Let your bosses do some of the work for once."

"I'll be fine. The bosses do their share."

"What's the charity cause tonight?"

"It's a mix of some women's charities: health clinics, childcare centers, shelters for abused women… and job training and other support for struggling independent mothers."

"That all sounds like good causes. And kind of aligns with your pro-life goals."

"Mostly. I know your opinions on that are different."

"I support all that. I'm for life, I just don't think any man should have a say about what a woman decides to do with anything going on in her own body. But the things in those charities you mentioned: good medical care, help during pregnancy, and childcare help for people with little kids all sound good. It sounds like you're trying to make it more likely people can manage to have kids if they want to. I'm for all that."

"Yeah. We should get some good donations from people with a range of policy opinions. And you'd be surprised; these people sometimes have good new ideas about how the money should be spent. Just because they are celebrities and have different politics than me doesn't mean they can't have good ideas. It's good for the foundation to network like this. Speaking of getting input from others, tell me more about what Randy said about your analysis model. Didn't you have a review with him today?"

"Oh. Yeah. He likes it. He passed a positive summary up the chain today to say we should keep pursuing this. He said my analysis revealed 'breakthrough patterns'. I'm not sure exactly what he meant by that, except that I think he liked it. It involves a very large data set that's getting bigger all the time. Finding patterns across multiple data dimensions. I can't talk about it, but imagine if it included things like financial transactions, various kinds of social media and dark web posts, as well as topics covered on cable shows and web blogs. Stuff like that and a lot more. A lot of data.

A shit ton of data. He thinks it may lead to tracking down financial sources for some bad dudes. I know this is vague but I'm probably saying more than I should."

"Yeah. Probably. Well, keep trying to save the world."

"You too. Your work is doing real good in the world. I don't really know how my work will be used."

"I don't know how much impact these charities have."

"Keep working it. I miss you. You sound a little down. I know we are both working on our own things right now, but I wish we could see each other more often and have more time to talk. I hope we don't grow apart."

"You think we're growing apart?"

"No. No. That's not what I meant. I hope not. I mean no. We decided we would each go our own way for now but keep in touch and see what happens."

"What do you think has been happening?"

"Good things. It was fantastic that first week in mountains just starting to get to know each other and even better the days after that when we were able to see each other a lot, especially that day at the beach house, but we both got really busy and since I moved here, we've only seen each other in person once. It's been like a month since we saw each other. We should at least do video calls."

"You know I don't like those."

"I know we are both really busy, but somehow, we need to get more time together. Bi-coastal relationships bite. I'm thinking I should have stayed at the university or looked harder for something in Silicon Valley. Anywhere on the west coast, closer to you. Talking on the phone once or twice a day is nice, I always look forward to it, but it's not enough. I'm jealous of all those rich beautiful celebrities you say you hang out with and a little worried you might find someone you like more than me."

"Well, you should be worried. I am pretty special."

"You are."

"I think you are pretty special too."

"Okay. So, tell me more about how you are feeling. A little off? Still positive about this path you chose? You could still change your job. You sounded a little down and, in a hurry to get off the phone when we talked his morning, and I couldn't reach you during the day. Is there something wrong at work?"

"Most of the time I'm good. Work is very busy, but fine. I just get down or anxious sometimes. And I think I might have some kind of stomach bug today. But it's not enough to stop me from gaining back the weight I lost on the hike. You won't like what you see if we get together again."

"Crazy talk."

"I lost so much weight on that hike! If you'd met me before the hike… I don't know. It's best we just keep doing our own things." I tried to convey calm determination in my tone of voice, but I think my anxiety still came through.

Perry tried to reassure me, "I really like you, Mara. Everything about you. Let's find a way to meet up again soon. You are beautiful, inside and out."

"Both of us will do fine on our own. Stay where you are."

"Where are you going to be this week? Santa Barbara or going back to LA or the bay area or somewhere else?"

"Tomorrow I'm in OC for a homelessness event."

"How long are you there."

"I don't know. A couple days maybe."

"I'll see if I can get away to meet you there."

"Don't. I gotta go now. Bye."

After the call, I finished dressing and drove myself to the charity event. What Perry did next he never completely explained, but I'll reconstruct what I think he did, based on things he told me later and what happened the next day.

He was worried that I was breaking up with him, which was true, I guess, and he wanted to meet face to face to persuade me not to. He called his team lead Randy and said he needed to take a few days off. He could do some work on his secure laptop, if needed, but he needed to go to California. Randy said that as a new employee it was not a good time. Maybe in a few weeks. He had told the big bosses Perry was close to delivering more results in his analysis. Results that could be actionable and important. It was important for Randy's career to deliver results soon and he was counting on Perry's work. Perry said, "I'll do what I can from there, but I've got to go. I'll be back in a few days. I'm online looking for a red-eye flight tonight or the first flight tomorrow. I'm going. I just wanted to let you know. I'm going. I'll accept the consequences."

Randy said, "Stay on the line for minute. There's something I need to do. I'll be right back."

Perry replied, "Okay," and he continued looking for flights. He found some that left early the next morning. The fares were higher than he wanted to pay, so he hesitated from booking and used another travel search engine to see if he could find something cheaper, or something tonight.

Perry wondered what Randy was doing. Did Randy know he had a relationship in California. He probably did even though Perry didn't talk about it. He was going to go whether Randy gave him permission or not. Randy had said earlier that Perry's analysis really did seem like something new and important. Others in the agency had read his papers, and tried to duplicate his analysis, but no one else on the team had the knack that Perry had for this kind of analysis yet.

It wasn't just the data models, which others could run using Perry's code, but Perry was able to see things in the data and tweak the models in ways no one else could. Randy probably also knew Perry had contacted some tech companies about possible jobs in California and he didn't want to lose him.

After a minute or so of silence on the line Perry was just about to hit the button to purchase tickets for a 6:30 AM flight. But first he asked, "Randy, Are you still there?"

Randy answered, "Yeah. I'm still here. Here's the thing. Don't book that flight."

"Oh?" Perry held off on pushing the button to book it and shook his head realizing that Randy could snoop on what he was doing on his laptop. He would have to find ways to block that.

Randy continued, "You can go, but I need you to keep working while you are there. I can get you on a Navy flight out of Andrews tonight that gets into Los Alamitos at around seven-thirty. We can have a rental car meet you when you get there. I'll secure text you the flight info. It's a business trip. You'll need to check in at our Irvine office and give them a talk about your analysis techniques. It doesn't have to be anything prepared, just be ready to answer their questions. Maybe an hour or two. I'll send you that address too. I'll arrange a workspace for you there. Can you be at Andrews in one hour?"

"At this hour traffic should be light. I think I can do that. Thank you, Randy!"

"Get moving. Pack. Go. Or you'll miss the flight."

Detailed instructions for getting into Andrews and catching the flight appeared in a new window on Perry's computer.

As Randy probably hoped, Perry was impressed by this little benefit from working for the agency, but a little spooked by the lack of privacy on his computer.

Friday, 12/06/2019, Around 7:30 AM, A Surprise

The next morning Perry called me after he got off the plane in California but didn't mention he was there. I thought he was still in DC. I had left the 'Perry' phone on overnight.

"How are you today?"

"Not great. My stomach is a mess again. I'll probably be fine, but flu-like symptoms kind of freak me out."

"I bet. I bet. I'm sorry. I'm sure you'll be fine. If it's the flu, there's a treatment for that if you catch it early. Maybe you should go to urgent care before your flight."

"No. I'm at the airport in SB right now. My flight leaves soon, and I should get to John Wayne by nine. I might get checked after I get there."

"Okay. I'll let you get on your plane. Text or call me as soon as you land."

"You are busy. You've got do those new breakthrough patterns and save America. I don't want to interfere with your work. I'll be fine. We can talk next week sometime."

"Work is no problem today. Promise me you'll call or text when you land."

"Yeah. Whatever."

"Say you promise."

"Don't be a jerk."

"You don't be a jerk."

"Bye," I said.

"I care about you. Talk to you soon."

Perry later told me he wasn't sure if I hung up before or after he said that, but I heard it. I considered turning off and throwing away my Perry phone but for some reason I didn't. The way I kept discouraging him,

Perry must have felt it better to surprise me at the airport rather than letting me know he was already in town.

He drove down the 405 from Los Alamitos to the airport in heavy traffic. He thought it should take about 20 minutes, but it was more like an hour. My flight from Santa Barbara was faster than his drive. Knowing how he responded to traffic when he was driving me somewhere I'm sure he complained repeatedly out loud to himself about the traffic and wished he didn't have to drive in it. He would often say things like:

"Why aren't cars self-driving yet? They've been saying self-driving is just around the corner for years now."

When he saw other drivers looking at their phones or shaving or eating or doing anything but paying attention to the road, he would say, "Those people should not be drivers, and neither should I. Besides the safety issues we could use all this time for something productive."

When he finally got to the airport, he parked in the parking structure and hurried into the terminal to find a restroom. After that he found and checked the Arrivals board. There weren't any Santa Barbara flights on the board. He went to an information desk to ask about it.

"A friend said she was arriving on a flight from Santa Barbara at nine, but I don't see any flights from there. Are there flights that don't show?"

"Nope. There aren't a lot of flights from Santa Barbara. Maybe you got the wrong time or the wrong airport. Did she say what airline she was on?"

"No. She didn't say."

"Well, that's tough then. She isn't flying on a private plane, is she?"

"I don't know. Maybe."

"These terminals are only for commercial flights.

"Where do I find out about private flights?"

"No idea. They don't come through here."

"But they do come into this airport, right?"

"Yeah. I suppose. Let's look at a map." He pulled out and unfolded an area tourist map and after studying it for a few seconds pointed to a spot a few blocks from the main terminals. "I think some private plane people come through here, but I'm not sure if all of them do."

"Thank you. Can I take this map?"

"Sure. For twenty-five dollars."

"Really?"

He held out his hand palm raised, while Perry patted his pockets looking for his wallet, then smiled and said, "Just kidding. It's free. Good luck finding your friend."

Perry had a bit of trouble finding his rental car. He had forgotten to take a mental picture of where he parked. But he had the key fob. He walked down a couple of aisles in two different levels in the parking garage clicking on the lock and unlock buttons until he heard the car honk.

"I guess I have to remember to memorize things. Maybe it's just because I'm distracted today, worried about Mara," he thought.

He must have missed an exit sign in the garage because he ended up driving in circles inside the garage before finally finding the turn that took him down to the lower level to exit. When he left the airport, he followed his mental image of the map to a small parking lot a couple blocks away and parked. It was after nine and he didn't have any calls or messages from me. He found an entrance to a building that looked promising as a private flight terminal. A small sign over the door said, 'Private Flight Terminal.' "This must be the place," he thought. He found a young woman inside.

"Is there a flight from Santa Barbara?"

"I don't normally give out information about flights coming through here, but for you I'll check. I'll also give you my phone number if you'd like."

"No thanks. What about the flight?"

"Bummer. There was a *Zzynnarji* company flight from Santa Barabara a little while ago."

"That would be it. Mara works for the Zzynarji Foundation. Her name is Mara Strong."

"I don't see a Mara Strong on the manifest. I think the passengers already disembarked and left the airport."

"Do you know where she was going? An address?"

"If she is your friend, you must know her address. I don't have that name on the manifest, and we would not give out passenger address info even if we had it. But I might give you mine if you want."

"I've been to her house once, but she drove us, so I'm not sure of the address. It was on a bluff over the beach."

"Nice. Why don't you just call her?"

"I'm trying to surprise her."

"Good luck with that. Most people don't like surprise visits. Although I wouldn't mind. I get off at noon. If you don't find her come back and surprise me. Maybe we can both get off."

"She was supposed to call me, but she hasn't yet. Okay. I guess I will call her. Of course, I should just call her. Surprising her was probably a bad idea."

"It's none of my business, you know, but I think you may want to reconsider and back off the lady. Give her some breathing room. It sounds like she may not want to see you as much as you want to see her. Don't be so pushy with her. Now me on the other hand. I might not mind pushy."

"Maybe I was wrong to come here. Which way is it to the houses on bluffs over the beach?" Perry pulled out the tourist map.

"You can take the coast highway south, but you're not likely to find a specific house just by driving around. Even if you could, don't just show up unexpected. That's not cool. Give her a call. And back off if she says back off. And if so, you know where to find me."

"Sure. Yeah. Thanks."

Perry went back to the parking lot and found his rental car by clicking the key fob again. He sat in the car and checked his phone. He sent a message.

I heard the buzz of a text on my "Perry phone."

Perry:

Did you get to OC OK?

I considered turning off that phone or throwing it away and just going back to my old life. But I decided it would be better to tell him to stop bothering me rather than just cutting him off. I called him.

He answered, "Hi, Mara. How are you? Still feeling sick?"

"Yeah. A little. Stopped at a drugstore."

"Good to get something for it. I hope you feel better."

"You don't need to keep checking on me. Concentrate on your own work and let me do mine."

I was getting ready to tell him we needed to end this. I was sitting in a stall in a bathroom at a local pharmacy checking a pregnancy test.

"I wanted to surprise you at the airport, but I missed you. I'm in OC now."

"Oh Crap. Oh Crap."

"I'm sorry. That's not the response I was hoping for. If you really don't want to see me, I guess I can go back."

He probably thought about going back and meeting the young woman at the private flight terminal.

"Sorry. What did you say? I was distracted. Did you say you are here? How did you get here so fast?"

"Yeah. I told you I'd be here. I'm at the OC airport now. I wanted to catch you when you landed."

"Really? How? Never mind. Since you are here maybe we should meet."

"The beach house like before? What's the address?"

"No. Somewhere else." I thought about options and then said, "Let's meet at the farmhouse."

"Is that a restaurant?"

"Maybe, but that's not what I mean. I'll text you an address."

"Thanks. I think the rental car has a GPS. Oh. And I have a map."

"You didn't bring your real-time video satellite-hacking mapping machine?"

"Not today."

"I'll text you the address."

"Okay see you in a few minutes."

"Yeah. We've got some things to talk about."

"Okay. See you soon." By his tone I could tell he was concerned.

"Bye." I hung up. I wondered if it was a bad idea to meet him. Maybe I should just ghost him. I could send him a made-up address. Then again, maybe it was better to break up with him in person. Let him know that I mean it. And that would be more polite than just cutting him off. My dad always said I should be more polite. I needed to think about what I should do. Meanwhile, I hadn't begun to process the implications of the test result.

I had to think for a few seconds to remember the farmhouse address. I had seen it in one of the papers from the accounting firm about the Strong Trust assets and had been meaning to check it out. It seemed like a good out-of-the-way location for a private conversation. I brought up mental images of various documents from the trust attorneys and finally found it.

After I got back in my car, I sent Perry a message with the address, the actual address. I also sent a text to another number to let the groundskeeper know we would be coming. I had texted him once a few weeks before when I first learned about the place, and he had said I was welcome to come by anytime. This time he texted back to say he would be away today, but I was welcome to come any time. He gave me the codes for the front gate and a key box for the house.

Perry and I each looked up directions to the address. It was in a part of the county near some hills a few miles inland from the airport.

I memorized the directions, and the relevant parts of the map and Perry put the address into his rental car's navigation system. We both started to drive. Traffic close to the airport slowed Perry down. I was ahead of him. We crossed the flat plain of the county towards the hills on slightly different routes.

Seeing the flat lands covered in industrial buildings and housing tracts, I wondered how there could still be a farm or farmhouse in the county. Just then some open fields near the old Tustin blimp hangars came into view. It looked like there had been farmland here recently, but now it was crisscrossed with grading for new roadways and construction projects. Some vultures soared above the hangars. Was that an omen? I still had a few miles to go. I thought Perry must know this area having grown up in nearby Santa Ana and gone to college in Irvine.

As I got closer to the hills I found an area of older suburban houses with decent sized yards, not a cookie-cutter subdivision like most of the newer neighborhoods in the county. Some were custom homes; some were large tract homes but most of those had been or currently were being remodeled or enlarged. I passed at least three homes in various stages of remodeling projects as I got close to the address. Most, but not all, of the properties were well-maintained. The neighborhood was nice: a step or two below the neighborhoods I had lived in and probably a couple steps above anywhere Perry had lived.

12/06/2019, Late Morning, News at the Farmhouse

When I reached the address the property appeared to have a brick wall along the street on one side and large eucalyptus and other trees on the perimeter blocking views into the interior of the property. An asphalt driveway with a gate appeared in a gap between the trees. I turned in, entered the code to open the gate.

The driveway curved past what looked like multiple small orchards of different kinds of trees such as avocado and citrus. There also were some flower or vegetable gardens. It seemed like a pretty large lot, more than ten acres, and it seemed to be well-cared-for. A couple of barns with weathered wood walls stood near an old farmhouse with walls that looked like adobe.

I texted Perry the driveway gate code. When he drove in I was standing near the front door of the house. I waved and pointed to a place to park next to my car. I must have looked upset. He parked and quickly got out.

"Hi Mara. What's the matter?"

"Let's go inside. You never know who's watching outside."

I glanced upwards. With all the tall trees around the perimeter it seemed like a very private space other than what might be seen from the sky above, but we both knew that was a possibility.

I had already unlocked the front door of the small house. We went inside. It was not fancy. The few furnishings were old, but it seemed to be clean and tidy.

"This is less fancy than I expected."

"Apparently, it's an old family property. They called it Rancho del Fuerte, Or "Strong Ranch." I didn't know about it until just recently. I think there was a plan build a big house or subdivide it, but that hasn't happened yet. This is my first visit. I think this house is used by the groundskeeper, Sergey, when he's here. He's not here today. But I didn't bring you here to talk about the ranch." I pointed to a chair and couch. "Sit down here, Perry. We have to talk."

"Okay. What's the matter, Mara. I'm here for you. You still look beautiful by the way. Even more than before."

"Thanks. Whether you mean it or not."

"Of course I mean it."

"Okay. Just let me say some things."

He was quiet and waited.

"First, I want to say it was really nice when we were together before—the week in the mountains, and the times we were together since then were special and I'll always remember them—but it's time we go our separate ways."

"I don't agree with that."

"Let me finish. There are things you don't know."

"Okay. Tell me."

"Where to start?" I considered what to say:

> *"I'm not who you think I am."*
>
> *"I don't feel a spark when I'm with you."*
>
> *"I just don't want to spend time with you anymore."*
>
> *"We're not right for each other."*
>
> *"We are too different."*
>
> *"I don't have time for a relationship."*
>
> *"I've got other things I need to focus on."*
>
> *"It's not working out."*

Looking at his eyes looking back at me I changed course and decided to reveal the more immediate news. This was one of those pivotal moments in my life when I went against my better judgement, like when I decided to follow him on the trail.

I hoped this wasn't a big mistake, as I said, "Remember I told you I lost forty pounds on my hike."

"Yeah. That doesn't matter. If you gain that back and more you will still look great to me."

"It was really more like sixty, but quiet and let me finish."

"Okay. Sorry."

"I didn't mention that all that exercise and weight loss stopped my period for a while."

"Okay. I guess that happens sometimes."

"And now it's been a few months since I cut back all that exercise, and I've gained back twenty pounds or so and it still hasn't started again."

"Okay. It probably takes a while. You still look great."

"Let me finish. I've been getting sick every morning."

"Oh… kay…"

"And now this."

I pulled the pregnancy test wand out of my purse and handed it to him, showing the little plus sign and watched his eyes closely, seeing them widen and dilate. I played back in slow motion my photographic memory images of the micro-expressions on his face; maybe exaggerating them a bit. It showed a series of different emotions: surprise, fear, excitement, disbelief, anger, confusion, determination, uncertainty, giddy elation.

I added, "I'll be fine on my own, but I figured you should know."

"Oh wow. Oh wow. That's a surprise. How did that…? Oh, Yeah. This is a lot to process. A baby? But we just did it that one time and we were careful. I guess not careful enough. I guess one time is all it takes."

"It's only a drug store test. I still need to see a doctor to make sure."

"Yeah. I guess so."

I continued, "Anyway, I don't think we should see each other again. If this turns out to be real, I'll handle this just fine. I've got money and people to help me. You don't have to do anything. You should go back to DC and do your thing. I just thought you should know, since you were here today, I decided to tell you."

I was already regretting telling him.

"Wow. No. Wait. Okay. Okay. I think it is a little early to say this, but I'm going to say it anyway because I believe it in my heart. I love you, Mara."

"You're right. It is too soon to say that. Please don't be stupid."

"I've never felt like I do with you."

"No. Don't."

"Okay. Okay. How about this? I know you like plans. How about: Mara, I plan to do what it takes to get us to love each other."

"Don't be stupid."

"Okay. How about this: I know you will do everything in your power to welcome this baby into this world and use your considerable talents to make it the best world possible for her or him, or them. I want to be part of that in whatever way you are willing to let me."

I wasn't sure what I was going to do until he said it, but I realized that he was right. I was going to welcome the baby and do what I could to make the world better for it.

"Oh Perry. That's nice. I won't hold you to it. But it is a nice sentiment. I'll be fine. We still hardly know each other. Let's both take some time to think about it. Maybe I'll let you be involved, if you want, but we'll see what happens. I don't expect anything from you."

"Oh wow. Oh wow. A baby?"

"Yeah. Not what you were expecting."

"I guess he or she is, they are what we are expecting."

He stood and gathered me in his arms and held me tight. I shook my head and resisted his hug at first and then melted into his arms and hugged him back. When I looked up in his eyes, they were tearing up, as were mine.

"Emotional day. Huh?" I said.

"Yeah, Maybe I got something in my contacts."

12/06 to 12/13/2019, Getting Reacquainted

That was a Friday morning. We talked together for hours, and it felt like that week in the mountains, but with some different tensions. I had work obligations and charity events to go to that night and the next afternoon and evening, and Perry was supposed to check in at the local agency office. He spent that night at his dad's old machine shop in Santa Ana and went to the local agency office in Irvine the next day. Even though it was a Saturday he ended up working into the evening because colleagues there had so many questions for him, and he knew I was busy.

Actually, he had not known that there was an agency office so close to where he had lived and gone to school. He had to go to DC for all the interviews for the job. His new colleagues at the local office said that most of the agency's satellite offices were covert. No need to let people know what kind of work was going on here. To the public it was an office of a non-descript consulting firm. The building looked like others in a newer office park, but with better security and inconspicuous shielding from electronic snooping.

I went back to the beach house Friday late afternoon to get ready for the charity events. I stayed there Friday night and again Saturday night. I took care of some company work-related meetings in the afternoon from the beach house, and evening charity events at a museum. Perry and I checked in with each other by text a couple times and agreed to meet again at the farmhouse on Sunday morning.

Perry got back to the ranch early Sunday before I got there, and he explored the grounds. He ran into Sergey who gave him a tour. Perry was particularly interested in the large barn buildings. They were mostly empty other than some of Sergey's tools, but he could imagine a nice workshop in that space. Perry had been wondering if he would need to let go of the leased machine shop.

Sergey had been surprised when he got word that one of the owners was showing up again after all these years. He explained to Perry that he had been hired by a young couple more than 20 years ago to maintain the place. He later said I reminded him of the woman, Ami, my birth mom.

He thought they were considering either subdividing the land into a few dozen home lots or maybe building one very big house, but they asked him to take care of the property until then, and then they just didn't come back. He still got a monthly check from some accounting firm, even though no one had talked to him for a long time about the property. He paid for farm maintenance expenses, like a truck and other tools, fertilizers, water and electric bills, and other farm expenses from the monthly check and income he got selling avocados, fruit, and flowers in local farmers' markets. He ran the ranch well and came out ahead, so he never complained about the lack of raises in the monthly fee over the years.

Sergey seemed to feel a lot of pride in the way he had been maintaining things. It was like his own small farm. If he was upset that I had showed up to claim ownership again, he didn't show it.

As they walked back towards the farmhouse, Sergey made a point of saying to Perry that he had not been living on the ranch, just maintaining it. Perry was pretty sure Sergey had been living there but didn't challenge him.

Late that morning I drove to the ranch and came into the farmhouse with a large bag with boxes of gourmet food for lunch. Leftovers from the event at the museum the night before. We talked all afternoon. Sergey gave us space while he worked around the farm. All that weekend Perry and I had long conversations about many different things we would like to see changed in the world that the baby would grow up in. It was like a continuation of some of the intense conversation we had when we were hiking together and afterwards. Now there was a new focus of fixing things for a specific new generation, not just for the generic good of future generations.

Perry got the okay from Randy to work the next week at the Irvine office. He spent 10 to 12 hours there each day, more on the days when I had evening events. During the hours when Perry was at work, I took care of my own obligations. I would go to the beach house for a few hours to work or to organize upcoming events. Both Perry and I ended up staying at the farmhouse most nights that next week, except one night when I had an evening event that went very late when I went back to the beach house instead. After feeling bad about missing that one night, I ended up coming back to the farm after my charity events even if it was very late. Our nightly conversations went very late each night. When we finally called it a night, Perry took the couch. I was no longer sleeping on the ground, so I took the bed.

By midweek I got confirmation of the pregnancy from a doctor's office. I wouldn't let Perry go with me to the appointment. The doctor said it was probably about 2 months along, which made sense, since the only time we had sex was about two months ago.

We didn't have sex during the week in the mountains or elsewhere the first few weeks after the hike. It wasn't until the weekend in October at the beach house that it finally happened, and then just the once. I thought I still had amenorrhea from the over exercise, but we still took precautions. Apparently, something didn't work. I think we were both inexperienced. I was anyway.

In the mountains, even though I liked him, and we were alone together, we had just met and didn't have protection, so it was a big no. My period had stopped, so I considered it, but another big factor was I felt I was too dirty even with the sun shower and Perry's big clean tent, thick ground pad, and fluffy extra-large sleeping bag. Plus, it triggered memories of some of the teachings from the catholic schools I had attended as a girl, even though I didn't think they made much sense at the time. When Perry asked to go further, I said no, not yet, and he backed off without complaint.

I slept outside on the ground during that week rather than in his tent. Although we did snuggle in the tent for a while each evening. I said it counted as my meditation time, but when he started to ask to go further I would say no and go back outside. He was always immediately respectful of my no. I appreciated his respecting my wishes, but I also wondered what I would have done if he had acted a little more eager about it. I kept the bear spray close by but probably wouldn't have used it on him unless he got violent, since it might kill him. Maybe he was shy. Or maybe he was just a gentleman. Or maybe he wasn't really interested in me that way even though he said he was. My mixed feelings confused me.

The night in the lodge room after the hike I still said no even though Perry brought protection. I was just not clean enough, and I also didn't feel well after eating so much greasy food at the snack bar after weeks of a near starvation diet. I guessed he was probably inexperienced too and didn't want to rush things even though he said he was very attracted and hoping for more.

A few weeks later at the beach house things did go a lot further. We met for brunch at a restaurant on a Sunday morning and I drove him to the beach house afterwards. That evening, our conversations, a little wine, and the sound of the waves outside led us to a bedroom and when he asked if it was okay to keep going, I said yes. It was awkward and a little uncomfortable, but overall nice. No real fireworks but nice. I worried maybe he didn't like it. Later I learned he wondered the same about me. So, both of us had some misgivings about it. Afterwards I thought maybe it was a mistake, but it was good to give it a try.

Early Monday morning at the beach house he was woken by a message that his security clearance was approved, and he should be in DC as soon as possible for a final interview before starting his job. The agency had booked a commercial flight for him that afternoon. I also got some messages that morning. My brother Douglas was on his way to the beach house. I was surprised he was coming on a Monday, but apparently his boarding school high school had some days off around Columbus Day / Native Americans Day that year. I didn't want him to run into Perry, so I told Perry there were problems with my work I needed to deal with, and I hurried him out of the house. I drove him back to where he left his car near the restaurant and then went back to the beach house to meet my brother.

Perry's final interview was really just a welcome to the job and getting read in on the first set of data that he would be working with. He had to find an apartment, move, and start working, which took most of his time for a couple of weeks. He tried to see me when he flew back out to get his things, but I was out of town, and one more time when he came out after that, but one thing or another got in the way. It seemed to each of us that the other was trying to avoid repeating the intimacy. If I was honest with myself, I was avoiding it.

There was always a complication that got in the way. Either I had to go to a meeting, or he got a call from his new boss demanding an urgent briefing on his work or an urgent demand to analyze one of his modelling runs. I was starting to think maybe he didn't really like me that much, which was okay with me. I guess he was worrying the same about what I felt.

After a few weeks I was planning to end it with him. Each day I would look at the Perry phone and decide whether to turn it on, leave it off, or smash it with a hammer. Some days I turned it on, some days I left it off, but I never had a hammer handy. That went on until the day I found out I was pregnant. I would sometimes answer his calls or texts, but I never called his number before that day.

When I found out, I still planned to tell him it was over between us and not tell him about the pregnancy, but something made me change my mind. If he hadn't been in town the morning I found out, I probably just would have never told him about it and just dealt with it myself. I was morally and politically against abortion, but the medication option seemed less drastic and real than having something done in a clinic and it was what first came to mind when I saw the test result.

The phone number he knew for me was on a disposable phone I had purchased for anonymously arranging my hiking trip. I had been planning to destroy that phone after the trip but had kept it around for contact with him. All I had to do was destroy that phone and he would have no way of contacting me.

But for some reason I told him about the pregnancy. Then we talked so much during the week at the farmhouse, I decided to give him another chance. Early that week, I rearranged some foundation events and work meetings so that I could stay in town longer and see a doctor as well as spend some time with Perry, but at the end of the week I had to go out of town, for foundation work, I said. I hoped his sentiments about wanting to be involved and make things work were real and not just out of some sense of obligation. I was still not sure if I trusted my own feelings and was still considering cutting it all off and going back to my old life.

We spent quite a few hours together that week at the farmhouse, most of the time talking about how we would like the world to be better for the baby. We now had a new focus for why we wanted to change the world. We avoided sex during that week, but I really enjoyed the intimacy of our conversations.

12/13/2019 to 1/15/2020, Life at the Ranch

After that week at the farmhouse, Perry had to go back to DC, but we looked at my travel plans and he booked several short trips west over the next few months, to coincide with days when I could be in OC. We planned a few long weekends, plus extra days around New Year's, Martin Luther King Day, Valentine's Day, and President's Day. I decided I should spend Christmas with my brother up north.

I offered to help with his tickets, but he said it was worth it to him.

During the days we were together we still avoided sex, although we got close a couple of times. We spent a lot of time talking and working. The sharing of ideas was more intimate for us than sex, at least for me. We were starting to build a list of things we'd like to change in the world for the sake of the baby. I told him I could try to persuade the foundation to fund some of the ideas. Others were just pipe dreams.

On days we were together at the farmhouse we also had to work. I arranged to upgrade the internet service to the farmhouse to a high-speed commercial connection. I spent some time on the phone, or the computer, and he would work on his secure laptop or go into the office. His colleagues at the Irvine office asked for him to be reassigned there permanently, but Randy did not approve the move. On each trip Perry brought more of his belongings back from his apartment in DC, either to the farmhouse or to his little apartment at the machine shop.

After about a month he floated an idea to me.

"I was thinking. There is a lot of room here in the barns. Maybe I could move my workshop, some of my dad's machines, to one of the barns. I could stop paying rent on the building in Santa Ana and have more money for my flights. I could fly here more often."

"I told you I can pay for those tickets."

"No. I want to, but then again, in a way you would be paying for them if you let me move the workshop. And then I would be able to use the machines more if they're right here. I could make some things for the house."

"Is Sergey okay with the idea? That's been his space."

"He suggested it. We could make things for the ranch too."

I thought about it. Letting him keep some clothes or personal items here was one thing but moving heavy machinery to the ranch that sounded more like a commitment. What the heck, I thought. If I get fed up with him, I could still go back to my other life and as long as he doesn't know me as Marta, he probably wouldn't be able to find me. I might lose use of this ranch and farmhouse but that would be small in the scheme of things. He was looking at me waiting for an answer.

"Then make it so…"

Sergey and Perry took the ranch's truck and made multiple trips moving some of the machines to the larger of the two barns. It was sad for Perry to think about giving up his dad's half-empty workshop. When the time came, he could not make himself get rid of the rest of the machines and turn in the keys. He ended up extending the lease and keeping the address. He would figure out the money later.

The pregnancy was proceeding without problems. I did my rounds in other cities for the foundation and the company without inviting Perry along. I still avoided letting Perry meet any of my colleagues or other friends. He was really busy too, so it wasn't all on my end.

One evening we were together in the farmhouse, and he confronted me on the question of meeting my friends or going with me to one of my events.

"It's like you are trying to live two separate lives and don't want me to meet them or them to meet me."

"You think so?"

"It's like parallel universes we've talked about. It's like you are trying to live in two different parallel universes. Are you embarrassed about me? I might not make a good impression with your celebrity or billionaire friends. What's up with you and your other life?"

"It's just the way things have worked out. Don't worry. Those people are not that interesting."

"Yeah. By comparison I'm just a regular guy who happens to be planning to get us to fall in love."

"How is that plan going by the way?" I moved closer to him.

"Not bad. I'm working on it. Making some progress."

"Okay. Let me help you work on that plan of yours tonight."

He let the topic drop, for one night. There were a few fireworks that night. Not a Fourth of July extravaganza with a massive grand finale, but pleasant, safe and sane driveway fireworks. Something worth repeating. Maybe.

January and February 2020, Perry's Work

Around that time his own work was really getting intense. Things were moving fast at work. He wasn't supposed to talk with me about it, but he did anyway. At least giving hints and talking about hypotheticals. But it was pretty obvious what he meant.

There had been some secret pinpoint strikes, some financial and some physical, on bad guys in other countries based on some of the analysis that he had done, which were not in the news. He didn't explain the strikes to me. He said he didn't know the details. But he did try to explain the math of his emergent hive intelligence models.

He loved the fact that I seemed to understand the math when he explained it. He said my questions gave him ideas for tuning the models. He said I understood it better than any of the people at the agency. Maybe in some ways better than himself.

When he explained the analysis models to his boss, Randy seemed to follow some of what he said, and his coworkers always had questions for him, but somehow didn't seem to get it. The higher-ups didn't care about the model. They just wanted the results. Through Randy, they asked him to use the model to explain how COVID got started and to prove that the Chinese had released it intentionally. Perry had to explain many times that his models didn't work that way, at least not with the data he had. They could show convergence points of questionable behavior by people who also happened to be involved in researching COVID, but it didn't prove anything.

His analysis looked for patterns of hive intelligence to make sense of data about many seemingly unrelated activities. Convergence points in the data pointed back to people or organizations that were influencing major events. This allowed other intelligence methods to focus there and verify targets or find specific actions that could be taken. Among other things, the convergence points highlighted physical and cyber locations where suspicious foreign groups were active. They also pointed out various people who influenced the overall negative behavior. This included a number of domestic politicians, media, and businesses who showed up as convergence points in the hive of interactions that contributed to destruction and violence.

Generally, the domestic points were not investigated by the agency because they had known roles in politics or government that could explain their impacts. Plus, they were Americans. There was some pressure to find and investigate bad actions by people who the current administration considered opponents, but generally the agency didn't do that. The convergence points were not necessarily doing anything intentionally conspiratorial. Additional investigation was needed to prove that. But the model showed where actions existed that contributed to eventual negativity or violence. The higher up people were very interested in his work since some of the convergence points it identified did turn out to be revealed as active terrorists or foreign agents that were previously unknown. Perry's technique seemed to be producing different results than other methods of investigation and analysis.

The modeling techniques were based on the idea of hive intelligence. Emergent patterns of behavior in the macro sense could be interpreted as a higher-level emergent intelligence that cannot be pinned down to any specific person. Individuals are more like bees or ants in the model. Looking for patterns that supported a destructive hive intelligence could find clusters of behavior that were like organs in a larger entity contributing to the bigger pattern. Those in turn could be broken down into smaller clusters and eventually down to individual behaviors of individuals. Strategically eliminating specific bees or sanctioning their actions did have some effect, but Perry's model revealed at a high level a malevolent emergent intelligence that seemed to be motivated to produce chaos and violence and provide subtle influences and reinforce negative messages and promote actions that were in line with its destructive goals.

I reminded him that any descriptive model is likely to find what it is designed to look for, and this evil ghost intelligence might be more an artifact of his model than of anything real. Also, even if the analysis did lead to taking out a set of bad guys, while satisfying to the powers above him, that might not have a positive overall effect, in fact, it might be contributing to the goals of the negative hive intelligence.

Following up on that idea, he reanalyzed after actions were taken to deal with bad actors, and he said I was right that the strikes themselves often showed up as convergence points of the negative macro intelligence. Perry and I talked about whether some new approach would be needed to influence things towards positive results. I suggested he change the model to look for evidence of a positive hive intelligence acting at odds with the negative one or figure out how to build a positive emergent intelligence. He said he would think about it.

02/14/2020, Valentine's Day

Weeks went by. On Valentines Day I gave him a card with pictures from an ultrasound I had gotten the day before. I had avoided learning the baby's sex so far. But everything was going well. I was starting to show, but I was still able to hide it if I wanted. At the ranch house I flaunted it, wearing halter tops with a bare midriff showing off my little bump.

I also had a surprise for him.

"You know it's a little tight in this farmhouse and it will be even tighter pretty soon."

"We're moving to your beach house? I'm ready. Let's go. Is there room for my workshop there?"

"No. The foundation has events there pretty often. It's more of a party house. I don't think it would be a good place for a baby."

"I've told you. I wouldn't mind going to your parties."

"Yeah, of course. I know. Still not a good idea. No."

"I know, no means no. But I sense you've got a better idea."

"Yes. Do you recognize this house?" I showed him a real estate flyer for a well-maintained, typical upper middle class suburban one-story ranch style tract house with a four-car garage, probably built in the 60's or 70's.

"Let me see. I don't recognize that specific house, but it looks similar to some of the houses in the neighborhood around here. Is it near here?"

"Yes. It backs up to the farm property not far from the barn with your workshop. Over that way." I pointed. "We can put in a gate or a path in back so you can get to the workshop from there."

"That could be nice. When can we see it? And can we afford it? I don't have a lot saved up, and I'd like to pay half. If we're going to buy something."

"Actually, I, or my family trust, already bought it."

"That was fast. Didn't want to look at it first?"

"I did. It's good. It has enough room. It's dated, and could use some upgrades, but it is clean and usable as is. And it's got room to expand. We might not find another opportunity so close like this anytime soon. I didn't want to let it get away. The escrow should close in a couple weeks, but it's empty and we can start using it right away. I paid rent until the escrow closes."

"Okay. Then I guess it is settled. It works for me. Let me know what I owe you. And, as a bonus, Sergey will be happy. Even though he said he didn't, I'm pretty sure he was living in this house before. He has a lot of his things stored in the loft in one of the barns. And I think I saw him one time when I drove past a homeless camp by the river. We should let him use this house again."

02/15 to 03/13/2020, Moving into the Ranch House

The next few weeks Perry tried to spend more time in town. He worked with Sergey on the plans to add a gate and some steps from the new house down the hill to the farm. Sergey got it done fast. We picked some new paint colors and flooring as well as all new appliances for the house. Sergey met with the contractors and got things done while Perry was in DC and I was traveling.

Since Sergey was doing more work for me and didn't have as much time for taking produce to farmers markets, I decided to raise his pay. I arranged a cost-of-living adjustment in his payments from the trust. Making it retroactive gave him a big one-time bonus.

When Perry asked Sergey what he'd do with the extra money he said he was moving his mom to a better assisted living long-term care facility. The one she had been in was farther away and not as nice. He was worried about the new virus that was affecting some convalescent homes and wanted her in a good one. Now she would be better cared for, and he would be able to visit her more often. She moved just in time before the state locked down all the nursing homes to protect them from COVID, and Sergey wasn't able to visit his mom for a while, except through a window.

I wanted to keep things simple and minimalist in the new house, so we started with just a few furnishings. When the new house was ready, we didn't have much to move. We had been living out of suitcases most of the time recently anyway. Sergey moved (back) into the adobe farmhouse. Perry started to think of ways to make more improvements to the house and the ranch. I told him to not to get carried away. One thing he did right away was extending the business-grade high-speed internet line from the farmhouse into the new house.

I let Perry attend my next ultrasound. I was about 22 weeks. Everything was still going fine. That's when we found out it was a boy.

3/15/2020, Mara, Marta

The COVID pandemic was now a thing. People were being asked to stay home unless their jobs were essential. We were both at the new house which we referred to as the ranch house to distinguish it from the old adobe farmhouse. Perry's work for the government was considered essential, and I was rich so everything I did was essential, but to be safe we figured we might stay at the ranch house a few days until this COVID thing blew over.

Up until then I had continued taking trips, telling Perry it was to deal with foundation charity job duties. Typically, when I went out of town, I would stop by the beach house first and change clothes and put on a wig that matched the length and look of my hair from before the hike. I chose clothes that helped hide my growing belly bump, but even with my weight inching closer to what it had been before, it was getting harder to hide.

Perry had nudged me repeatedly about keeping him out of my other life and, finally, after seeing the ultrasound together and being stuck together for the next few days during the pandemic lockdown I decided to tell him more. It was a big deal for me because once he knew about me being Marta I wouldn't be able to get him to unknow that.

He was sitting at the table near the kitchen, and I sat in the other chair and said, "There are some things you should know."

"You're not pregnant, are you? Wait, you already told me about that."

"Ha ha."

"Maybe something about why you don't want me to meet your friends and co-workers?"

"Yeah. Maybe something about that."

"Finally. Do tell."

"I told you my parents died from the flu. That's not the whole story. It's kind of complicated so this might take a while."

"I thought it was odd that a well-off couple could both die from the flu nowadays."

"Yeah. They did come down with a pretty bad case of some bug a year ago. They never found out exactly what. It probably wasn't' COVID-19 because that wasn't a thing yet. They were out of the country when they got sick, and when they went to a local clinic to see if they could get an antiviral, they caught a drug-resistant infection at the clinic. My mom died pretty fast from the secondary infection. They got medevacked back to the US, but her infection moved really fast. My dad started getting better from the virus and the other infections, but he always had trouble with depression. He refused to get any treatment for it, so life with him had been scary on and off for a long time. He had come close to suicide a few times. Anyway, he gave up when my mom died, and he took an overdose of elephant tranquilizers that he brought back from overseas."

"I'm sorry. I can't imagine what you went through."

"The public story was they both died of a drug-resistant infection. It didn't mention the suicide."

"Oh. So now I remember news about that. Your parents didn't just work for Zzynarji. Your mom was Sandra Zynn?"

"My adopted mom, yeah."

"Your parents were the Zynn's, like the owners of Zzynarji?"

"Sort of."

"Why couldn't you just tell me that? That's not complicated. I knew you were rich; What would a few extra tens or hundreds of billion dollars matter? You really thought it would matter to me? Or are you really just embarrassed by me?"

"Well, it's complicated."

The look on his face implied the 'embarrassed by me' explanation was starting to make the most sense to him. I wasn't sure he was wrong.

"Okay, so Mara Strong is not your real name either? Mara Zynn?"

"No. I'm Mara Strong. But I'm also Marta, Marta Zynn."

"I'm confused."

"Yeah. So am I. It's complicated. I'm still trying to figure some of it out myself. I'll try to explain what I know."

I explained that soon after my parents died one of their attorneys gave me access to a number of safe deposit boxes with my mom's private records. One had a foreign birth certificate and an old passport for baby Mara, daughter of Ami Narji and Ben Strong. Apparently, Mara was born while Ami and Ben were in Malaysia, and they got her Malaysian and US passports.

It wasn't clear why they were there, but maybe Ami Narji's family was from there. The passport records for Mara showed her birthday as March 4, 1997. I had always thought my birthday with April 3rd. There was also an envelope with some adoption paperwork that showed the name of Marta Zynn and said "unknown" for birth parents.

The records for the adoption showed my birthday as April 3. I wasn't sure if that was just a sloppy mistake transposing month and day or for some intentional reason. 03 / 04 versus 04 / 03. In an envelope was a note from someone named Alex saying he had found this in a box of stuff Ben had sent to him from overseas to store and said he was sorry to not send it to them sooner. Inside was a photo of a black man and pregnant South Asian woman labeled on the back "Ben and Ami with baby Mara". There was also a social security card for baby Mara Strong with a different number than mine as Marta.

"Okay. You're right. That is getting complicated. Maybe you had a different name and social security number when you were born. I guess that could happen. People sometimes pick new names when they adopt babies, and I supposed mistakes can happen with birthdates, but why are you using that name with me?"

"It gets even more complicated. But let me try to answer that question first."

"More complicated? Yeah. Okay. You were saying…"

"I'm not completely sure why I did it. I was already really stressed and depressed even before they died. My mom and dad wanted me to take on a big role in the family charity foundation since I didn't find a job I liked in their company. They were committed to eventually giving their fortune to charity, so their foundation was important to them, and they wanted me to run it until they got ready to retire. I wasn't sure I wanted to do that job either.

"But my parents died suddenly, and I had to take on responsibility for their company too. Then I found out that I had a second name and identity; it seemed like an opportunity to try to get away from the stress of being their daughter and all the politics that was swirling around their company and their money and try to be someone else for a while. Other people could run the company and the foundation just fine without my help. The executives would prefer to run it themselves anyway.

"Anyway, I decided to take a month to get ready and then disappear for two or three months of solitude to try to sort things out in my head. I tried to be as anonymous as possible when I made the arrangements for my trip, but when I had to use a name, I used Mara Strong instead of Marta Zynn. I figured I would just go back to being Marta when I was done, but I met you and I was Mara Strong with you."

"Okay. I think I follow."

"I wasn't sure why my parents didn't tell me about it before. Why wouldn't they just tell me what they knew about my birth parents? It didn't make sense. There must be something else going on. And then, also, I liked having a secret identity. You knew me as Mara, so if we socialized with people at my work, my old friends, or my parent's friends that might spoil the secret, so I found excuses. We went to places where people didn't know me, and that one time to the beach house when no one else was around and the housekeeping staff was off work, but I was afraid someone would catch us there and call me Marta, so we didn't go back."

"You could have just told me. It's been months now. I'm used to calling you Mara, but I could have adapted. I don't get it. I can start calling you Marta. How are you, Marta? Nice to meet you, Marta. See."

"No. Yeah. Probably. Well. I said it gets more complicated."

"More? So, do you have a fiancé or another boyfriend or girlfriend or both that you don't want me to meet."

"Sure. All of the above. No. Actually nothing like that."

I moved my chair closer to his and squeezed his hand which was gripping the arm of his chair.

"There were more things that didn't seem to make sense, and I didn't want to open up a can of worms. I should have been honest with you from the beginning, but I didn't know you as well back then. I had kind of made up my mind to break it off with you and just go back to being Marta, before I found out about this."

I gently rubbed my bare belly with its small bump.

"I'm glad I didn't break it off. Now I'd like your help to figure this out. Until we do, though, I'd still like to keep my Mara life apart from my Marta life. Maybe I'm just being paranoid. But can you humor me?"

"Sure. I don't understand, but I am intrigued."

I explained more of what I had done so far and what I had found in my research about my birth parents Ami Narji and Ben Strong.

"It was easier than I thought to open bank accounts and get credit cards with the Mara name and social, and to get a second driver's license. I didn't think an expired passport from when I was an infant was going to fly. But with help from an attorney who charges a lot, I was able to get an updated passport and driver's license in the name of Mara Strong. I didn't even need to go to the DMV. It was easy but pretty expensive."

"I'd hate to think what pretty expensive means to you. But you managed to avoid the lines at the DMV, so maybe it was worth a few million."

"Yeah. It was. This was all before we met on that hike. I had an ID then that said I was Mara Strong. As far as I can tell it's real."

"Okay I can see you had some thrill from creating a second identity, which is probably illegal, by the way, so admitting to that might be one complication for you."

"Yeah. There's that. But that's not the main thing. I'll get to that. Let me catch you up a little more first."

"Okay. Okay. Go on. Please go on."

"I used some of the contacts in my mom's records to find the accounting firm who did bookkeeping and taxes for the Strong Family Trust, and when I showed my ID as Mara Strong, they were able to provide me a list of accounts and properties owned by the trust. That's where I found out about Rancho del Fuerte."

After a couple hours of back and forth, Perry said. "Okay. This is exhausting. Let me summarize the history I think you have laid out. Ami Narji and Ben Strong started the Zzynarji company along with their college friends, Sandra Zynn and Carlos Anderson. The women were the technical brains, and each had 30% stakes in the company, and the men each a 15% stake for their design and finance expertise. Ami got an extra 10% because she and her family had contributed a lot more cash to get the company started.

"They named the company after the two women's last names, Zynn and Narji. Zzynarji. No explanation why they added an extra Z and fewer N's. Later Ami married Ben and Sandra married Carlos. And I guess Carlos took Zynn as his last name. That gave Ami and Ben a combined 55% of the company and Sandra and Carlos 45%, but they ran it together.

"The company was becoming successful and making money when Ami and Ben set up a trust and bought the Strong Ranch, *Rancho del Fuerte*, before they moved to Malaysia for a while, where Mara was born. They were reported to have all died in a small plane crash, but later it turned out Mara was in some kind of daycare that day. The reports that the baby also died in the crash were apparently not true."

He looked at me for confirmation. I nodded and then he continued.

"Sandra and Carlos found Mara in an orphanage and brought her back to the US as her god parents and guardians. They eventually adopted her and changed her name to Marta Zynn. The Zzynarji company continued to grow even faster under Sandra's brilliant and cut-throat leadership into a multi-billion-dollar business. Meanwhile the Strong-Narji Trust had successor trustee terms that were a little ambiguous but allowed Sandra and Carlos to manage those assets at least until after Mara/Marta turned 18 and was ready to take over the role.

"They apparently focused on the company and ignored other Strong Trust assets like the ranch and some other properties. Marta—you— turned 18 about three years ago, and your Zynn mom and dad didn't mention the Strong Trust to you. Maybe they thought you were not yet competent or ready to manage the assets? Anyway, technically, you may have been the majority owner of their company for three years without even knowing it. And now, after their deaths, you are the sole owner of the company, or you as Marta own 45% and you as Mara own 55%. And you as Mara did some kind of power of attorney to let Marta Zynn manage both parts for now."

He looked at me for acknowledgement. I nodded again, and he continued.

"But it sounds like you have some concerns about the ambiguities in the trust, why your parents kept it from you, whether you really are Mara or just a similar-looking kid from an orphanage, and maybe whether someone may try to declare you incompetent. Does that sum it up?"

"What's all this about incompetence. I don't think I ever said that. You think I'm not competent?"

"No. No. No. I was just interpreting and paraphrasing what you said. Maybe I should have chosen different words. I'm not concerned about that. I don't know, maybe someone would say multiple personality disorder would be an issue."

"Ha Ha! Don't say that. And I'm not sole owner. The Zynn part is tied up in the Zynn family trust. The Zynn Foundation already controls part and eventually gets most of it. And I didn't mention I have a younger brother, biologically a stepbrother, I guess, Douglas, who is also a beneficiary of the Zynn Family Trust. He can have a say in the company when he turns 18 in a couple years."

"A brother? The ghost Navy SEAL from the hike is real? I thought you made him up. And I thought you called him Chuck."

"No. Douglas is not Chuck. The SEAL part I made up to scare you into behaving, and obviously Douglas wasn't on the hike, but I do have a brother. He's very independent for a kid. He lives in Palo Alto most of the time. He goes to a boarding high school near there but spends a lot of time at our house. I usually see him when I go up there. I guess technically I am his guardian until he turns 18. We almost ran into him when we were at the beach house that one time. He texted me to say he was showing up that morning. That's why I got you out of there so quickly."

"I thought that was because I got called to start work. Did you have something to do with that too?"

"No. That part was a coincidence."

"Does Doug know about Mara, and me, and the baby?"

"Douglas. Not Doug. He doesn't like anyone to call him Doug. About Mara? Not yet. And I'd like you to help me keep it secret-from him and everyone else a little longer until I understand better why my parents didn't tell me all this before."

"How is he coping with your parents' deaths?"

"I'm not sure. He acts like it doesn't affect him. Makes jokes about being happy to be free, out from under their thumbs. But I don't know. We're not super close. We are six years apart, so we always had different interests. He has his own friends. Sometimes he'd say he's their only real kid, since he knows I'm adopted and he's not. But most of the time he's okay. He's a little brother."

"Siblings can be jerks. Some time I'll tell you more about my sister. In any case, you are probably going to have to tell everyone about some of this pretty soon."

He brushed his hand over my belly and tapped very gently.

"Some things are going to be hard to keep secret. Plus, I really don't think any of this is going to be a problem when it all comes out. It's better to be honest with everyone. And you can afford attorneys to make it all good."

I looked at him with one of my looks and said, "No."

"But…I'm willing to humor you and keep calling you Mara and stay out of sight of your rich friends …for now."

"I'd feel better if we did. For a while. Thanks."

"We'll figure this stuff out. Meanwhile, maybe you can find a way to let a PhD data scientist from UCI visit Marta at her beach house? And go to one of those celebrity-filled charity parties?? That is a really nice beach house. We could come up with a reason for Marta to meet Perry."

I considered it for a few seconds and said, "We'll see. Not right away."

Spring 2020, Marta's Charity

In the following weeks Perry and I spent more time together during the pandemic lockdown. We each spent time on our jobs, but also speculating about why my parents had hidden things from me, and in general getting to know each other more.

As Marta, I used phone and email to stay involved with the foundation and the company. Most in-person obligations were cancelled or done virtually during the first few months of the pandemic.

Soon the foundation started to use Zoom video conferencing, and the company installed secure video conferencing equipment at all the Zynn family beach houses for my meetings with Carl and other company executives. When I had to, I could do phone calls and foundation zoom meetings from the ranch house, but sometimes I had to go to the Corona del Mar beach house for company video meetings. I opted for audio only as much as I could for both kinds of meetings.

Since Marta was technically the guardian for my brother Douglas while he was still under 18, it would have probably made more sense for Marta to move back home and be in a COVID bubble with him during the pandemic lockdown rather than leaving him unsupervised. But I didn't want him to see me pregnant, and I worried he might bring COVID home, since he was not big on following rules. I did call him a few times each week. In June he got sick with mild COVID symptoms. He lost his sense of smell for a few weeks and had a bad cough, but he said he never got really sick. He refused to get tested, but I'm sure he had COVID.

I had the HVAC on the beach house and the house by the ranch both upgraded with hospital grade filtration. I started wearing N95 masks whenever I had to leave the house and made Perry wear them whenever he went to the office and for a few days after he came back. Over time I started to show more, but it was easy to cover it up during video meetings by a combination of camera placement and the clothing I chose to wear.

Given that almost everyone was working virtual I never got flack for being less visible at work. Carl was grateful for the extra power I had given him, but he and other executives in the company and the staff and other directors in the foundation still considered me a neophyte. They needed my approval for some decisions, and they generally followed my orders when I gave them, but they preferred when they could run things without my input.

I let Perry give me input on some of the decisions I had to make for the company and the foundation. The foundation funded other companies to increase manufacturing of ventilators, surgical and N95 masks, and UV lights for disinfecting interior spaces. I got Zzynarji to invest in a couple of drug research startups to work on vaccines and treatments for COVID and other potential new diseases.

I also had the Zzynarji company redirect some of their business to help with some of the shortages during the pandemic. They started making personal protective equipment for healthcare workers. They already made small quantities of extreme protective equipment for use in clean-room satellite manufacturing, and lab or manufacturing areas that involved toxics, as well as some space gear. They were able to make larger quantities of those, as well as simplifying them to be more affordable for merely protecting against an airborne respiratory pathogen. The foundation bought most of the extra PPE the company manufactured and donated it to hospitals.

Zzynarji had technology for making super-cooled liquids, which they adapted to make ultra-cooling freezers for some of the vaccines that were expected to need to be kept ultra-cold. They also started a new ventilator factory and made a few hundred ventilators, but other manufacturers were able to fill that need at lower cost, and they didn't scale up for making larger numbers. The foundation bought and donated what was built and the company saved the designs so that they could ramp production back up and make more if needed.

Their materials division developed coatings that made surfaces resistant to all viruses, while being safe for human touch and food preparation. They provided a few prototypes to some restaurants, hospitals, and for use in seating and handholds in public transportation vehicles, but the cost of manufacturing them made them impractical. They worked on a lower cost spray-on anti-viral coating that could be added to any hard surface, but it didn't have a big impact. When it was learned that the corona virus primarily spread through the air and not through surfaces the demand for the coatings didn't grow like they expected.

In addition to the PPE, they had technology from their satellite and space divisions for sanitizing objects and spaces. They had UV light and other wave-length EMF systems that could be adapted for sanitizing hospital rooms and other spaces, but their versions were too expensive to be widely used.

The company lost money on many of these COVID-related projects but also got a windfall from COVID relief funding. The paycheck protection program was aimed at small businesses that kept paying their employees during the pandemic, but Zzynarji's attorneys were able to make it apply to many small parts of the big company.

Overall, the pandemic led to a faster shift of the Zzynarji company from a profit-making enterprise to one that focused a larger portion of its energies on charitable efforts. This was formalized in a transfer of ownership of certain divisions of the company to the Zynn Foundation.

Spring 2020, Perry's Work and Hobbies

Perry was putting in a lot of time on his job as well. He was still going into the office because his work was considered essential and he was not allowed to access some of the agency data from outside the office. He could do some work from home on his secure laptop, but he needed to go into the local office or to DC to run some of his analysis models.

He used the local office as much as he could, but still made a few transcontinental flights, sometimes on nearly empty commercial flights and sometimes on government planes. He was pretty sure his analysis led to more targeted actions. He had mixed feelings about that. Bad people may have been stopped, but he was getting more skeptical about the big picture effectiveness of the strikes.

We bounced around ideas about alternative approaches to changing the growing negativity or destructiveness of the world's negative hive intelligence. When he floated some of the ideas to Randy at work, Randy listened but told him to concentrate on the analysis and let others decide on policies. Their agency focused on analysis. They passed the results to other agencies or other parts of the government that took actions.

Besides work, Perry was dabbling in making furniture in his workshop when he was in town, but he also started another hobby. I didn't know it at the time, but on flights when he couldn't work on agency work or building things Perry started documenting the stories about my hike that I had shared with him during our week in the mountains. He wanted to capture what I had said about my minimalism philosophy and the adventures I went through during the first eight weeks of my hike. He had memorized every word I said to him about it and was typing it up, with some embellishments of his own.

In his retelling I was even more self-reliant than in my own telling. And I exaggerated some points myself. He wrote that I made do without resupply drops and ate completely off the land. I didn't have any high-tech equipment. He illustrated it with cartoon-like pictures. The only photos he had of me were from the satellite images during the hike, which were a little fuzzy, so he edited them to make stylized cartoons of me without showing a clear view of my face to illustrate the story. In the story he referred to me as Min Strong instead of Mara Strong.

June 2020, More Secrets

We continued to look for more answers for why my parents had kept things from me. One theory was they had tried to take permanent full control of the company based on the ambiguities of the Strong Narji Trust and intended not to let me ever know about my rights. That wouldn't necessarily be out of selfish motives; it's possible they thought they were looking out for my interests by keeping control of things. Another thought was that since the value of the company had skyrocketed after Ami and Ben died there was an argument that the share of the company owned by the Strong Trust might be negligible and therefore it was not relevant. Not being lawyers we weren't sure how that worked, and we didn't want to ask one.

We wondered if they were concerned that there were other Narjis or Strongs who might make a claim on part of the company if I reached out to them to find out about my birth parents. Or maybe they had other reasons to keep me unaware of them. We tracked down some distant relatives in both the Narji and Strong families but didn't reach out to them out of concern about my parents' reasoning. Maybe there were good reasons my parents and some lawyers were the only ones who knew about the trust and that Mara Strong was still alive.

We couldn't find anything to prove my parents had intentionally changed my birthdate, but also, they apparently never tried to correct it. It looked like they may not have known that Ami and Ben had already applied for a social security number for Mara when they got one for Marta, but they never resolved that duplication.

Perry and I could see a resemblance in myself to pictures of Ami and Ben, so we were pretty sure I was their Mara and not just a kid of about the same age with similar coloring whom Sandra and Carlos found to replace her. We considered doing some kind of DNA analysis but didn't know where to get samples for Ami and Ben and wanted to hold off on contacting their relatives.

Perry still said, "Maybe your parents hid some things, or were sloppy, and maybe they were trying to take advantage of mistakes to get the best result for themselves but just tell everyone what you know and let the chips fall where they may. It will be fine. It's not like you are going to be poor afterwards."

But I was still nervous. And the longer we hid Perry and the pregnancy from my Marta acquaintances the easier it was to continue hiding. The pandemic made hiding easy.

It had been a few months by then and we didn't hear of any new issues about the ownership of the company or the trusts. As Marta, I was in charge, although I had to assert my authority from time to time with the executives. Carl humored me because he owed his power to me, but I could tell even he really didn't want my input.

It would be another couple of years before Douglas would come of age and there could be some issues when he found out he owned less than 25 percent of Zzynarji rather than 50%, but so far he seemed to be happy getting a generous allowance and having use of a couple of houses in Palo Alto and Santa Cruz mostly to himself while he did high school virtually during the pandemic. From background sounds in some of my phone calls with him, I got the impression he was not socially-distancing but was having friends over to party with him at the houses.

7/13/2020, Baby Boy

My baby boy was born to Mara, not to Marta. We had a COVID-tested midwife, wearing hospital-grade masks and other PPE come to the house for the birth with a lot of disinfecting afterwards. We planned to have live-in nannies to help afterwards. We got a couple of self-contained tiny houses installed in the farm for the nannies. We had two different nannies isolate in the tiny houses before the baby was due and had them both tested for COVID multiple times during their isolation so that we could be sure they weren't carrying COVID before joining our bubble. We were going to have them trade off, but when I explained that they needed to stay on site even on their days off one of them backed out, saying she had her own family she needed to spend time with on her days off. We ended up with Maricela staying on site with us seven by twenty-four for almost a year. Sergey offered to help out from time to time so Maricela could take more days off in her tiny house, but I was nervous he also might not be social distancing enough. We did give her some hours off when we were not super busy with work. That didn't happen often. Perry used the other tiny house a couple of times to quarantine when he had symptoms after flying back from DC.

Since the baby was born to Mara, daughter of Ami Narji Strong, I decided to find a name related to Ami's south Asian heritage. It seemed like her family had connections in India as well as Malaysia and Indonesia. I looked up possible baby names and found one that seemed to have a connotation of strength, or "Strong" like my birth dad's last name. I wasn't sure if it really fit and didn't ask anyone who would know, but I also liked the sound of it. Balaji. Perry immediately started calling the baby Billy Jay, which I didn't like, but tolerated and eventually got used to. We went around in circles about the last name to give the baby. Mine or Perry's or make one up. Finally, I put his name as Balaji Lee with mother Mara and left the father's name blank on the birth certificate.

To stay more private, I asked Perry not to put Balaji on his insurance at work. I could cover any medical costs. Perry had a hard time not telling his coworkers about his family. He didn't socialize with people from work much, but people did ask about his life outside of work from time to time.

Most of the time he wanted to get home as soon as he could to spend time with his Billy Jay and me so there wasn't a lot of time for socializing. He also had some friends from growing up and from college that still lived in the area. He got together with some of them from time to time on his own while keeping good social distance and was careful not to say anything to them about me or Balaji. During the first year or so of COVID I didn't go out of the house with Balaji other than in the back yard and down the path into the farm.

I had a trust created for the benefit of Balaji and arranged it so that ownership of the ranch house was under that trust, with trusteeship through attorneys and shell companies that eventually came back to my control.

9/13/20 to 11/15/20, Still Marta

After a couple months I had lost enough of my pregnancy weight that I could have resurfaced as Marta, but it was easy to stay isolated due to COVID, and I was comfortable the way things were. I was in no hurry to start traveling again. I continued communicating remotely with the foundation, the company, and occasionally my brother. He seemed to be high a lot of the time, but as he started his senior year his grades were still pretty good. I got on his case to keep them high while he applied to colleges. With the family connections and donations at Stanford I thought he could get in there, but only if he kept up his grades.

2020, Life at the Ranch House

Perry and I made some acquaintances with neighbors, but mostly we stayed home with Balaji. When we left the house, we routinely wore masks, both for the health protection and to avoid having my face visible where it might be recognized as Marta Zynn. We had food delivered from restaurants in the area but also did some cooking with easy prep meals from local stores or meal services.

Perry pushed on Randy to find technical solutions for securely allowing more work from home or at least from the Irvine office. Randy resisted, but eventually someone above him in the agency, in a nod to COVID social distancing accommodations, authorized a secure line to Perry's permanent address at his dad's machine shop, where he could do some work. But Randy still made him travel to DC a few days a month to tweak some of his modeling runs.

Without telling him I had one of my shell companies buy the block that included the old machine shop in Santa Ana and modified Perry's lease to be a lease-to-own arrangement.

2020, Saving the World?

As we looked for ways to make the world better, I again suggested to Perry that if his analysis showed a negative emergent intelligence pervading the internet and human behavior, maybe he could search for emergent positive intelligences also. I pointed out again that you are likely to find what you are looking for. Maybe my foundation could do some funding to help some of those positive convergence points to counteract the negativity. Perry said he had some ideas for how to do that.

I also suggested a wild idea. Maybe Perry and I could figure out how to construct an alternative positive emergent intelligence to overpower the negativity monster. His mathematical hive intelligence model was a descriptive model. He thought he could adjust it to look for a positive emergent intelligence, but he didn't know how to turn it into a prescriptive or generative model. I reminded him that the Zzynarji satellite network was a generative emergent intelligence that worked. He reminded me that it was overly simple and subject to hacking.

We discussed the modeling techniques to search for positivity and brainstormed about what it might take to create a robust positive generative model. Perry adjusted some of the models at the agency and included some positivity searches along with the negativity search model runs. They showed a number of potential candidate organizations and individuals as agents for positivity. Like with the negative convergence points, these needed to be investigated by other techniques before taking action. Some of them were already groups that the Zynn Foundation was funding. I had the foundation increase the funding for those and suggested the staff at the foundation look into the others as potential beneficiaries.

The foundation was able to arrange for early COVID vaccinations at a number of healthcare and convalescent facilities including the one with

Sergey's mom, and some door-to-door vaccinations in a number of neighborhoods, that happened to include the neighborhoods around the machine shop and the ranch house.

11/15/20 to 1/31/21, Introducing Min

After one flight to DC, Perry was about halfway through transcribing and illustrating with cartoons his memories of what I had told him about my first weeks on the trail. When he got to his apartment, he uploaded that half of the story about Min Strong from his personal laptop to a free storage website to later share with me. He also wanted a backup copy in case something happened to his laptop. Somehow the files he uploaded got indexed by a search engine and within hours someone found it, made copies, and moved it to a more accessible part of social media. Soon others were sharing the link, making copies, and talking about it in discussion groups.

The things Min said about minimalism in Perry's comic book version, and what she did to show she could leave everything behind on the hike caught a lot of attention. It appealed to environmentalists who wanted to encourage people to get by with less impact on the planet. It appealed to survivalists who took inspiration about how they could survive when civilization falls apart like they thought it was doing. Some of Min's philosophical comments appealed to new-age people who wanted to promote ancient traditions of indigenous peoples. Some appealed to tech people who figured out Min must have been using breakthrough technology in some of her clothing and tools even though that wasn't mentioned. It appealed to anti-tech people who applauded Min for going unplugged and off-the-grid for two months. Many disagreed with one another about what lessons to take from Min's quest, but nearly everyone admired the grit and determination to put herself through a grueling ten-week ordeal and come out stronger. Perry's illustrations of the transformation of a pretty but plump girl into a very fit and barely dressed young woman also were popular.

Specific stories, which I had embellished a bit and Perry had embellished even more, of Min's encounters with animals and the tricks she did to avoid contact with people entertained. Stories of Min's first days on the trail were particularly enchanting since she started as a plump non-hiker with no experience, but a lot of book knowledge, a lot of smarts, and a plan. Perry's telling of Min had a lot more brushes with potential disaster than I had told him, which in turn were more than I actually had. The story of Min's transformation from her early struggles with the discomforts of austerity to a celebration and mastery of minimalism and a saintly coexistence with nature was extremely popular. Unknown to Perry, Min Strong was an internet sensation almost overnight. After other flights, as Perry posted additional segments, the buzz grew even greater in anticipation of each new segment.

One day when Perry was working in the barn workshop to help Sergey make some more efficient water sprayers for irrigating the orchard, and bragging how efficient they would be, Sergey asked if he liked the Min Strong website, since Perry liked to be so efficient it seemed like something that he would be interested in. He said lots of people he knew loved Min and couldn't wait for the next episode.

Perry was aghast. He had heard people at work debating about minimalism in some of the same terms that I had used, and he thought it was just a coincidence that I must have read some of the same books that were popular now. He didn't realize until he did a web search that it was his postings that people were talking about. Min Strong was trending.

He took a deep breath and went to talk to me. I had just finished nursing and handed off Balaji to the nanny to put him down for a nap.

"Come in here. Mara, there is something we need to talk about."

He motioned me into my room and closed the door for privacy.

"You're not pregnant, are you?" I asked.

"Kind of."

"What???"

"Well, I didn't mean to do it, but it looks like you and I are giving birth to an internet phenomenon."

"I don't know what you mean."

"Have you been reading about minimalism recently?"

"Too busy lately. That was a last year thing. Why?"

"Do a search for minimalism."

She went to her laptop and typed a few keys. Then said "Oh shit. What have you done?"

The first 10 entries were related to the Min Strong phenomenon and one of them included a stylized cartoon picture of her coming out of the water in the mountain stream in her underwear, but with her face mostly turned away.

"What have you done?"

"It was supposed to just be for us. I don't know how it got out on the internet. I saved a copy on a free personal storage website. I didn't think anyone else could see it."

"How long has it been out there?"

"I uploaded some files a few weeks ago and have been adding more every week or two. I didn't know. It's mostly just things you said and some illustrations. I called you Min Strong in the stories."

"Shit. Let's do damage control. Let me read this and see what people are saying about it."

A few hours later I said, "I can't believe you did this, but there might be a positive side."

"Really?"

"Probably not... Idiot. But it may not be the end of the world either."

"I'm so sorry. I don't know how I misunderstood about the files being visible to others."

"Seriously? Mister cyber security spy guy?? Okay, you don't mention either of us by name, nor anyone else we know, nor any company name. You don't give specific dates or locations. Only you and I know I was hiking for ten weeks. My brother and others thought I had been at fat camp or getting lipo or something since I was a lot thinner when I came back."

"You don't think they will put the pieces together and recognize you as Min? You went away for two months and came back really fit. You've probably talked to them about minimalism before, so they are bound to recognize some of the stuff you said."

"Maybe not. I was kind of a loner after my parents died when I cooked up those philosophical opinions before the trip, and I haven't talked much about them really with anyone but you. I think the biggest risk is that people will track you down for posting it."

"I made up a fake name, Rex Max, for signing up for the free file storage space, so we might be safe there."

"Maybe. Still, we should probably think about how to make it more anonymous. Another risk is that people at Zzynarji might recognize a couple products I used that came from their research labs, but that's probably not a real big risk."

"I didn't talk about the tech stuff."

"No but it's there between the lines. And people are speculating about it. There are also the supply drop services, and the wilderness permits. Even though you don't mention the supply drops the people who did them might remember. I arranged supplies anonymously, but someone might be able to track permits and payments back to Mara Strong and make a connection.

Only you and some lawyers know me as Mara Strong now so the chances of it coming back to us here are not high."

"So, you're not mad?"

"I'm furious. Why did you make this at all? And posting it–that was such a stupid mistake."

I paused to let him suffer and then continued, "But it's also interesting that so many people like it. What I said and did. Your exaggerations are kind of funny too. And your artwork is not bad. Min looks hot. How many times did Min stare down a bear? And did hawks really bring her gifts of small game? We might be able to use the popularity of Min to get some ideas out into the world and do some good. When it comes to influencing the world, your modeling can interpret patterns, as Marta Zynn I can spend money, but maybe Min Strong can get ideas to people's heads. Ideas could be more valuable than money."

"So, you're not mad?"

"I am near apoplexy. You don't post anything else without me editing it first."

"You know. I still think it would be fine if we just went public that Mara and Marta, and now Min are all the same person. What would be the worst that could happen?"

"No. I'm still not comfortable with that. Maybe people will forget about Min if you stop posting. Internet fame fades really fast. Maybe it will just go away."

"Yeah. Maybe."

"And if we decide to post more it will be better if Min Strong is mysterious."

"I can see gears turning in your head. What are you thinking of doing?"

"Let's think about it."

7/13/2021, Baby Boy Turns One

Baby boy Balaji was healthy and growing and developing at a normal pace. Because of the pandemic he spent all of his first year at home. I paid for medical house calls for his well-baby exams and shots. Most of the residents in the neighborhood were older people whose kids had already grown up, so there were not a lot of neighborhood kids for him to meet. There were two teenagers next door, who offered babysitting, but that wasn't an option during the 2020 pandemic lockdown nor 2021.

There were no parks close by. But the farm downhill out back was almost like a park. One of us or the nanny would sometimes take his stroller on walks in the farm, and rarely the nanny would go on longer walks in the neighborhood to meet on the street with some of the few other nannies and babies. The neighbors mostly kept to themselves.

I sometimes complained that Perry was away too much. I thought Balaji needed his dad home more. Perry argued that he had managed to be home more days than he was away, but he agreed that he would like to be able to spend more time with his Billy Jay and me. I decided to start getting out again as Marta, first through video meetings from the beach house and then some trips to Zzynarji offices by way of private jet flights. We depended a lot on the nannies and later also on Sergey during those first couple of years.

2021, Marta, Mara, and Min

The Min Strong phenomenon seemed to get stronger rather than fade away. I waited several weeks without letting Perry post anything new. I had him remove the original postings from the file sharing site hoping it would fade away. A 'Where is Min?' movement seemed to be catching on with various conspiracy theories about who was trying to suppress her ideas. Copies of the original postings were still out there on other websites.

After a few weeks I decided to post again. First, we found a reasonably secure way of setting up a web presence without revealing our own identities. I edited the format and wording of all the postings before reposting them along with a promise of a next episode coming soon and warnings about copyright infringement. I added a 'What Would Min Keep?' section in which I would respond to some of the questions people posed about their own challenges in downsizing and achieving minimalism in their own lives.

I started to enjoy the fame and the mystery of my second secret identity. Min got a lot of questions from companies who wanted her to recommend their products or let them put ads on her site. I resisted, at least at first. But that didn't stop others from creating an unauthorized Min-ism industry of websites, merchandise, and conventions. I didn't pursue legal action against them, so they multiplied.

Months started to pass, and I continued enjoying the Min fame as a distraction from running Zzynarji and the foundation and being a mom. I even started joining live online events at some of the Min-iverse conventions. The conventions started as all virtual but evolved into in-person events as vaccines and treatments became widely available. During those live events I was still virtual. I used software Perry found that altered my voice enough to prevent voice matching analysis and presented my image as an altered animated cartoon. Min didn't take any direct compensation but asked the organizers to give donations to certain charities in return for her participation.

When fans asked Min for details about where, when, and how she did her long minimalism hike of self-discovery or "MinQuest" as it was now known, I resisted giving any more information other than what was shown in the comic strip episodes. Min said her journey was hers alone and others would have to find their own quests. Disregarding that advice, fans worked together to test theories about Min's quest. Many attempted to recreate the trek and shared information about their efforts and their guesses about the trails Min took. In the process of traveling in the wilderness with virtually no food or equipment, some were injured, and a few died. A few got so good at living off the land minimally that they were able to complete treks even more spartan than the exaggerated version that had been posted about Min Strong and some of those became professional MinQuest guides.

Min Strong herself was a cartoon mascot for minimalism. The opinions she expressed were extreme takes on minimalism. The images of her that were posted were abstracted to the point of being more of a cartoon superhero than a photo. Perry had some artistic talents, but we also had software for manipulating pictures. Perry got some software from work that was used to recognize people in photos and to alter or mask images to make them unrecognizable. Then there was commercial software to make cartoons out of photos. Most of the pictures we used emphasized Min's strength and fitness like she was at the end of her hike rather than how I looked before or after. A year after giving birth I was a lot softer and rounder than Min. Also, Min didn't age.

I occasionally dressed up as Marta to go to some work events and meetings again, wearing surgical masks most of the time, both for safety and to limit photos. When pressed about my previous absence I referred obliquely to some medical challenges and let them draw their own conclusions. Most speculated that I had suffered a lingering case of COVID.

Between wigs, makeup, clothing, and jewelry I was able to cast a distinct image as Marta that was different from how I looked at home as Mara. I behaved differently as Marta also: very businesslike and a more abrupt than Mara. I tried to channel my mother, Sandra Zynn. I would get into character each time I was going out as Marta.

Late 2021, PATH & INCA Projects to Save the World

Organizations that got donations from the Min-iverse conventions also tended to be among those that the Zynn Foundation provided with funding. Among them was one which was aiming to provide thousands of easily movable tiny homes for addressing the stubborn homeless crisis. The charity wanted to provide both shelter and mobility to give people better chances of finding jobs. Perry recommended it to me after it showed up as a small positive convergence point in his analysis.

The project wanted the homes to be small, stylish, simple, and standardized so that they could be easily moved to new locations if their residents had a new job or educational opportunity. They also planned to create a network of small *garden villages* or communities with very low ground rental rates where the tiny homes could be hooked up and removed easily as residents came and went. They planned to provide counseling in the villages to steer residents towards training, job opportunities, mental health, and substance abuse treatment. This project was having some positive impacts on a very small scale before the extra funding, with two *garden villages,* each with 20 hookup spots. The extra funding was intended to allow them to expand quickly to 100 larger villages across three different metropolitan areas.

With our experience with a couple of tiny homes in the farm, the idea of tiny homes was appealing, but I asked Perry how these were anything but cheap trailers and trailer parks. Perry said, "That's probably true for the first two villages, but the vision is different." He explained that eventually with thousands of hookups in dozens or hundreds of villages people would be able to move easily to follow job opportunities. They would have free or subsidized towing between villages and simple standardized hookups making it easy to disconnect and reconnect to utilities, almost automatically. No packing needed to move. Just go with your tiny house to the new village. I was skeptical about that. If they want RV's, why not just give them RVs? They would be even more mobile. Still, I supported the project because tiny homes fit in with ideas of minimalism and because Perry liked it. And with the endorsement of Min Strong, the tiny homes project got more acceptance than they would have otherwise.

An important factor was that not all the units would be given to homeless people, but more than half were to be leased to young minimalists wanting to get out of their parents' houses but stuck by the high costs of housing. That made the *garden villages* self-supporting and more acceptable in various neighborhoods. They were not homeless camps, but cool enclaves of minimalism that happened to house some previously homeless people too.

Another investment for the foundation was academic research related to emergent hive intelligence similar to Perry's PhD work which Zzynarji had previously funded because of its similarity to principles they used in their satellite network. Perry convinced me to expand the funding at his university to create a research center.

The center was to be a hub for hive intelligence research, supporting faculty and graduate students and coordinating funding for researchers at other universities, and it took the name of INCA, Institute for Nested Cellular Autonomy. The term Nested Cellular Autonomy was coined by one of Perry's faculty advisors. Autonomous entities with intelligence could be seen as a nested collections of independent components communicating and combining into successively more complex independent entities until intelligent behavior emerged. Perry's dissertation and postdoc work focused on recognizing such emergent intelligences.

Perry was asked to participate in conferences and seminars at the center. He could not share what he was doing for the government agency, but he could explain his previous research and some papers he had written since then that were not based on the government work. But more importantly he could network with others around the world and look for ideas that could support fighting the growing emergent negativity.

At one of the conferences, Perry was particularly interested in a new research project at an Australian university that planned to use NCA principles to design human-like artificial intelligence. If they could really generate an emergent hive intelligence that would be significant. It might give us clues about how to build a positive emergent global intelligence to counter the negative one that Perry's analysis revealed. Perry spoke briefly with one of the researchers, Geraldine Atwood, who Perry described as a loud and large woman with possibly some aboriginal ancestry. She presented a poster session about the Australian project, and she seemed receptive when Perry told her he'd get in touch with her about it later. Since their project was just getting started we decided to wait and see if they had any success before following up.

Perry also wanted faster progress on self-driving vehicles. The Zynn Foundation supported related academic research and Zzynarji acquired and expanded a couple of autonomous vehicle start-ups.

Early 2022, Need for a Data Center?

Despite the actions the foundation funded to promote positivity, and any interventions government agencies may have taken based on the models Perry ran for the agency, his models continued to find growing strength of a negative emergent intelligence. He could also find some growth in scattered clusters of positivity, but those were overshadowed by the negativity.

We wanted a way to predict which investments would have positive, or negative, results without waiting months or years for their impacts to play out.

We needed a good simulation, where we could try out different actions. Perry tried running some limited simulations at the agency, especially to predict impacts of some of the government's own planned policy actions, but he was restricted there in what he could put into his analysis models. The INCA institute had possibly enough server and data capacity to run the simulations, but it didn't have access to the data that Perry was able to access at the agency.

Perry and I figured out a possible way he could copy some of the agency's data. We couldn't risk housing it in the INCA server farm, so we decided to build our own private server farm where we could have full flexibility to do our own simulations. We didn't trust commercial cloud computing services, because we knew from Perry's job that some government agencies did have access to all of the supposedly private and encrypted data in the big commercial cloud computing services.

We thought about different locations for such a server farm but ended up deciding to make a small first version of it out of sight in the farm next door. We got the property zoning changed from agricultural to something that also allowed development. Neighbors who were nervous about increased housing density, relaxed somewhat when they learned there were no immediate plans to subdivide the property. Permits called for the farm to add a hydroponics facility and expanded machine shop, but it would leave most of the farm intact. We reasoned that a small server farm had similar electrical and mechanical requirements to a hydroponics building. The utilities would be upgraded and there would be some construction.

I had Sergey contact a number of different contractors that I knew had done projects discretely for Zzynarji. We didn't want to disturb the neighbors. We had Sergey be the face-to-face contact with the contractors, but he would get Perry or me on the phone sometimes to help answer questions and we had a number of surveillance cameras installed around the farm to allow us to monitor the work.

The project added a steel framework inside the wooden exterior of the larger barn and multiple basements extending into the sloping ground below the barn and into the hillside towards the ranch house. We made the basements and interior of the barns secure and climate controlled. On the ground floor we upgraded Perry's machine shop and included arc-welding equipment as a cover for occasional power surges.

We added solar electric shingles on the barn roofs and scattered clusters of solar panels through a couple acres of orchards. The solar panels looked about the same as any others but were actually higher in output and durability than what was typically used on homes at that time. Through Zzynarji I had connections. We also added a couple of massive grid storage batteries and natural gas backup generators.

The goal was to operate a server farm primarily from solar power, without drawing much energy from the power grid, at least no more than a hydroponics facility.

The work was all done out of sight of the neighborhood behind the barrier of trees that lined the perimeter of the ranch property. Dirt from the excavation for the basements was partly redistributed on the site.

Different contractors did phases of the work so that no one had a full picture of all the work being done. Sergey also got day laborers from other areas for some of the work.

I got good at moving funds around from my Strong Trust accounts through shell companies to provide Sergey with the money to pay for all of it without leaving an obvious financial trail back to the two of us. I didn't let Perry see the actual costs. I told him not to worry about that.

02/24/2022, Events in the News

While we were planning our server farm, Russia began its special military operation in Ukraine and Perry was asked to use his analysis to find areas where sanctions could provide leverage to stop the Russians. While he complained that his analysis didn't work that way there were a number of Russian oligarchs, companies, and officials identified by his analysis as participating in part of the negativity hive intelligence that his model described. Some actions were taken based on that assessment even though he protested that his analysis didn't work that way.

04/30/2022, Marta and Douglas

I was worried that my stepbrother Douglas would demand more control of the company and the foundation when he turned 18. The text of the trusts gave latitude to the current trustees, Marta and Mara, both me, to decide when to share control. I realized that both trusts must have been written at the same time by the same attorney. My Zynn parents had used that same latitude in the Strong Trust to keep control when I turned 18 a few years before. But I worried that Douglas could make trouble and that might lead to revealing that there was a second trust and the existence of Mara Strong. If Douglas thought he was being excluded from a majority of the family assets he might make even more trouble. Perry kept saying it didn't matter, and I should just tell everybody everything. I repeatedly told him "No!" and to stop saying that. He would drop it until the next time.

I made a point of visiting Douglas a week before his birthday to sound out what he was thinking. I also had a foundation meeting in the city that evening with funding recipients, so it was convenient to meet Douglas on the same trip. I was dressed in my professional Marta costume when I found him at our family's Palo Alto house.

"What brings the fabulous reclusive Marta Zynn back to her humble home?" he asked as he sat in the family theater room playing a video game on the large screen. He continued playing but backed away from an intense battle so that he could give me some of his attention.

"I wanted to wish you a Happy Birthday, Douglas. You are turning 18 next week. And graduation soon after that. Adulthood. You can vote in the next election. What do you want for your birthday?"

"I want to travel."

"Yeah. We couldn't travel as much because of COVID. Where to this time? Big trip?"

"Everywhere."

"Okay. Yeah. You should have time to do a few trips before starting at the University in the Fall? Congratulations again on getting in there by the way."

He didn't even try to get into Stanford where all four of my parents and I had gone. He said it was because it seemed too close to home in Palo Alto, but his senior year grades were not great and he had been wait-listed even at his first choice, Cal. Recently a spot opened up for him, coincidentally after the Zynn Foundation paid to upgrade a science building on campus.

"Thanks. No. I'm taking a year delay on starting. I want to see the world first."

"Really? I thought you couldn't wait to get into college campus life."

"A few friends and I are gonna take a sailboat and see how far we can go. We've been following the stories of that Min Strong lady and her minimalism challenges. We want to sail around the world in a minimalist way in a personal challenge kind of like her vision quest hike. I'm not going all alone like she did. I plan to take different friends on parts of the voyage, but it will be my personal voyage of self-discovery."

"Really?"

"You don't approve?"

"Seems dangerous. Have the captain make sure the family boat's in really good shape before you go and check in a lot. But if that's what floats your boat…"

Douglas laughed. "I don't need a captain. I know how to sail. I'm not taking the family boat. Too big. I'm going to get a smaller boat. I knew you wouldn't understand. You're nothing like Min Strong. You always hold on to so many things. You never even cleaned out your room here.

You have so much stuff. I almost never see you and you keep so much stuff here. You should see my rooms. I'm trying to lighten my load. You should listen to Min's stories. You would learn something."

"I am lightening my load. Mom and Dad wanted to give away their fortune to charity. I'm working on that with the foundation."

"Yeah. I like some of what you have done there so far. I'd be happy if you went faster. We don't need much. I'll send you a link to Min's stories."

"I'll have to try to find some time to look at that. Did you say her name was Mindy Strange?"

"Min Strong."

"Minestrone?"

"Min Strong. Don't make fun of her. She's important." He looked at my skeptical expression and continued, "Never mind, Marta, Mortal, Mortal Zynn. How the hell have you been?"

"Douglas, Dog Gas, Dog-less Zynner, What the frick did you eat for dinner? I've been good. Really busy. But good. It's good to see you too,

"How about we never use those nickname jingles for each other again. Ever." Douglas suggested.

"Agreed," I patted him on the head.

"Don't do that. I'm not your kid brother anymore. I'm turning 18 next week."

"Okay. Okay."

"Do you want to go to dinner? There is a new place on University that is pretty good, and they have outdoor seating if you want it." He noticed the designer N95 mask I was wearing pulled down under my chin.

"No. Can't stay for dinner. I've got to be in the city for a foundation event tonight. There will be plenty of food there."

"You should blow it off. Other people can cover for you. From what I hear you are always working. I check on you sometimes. With the foundation and the company, seems like you are trying to do everything both Mom and Dad did. You need to find a life."

I sighed and said, "Gotta go."

"See ya later, Mortal." He rejoined the battle in the game he was playing.

"Smell you later, Dog Gas."

05/07/2022, Douglas Turns Eighteen

When Douglas turned 18 he did not immediately push for more control. He didn't mention the company or the trusts at all. He was too busy with high school graduation activities and planning his sailing adventure. Due to supply-chain issues the custom boat he wanted would take several months to be built so he decided to do some backpacking after graduation, start school at UC Berkeley in the Fall, and do the sailing adventure the following summer.

For his birthday, to help him pay for the boat, I offered him a one-time $20 million coming-of-age payment from the Zynn trust along with an increase in his annual living stipend to $4 million. I told him even if he was aiming for personal minimalism, I wanted to make sure he had enough to stay safe on his world-wide adventure. He said I just didn't understand minimalism, but he accepted the money.

I paid myself a similar annual stipend in lieu of salary. And, in line with my parents' stated wishes, I continued to move assets to the foundation to fund charitable causes. Douglas didn't seem to object to the choices that I pushed the foundation to support, if he paid attention, nor did he object to letting me do all of the trustee work as long as he got enough money for himself. I did get some pushback from Carl who said I should be careful because some of the Zzynarji executives thought I should go slower about giving away parts of the company.

Summer 2022, The Strong Server Ranch

The big barn was rebuilt by the end of June, looking old outside, but fully new inside. Perry was impressed by how fast so much could be done especially with the supply chain shortages that were still happening. I wasn't surprised about it when cost was not an object. When the new building was almost ready, I started purchasing computing equipment through shell companies, which was delivered in batches to a leased light industrial building a few miles away. Sergey and Perry took a rental truck to bring back a couple pallets of equipment at a time. With some help from me and Perry at first, Sergey and some his day laborers got good at hooking up the computing equipment. Just a few months after we started, and after Perry spent a few long nights debugging mistakes that Sergey had made in the installation, we had a functioning server farm, or Strong Server Ranch, as we called it, that could support running some of Perry's simulations.

Getting the right data, however, proved to be a challenge. Perry could access massive amounts of data in the agency's systems at work, and he was able to pull a few hundred terabytes at a time from there to use attached to his upgraded secure laptop, but it was illegal transferring that data to equipment not owned by the agency and they had tracking software on all the equipment that would show if it was copied to an external device. He eventually figured out a way to adapt the antenna technology of his satellite-hacking machine to capture the data flowing between storage units in his secure laptop. It was supposed to be shielded from that kind of snooping, but at very close range he was able to make it work. This allowed transferring data without leaving a record of the transfer.

He started transferring data a few terabytes per hour into the server ranch, picking up a fresh batch of data on each of his trips to the office. In a few weeks he had a decent-sized sample of data representing information from social media and other sources for a few hundred million people–still only a fraction of what the agency had access to–and started doing some simulations of effects of different choices for charitable actions.

Perry could analyze the negative and positive hive intelligence patterns in the initial data and then the simulations would try to predict how those emergent intelligences would change after certain actions were taken by the foundation.

We struggled with how best to run time forwards and generate new data on millions of people to see how the positive and negative hive intelligences would change. Our simulations depended on heuristics to predict how individuals and groups of people would respond and behave in different circumstances and generate a new set of behavioral data for analysis. The heuristics were based on expert opinions and historical trends using the current and past data the agency had about individuals. We felt they were good models, but worried if they were good enough.

We decided we would keep working on improving the heuristic model of people's behavior to predict actions of the population as a whole, but what we really wanted was feedback from a sufficiently large group of people interacting with the simulated situations. Two ideas that came to mind were using AI to create a population of simulated people or creating some kind of popular massively parallel game in which different scenarios could be tested by large numbers of real people playing the game. Both ideas seemed impractical. But then again if cost was not a concern, who knows.

In the meantime, we created software tools for building more simulated potential worlds with different assumptions about charitable investments that we could in turn analyze with whatever analysis tools were available. We started to build a variety of variations of possible worlds. Some were based closely on the current state of the world and others were based on assuming various changes had already been implemented.

Summer and Fall, 2022, Douglas

Douglas headed to school at Cal in August. In the weeks before that he did a few backpacking trips in the Sierras, some with high school friends and some on his own as his first try at doing a Min Quest.

He seemed to do okay in his first semester at the university, but he concentrated as much on partying and drugs as on academics.

11/24/2022, Thanksgiving

It turned out that Sam Muller, one of the kids next-door to the ranch house, was attending Cal and became friends with my brother Douglas. Sam's mom, Camilla, insisted that Sam invite Douglas to visit for Thanksgiving when Sam told her that Douglas didn't have any family but a sister who was out of town and he was going to be alone at home in Palo Alto for the holiday. Camilla told Perry we were welcome to share their Thanksgiving dinner also, but he declined and said we had our own plans.

I told Douglas I had business trips I had to make. I kept out of sight at the ranch house when Douglas was visiting next door. I didn't want to chance him seeing me. He went back to the Corona del Mar beach house each night and partied with Sam and some of Sam's local friends and other friends from Cal who lived in the area.

12/25/2022, Christmas

I was feeling guilty about blowing off Thanksgiving with Douglas but also didn't want to miss holidays with Balaji. I managed to meet Douglas at the Palo Alto house a few days before Christmas after the end of his first semester at Cal and offered to come back and spend part of Christmas Day with him there, but he said he would be in Tahoe. Some of his college friends were joining him after Christmas for skiing and winter backpacking, and he was going early to check out some cross-country ski trails. He said if I got a room at the same resort, there was a chance he would be able to meet me on Christmas Day. I thought about it but declined and wished him and his friends a good holiday. Douglas still didn't say anything about taking a bigger role in the company and the question of the ownership split between the Zynn and Strong trusts did not come up that year.

Almost every week when Perry took out the trash bins to the street, Camilla, the single mom next door, would hurry out to meet him at the curb and talk. That week she asked about our Christmas plans. He said we would probably have a quiet family Christmas at home. She said that it would probably be the same for her on Christmas day with her two kids. But both of her kids, Sam and Josephine, were going to Tahoe right after Christmas with a college classmate of Sam's. She was off work until after New Years and Perry was welcome to drop by for coffee anytime that week. He said he'd think about it.

Perry, two-year-old Balaji, and I enjoyed a low-profile Christmas and New Year's at the ranch house. Perry did go over to Camilla's for coffee at least once that week.

3/25/2023 to 4/2/2023, Douglas' Spring Break

Douglas flew down on a Saturday to stay at the beach house for Spring Break week. His new sailboat was supposed to be ready in Newport Beach harbor on Monday. He said he wanted to take it on a test sail to Catalina before accepting it and having it moved to a marina near Berkeley for final delivery.

I kept out of sight at the ranch house that week in case he visited his friend Sam next door, but I decided to take the opportunity to visit him while he was staying at the beach house. I figured I could spend a few hours with him without having to travel north, and I could be back home to Balaji and Perry at the ranch house by dinner time. It would give him a chance to wish me happy birthday a little early while he was in town.

I dressed in my Marta clothes and wig and drove down late Sunday morning, changing cars along the way at the airport. The car I used at the ranch house was a Land Rover registered to one of the Strong Trust shell companies, not connected to the Zynn Foundation or the Zzynarji Company. The BMW I picked up at the airport was kept ready for Marta Zynn by one of the car rental companies there. They would also bring it to any address near the airport if I called and asked them to, but I never called them from the ranch house.

I parked my Marta BMW in the beach house's underground garage. There was a rented Tesla Plaid Model X parked there already. Douglas was into electric cars at that time. No other cars were there so I thought that if Douglas had friends over the previous night, they must have already left. That was good. I didn't really want to meet his friends.

From the garage I entered into the basement level of the house and had to step around bottles, cans, and empty drink cups on the floor in the hallway. I looked into the home theater room on that level, and it was also trashed with party remnants, including several empty pizza boxes and some pizzas that looked like they had been flung like frisbees against the wall. Douglas must have had quite a party here last night. But so far, no sign of him or anyone else still here.

The housekeeping crew would have some extra work to do to clean this up. I would probably have to authorize extra repairs and repainting before the next fund-raising event. I planned to talk to Douglas about taking better care of the house.

I looked in the elevator, and it had a puddle that looked like a combination of pee and vomit. I decided to take the stairs instead. They also were stained with something unidentifiable and foul-smelling. I stepped carefully up the stairs. Yes, the house is going to need a major cleaning. Damn it, Douglas. Can't you control yourself and your friends even a little bit?

The great room on the ground floor was also a mess. Trash from food, drinks, and drug pipes were all over the place, but no sign of people. The glass patio doors were open to the pool and deck overlooking the ocean. I didn't see anyone out there. I didn't want to see what they had done to the pool, so I didn't go out.

I figured Douglas was probably still asleep upstairs and started up the next flight of stairs. After a couple steps I heard a coughing noise behind me. I turned and looked down and saw the extended arm of someone lying on one of the couches, stretching and waking up. I was about to say hello to Douglas as they started sitting up when I realized it wasn't Douglas but was a teenage girl. Some of his party guests were still here, even without extra cars in the garage. I quietly but quickly went up the stairs to the bedroom suite Douglas usually used. I peeked into his rooms and saw he was asleep on the bed, apparently alone. I went in.

"Douglas. Are you alive?" I whispered as I nudged his arm.

"Butterflies," he said in a groggy voice without opening his eyes.

"What's that?"

"Huh? Mom? I don't want to get up yet."

"Do you think I sound like mom now?"

He opened one eye and looked at me and said slowly in a whisper, "Hey, Mortal. What are you doing here?"

"Hey Douglas. Had a little party here last night? What was that about butterflies?"

"What???"

"I'm surprised you're sleeping alone. I saw a girl downstairs sleeping on the couch."

"Yeah. Whatever. That must be Sam's sister, she's pretty nice. But she's Sam's sister. Still in high school. Sam's around here somewhere too. I gave them a ride here yesterday and they are probably expecting me to give them a ride home later. They should get an Uber or something."

I had a speech I was getting ready to give Douglas about being responsible for the beach house but when I realized that the friends who stayed over included Sam and his sister Josephine, who might recognize me as their neighbor, Mara Lee, even though I was dressed as Marta, I quickly changed gears.

"I was on my way between two Zzynarji meetings so I had the plane do a detour and stop here so I could say Hi. But I'm actually running late and need to get going again. Hi and Bye."

"Really? You work too hard. Stay and meet Sam."

"No. I really have to run. You get your new boat tomorrow, right? Good luck with that." I started back towards the door.

"Yeah. But I should get up and introduce you to my friend Sam–and his sister–before you go."

"No need." At the doorway I saw Sam in the hallway walking towards Douglas's room in his boxer shorts. He was looking down to avoid some broken glass on the floor and probably didn't see me. I ducked back inside Douglas's room and partially closed the door. "Can I use your restroom?" I stepped quickly into the restroom and closed and locked the door.

"Uh. Sure," said Douglas.

I listened through the door as Douglas and Sam talked.

"Hey Sam," Douglas said.

"What do you have that's good for a headache?" said a voice that must have been Sam's.

"What do you want? Tylenol? Beer? Tequila? Or something stronger?"

"Probably best to start with the Tylenol."

"My sister's here. In the bathroom. You should meet her. Wait a sec." He raised his voice to talk through the bathroom door. "Hey Mortal, can you find the Tylenol in there for Sam?"

I turned on the fan and flushed the toilet. "What did you say, Douglas?" I made my voice sound raspy just in case Sam might remember Mara's voice.

"Tylenol. In the medicine cabinet."

"What's that?" I rasped.

"TYE-LEN-ALL!"

"Check the other bathrooms. I'm going to be a while in here," I rasped in a stage whisper.

"You had to use my bathroom for that.? You've got 10 other bathrooms in this house."

"Sorry. It came on kind of urgent." I flushed the toilet again. "You might not want to use this bathroom today."

"Oh Shit! Really?!"

"I can look in another bathroom," said Sam's voice.

"I'm awake now and I should probably take some too. I'll go with you" said Douglas's voice.

I listened for the sound of steps going out into the hallway then quickly unlocked and opened the bathroom door and peeked into the hallway. I saw Douglas and Sam step into another bedroom. I walked quickly towards the stairs. I turned around when I saw Josephine starting up the stairway. She was looking carefully where she stepped so she may not have seen me. I walked away from the stairs and summoned the elevator. It arrived just in time, and I stepped in, keeping my feet at the edges of the floor, trying to avoid the puddles in the middle. I kept my face averted from Josephine on the stairs. I pushed the button to go to the garage level. As the door closed and the elevator descended, I caught part of the conversation I left behind.

"Sam, Douglas, Who's that? Did one of you have some older woman in your room last night?" Josephine asked. "That's gross."

"Where'd she go?" asked Sam's voice.

"Elevator," said Josephine's voice. "Your lady is sneaking out?"

"It's just my crazy sister. She's too rushed and selfish to say Hi," said Douglas's voice.

"It's okay. Jo-Jo. She's just embarrassed about stinking up his bathroom," said Sam's voice.

When I was a few blocks away I texted Douglas to apologize for leaving so abruptly. We texted each other back and forth a few times that day. He said that Sam was going with him on the test sail to Catalina tomorrow.

Later that week I learned that the test sail went well, and Douglas agreed to accept the new boat. He also said that Sam was going to accompany him on the first leg of his round-the-world sail starting in May or June after school got out.

He never mentioned my birthday.

April and May 2023

The sailboat was delivered to a marina near Berkeley after Spring Break and Douglas made a number of short trips on it from there around the Bay and longer trips on weekends, like out to the Farallon Islands or up and down the coast. He took Sam or other classmates with him to get ready for the planned big voyage.

After classes got out in May he did a few more overnight test runs. Douglas wanted to be sure that each of his potential co-pilots knew how to operate the boat and that all of its systems worked properly. I told him I was impressed by his preparations.

He had the boat hauled out for inspection one last time and the trip was delayed by two weeks when a small leak needed to be repaired in the thru hull for dumping waste. During that delay Douglas did some backpacking in the Sierras with his friend Sam. Sam's sister Josephine also came along on part of the hike. Because of crazy heavy snow that winter there was still snow in the Sierras at that time, but Douglas and Sam wanted to do a Min Quest hike while waiting for the sailboat to be ready, so they went anyway. Douglas bought all the gear. Josephine apparently took every opportunity to spend time with Douglas.

June 2023

Finally in mid-June he and Sam started on the first leg of the voyage that was supposed to make it to Hawaii in two to four weeks. Douglas arranged for another friend, Brock, to fly to Maui and wait for them at a beach house in Kapalua north of Lahaina. Brock would take over for Sam and join Douglas for the sail to Tahiti.

07/13/2023, Douglas and Sam at Sea

After three weeks at sea, Douglas and Sam were still a couple hundred miles from their destination. I checked their progress each day on a website that showed the location of their GPS beacon. I also called Douglas on his satellite phone a few times a week. On Balaji's 3rd birthday, after an early dinner, while Balaji and Perry played a game that Perry game him I gave Douglas a short call.

"Any sign of land yet, Douglas?"

"Everything is a sign, Mortal. Every swell tells a story."

"Are you drunk again?"

"No. No. No. No. We are high on the universe."

"And a few chemical gifts from the universe?"

"And chemicals from the universe. Yes. Yes. Yes. The universe is nothing but chemicals, or waves. As are we."

"Be careful out there. Is Sam navigating today?"

"Sam is dream navigating. He is my spirit guide."

"Douglas. You're not far from shipping lanes. You need to stay awake especially as you get closer to the islands."

"Islands are like stars in the sky. Or clouds. Or birds. Or fish. Tiny fishes. Billions of tiny fishes eating other fishes."

"Okay. Okay. Douglas. Stay safe. I'll check in again tomorrow."

07/14/2023, Lost Contact

The next morning, I checked on the website, and it showed no current location. I tried calling their satellite number and it didn't connect. Douglas's incoherence in the previous call hadn't worried me too much at the time because it was typical of many calls I had with him in recent months. But with the subsequent loss of contact, I was very concerned.

As Marta, I authorized a search. Dozens of planes and ships searched the area around the last coordinates for six days before the boat was found a hundred miles from the Big Island upside down and tangled in drifting trash debris. There was no sign of bodies, and the inflatable life raft was not found with the boat, so the search changed to looking for the raft or people in the water.

The search continued for another week until torn remains of the life raft were found on a remote part of the shore of the Big Island. There was some blood on the raft but no other sign of the two.

After additional searching on and offshore in the area they were found at a bar a few miles down the beach. They had no ID and no money but apparently Douglas was able talk his way into free drinks and food. He was still carrying a first aid kit half full of drugs which helped to keep up their spirits and may have been involved in some bartering.

I was relieved they were alive, and I arranged to replace Douglas' passport, satellite phone, and credit cards, but I didn't immediately go to Hawaii to see him.

His friend Sam had a deep cut in his leg, although some of the drugs they were taking helped with the pain. I convinced Douglas to take him to a clinic on the Big Island where his wound was cleaned and stitched, and he got more pain pills. Then Sam and Douglas flew to Maui to meet up with Brock.

Douglas wanted to get another sailboat to continue the voyage, but Brock backed out. The sinking of the first boat probably didn't inspire confidence. Instead of the South Seas adventure, he decided he wanted to get back after all for an interview for an internship in DC for the next summer and the start of classes for the Fall semester.

Sam and Douglas stayed at the Maui house. Sam recuperated there while Douglas tried to arrange the next leg of his voyage. He couldn't find a copilot and was pretty much set on taking whatever boat he could get and going solo for the next part.

While at the beach house both Sam and Douglas indulged in Sam's pain killers and some of the other drugs. Douglas also did some backpacking in the mountains on Maui as another personal Min Quest. Sam's leg hurt too much to hike so he went back to the beach house while Douglas hiked. Douglas cut his hike short because the island was unusually dry and there were fire restrictions. When he returned to the beach house after the shortened backpacking trip he saw Sam's leg. It was turning colors. Douglas took him to another clinic. The nurse practitioner there sent him straight to a hospital on the other side of the island.

After a few days, Sam was released from the hospital back to the beach house to rest after the amputation. Douglas got my help to arrange for a private flight from Maui back to John Wayne. He was bored staying with Sam, so he said he was taking one last overnight backpacking trip before going home.

08/08/2023, Near Lahaina

Shortly after Douglas returned from his backpacking trip he and Sam packed their things in the rental jeep and started driving from Kapalua heading to the airport on the other side of the island. As they were approaching Lahaina they were confronted by a traffic jam. Someone said the road was closed ahead and billowing clouds of smoke were rising. Douglas tried to convince people to let them through but confronted by throngs of people heading away from Lahaina, they finally gave up and turned around and went back to the beach house.

He called me on his satellite phone after they got back to the beach house.

"Mortal, we're not going to make it to the airport today. Or maybe for a few days. Tell your jet people. There's a fire."

"I see it on the news. Are you okay?" I asked.

"I'm okay. Sam is the same. It seems safe here at the beach house," Douglas replied, "But we need to find a way to get out of here."

"I'll arrange something," I said. "Your backpacking didn't have anything to do with the fire, did it?"

"I know how to have minimal impact."

I suspected he might have had something to do with it, since he was unpredictable when he was using drugs, but the reports later seemed to blame it on power lines. He wouldn't ever say exactly where he had been backpacking so I still had some doubts.

I convinced him to take in some refugees from Lahaina and stay at the Kapalua beach house for a few more days. With phones and cell service down in large parts of the area the satellite phone was helpful for getting news in and out. I arranged for a larger, private jet to bring in supplies for the fire victims and to take Sam and Douglas on the return trip back to California. I also arranged a helicopter to take Sam and Douglas from Kapalua to the airport to meet the plane to avoid the roads through Lahaina.

After they got back to California, Sam wanted to recuperate at home, so Douglas accompanied him there and visited him off and on for a few days, while staying at the Corona del Mar beach house. I stayed out of sight indoors at the ranch house during those days, talking to Douglas by phone each day to see how things were going. Sam's mom Camilla was upset about Sam's injury and made Douglas feel unwelcome. Through my foundation contacts I found a good prosthetics service, that made limbs for military veterans. I arranged for them to help Sam get fitted with a prosthetic leg.

Sam took the semester off, and Douglas went back to school after all. He drove a rental sports car north, taking the coastal route, but making detours on any winding roads he could find. He left on the 20th and ended up staying overnight at Zynn houses in Santa Barbara and Carmel. He managed to get back to his condo in Berkeley just in time for the start of classes on the 23rd.

That Fall Douglas made frequent trips south to visit Sam while he convalesced at the house next door. Douglas would take Sam away from the house so as to avoid Camilla. I don't know all the places where they would go but they spent some time at the Corona del Mar beach house. Reports from the housekeeping crew said that they had some parties but didn't cause as much damage as last Spring.

Sam used a lot of pain killers and other drugs. Douglas brought some with him every time he visited. I got in the habit of staying out of sight when I was home at the ranch house because I never knew when Douglas might be showing up next door and I didn't want to chance him seeing me. Sam's sister Josephine was a senior in high school at the time and apparently Douglas and Josephine became close when he visited.

Late 2023, A Generative Hive Intelligence

Perry and I continued to have doubts about the value of our simulations for predicting changes to the negative and positive emergent intelligences in the world. While I was busy dealing with Douglas's shipwreck, Sam's amputation, and the Maui fires, I suggested that Perry should follow up with the Australian project from a couple years ago and see if they had any success generating an emergent intelligence using NCA principles. I didn't expect success, but they should have some results.

He came back to me a couple days later and said, "Do you remember Dr. Geraldine Atwood?"

"I don't think we've met. Remind me."

"You haven't. I mentioned her. She did the poster session at one of the INCA conferences a couple years ago before she finished her PhD claiming to be able to create a simulated human personality using hive intelligence principles."

"Now I remember the name. Geraldine Atwood. You did mention her once. The Australian work I asked you to check up on. Okay. If she finished her PhD she must not have failed miserably?"

"I think she's got a couple ideas that might be useful."

"Tell me about it."

Perry explained, "I emailed her the other morning, reminding her that we met at the INCA conference and saying I was interested in learning more about her work. It was the middle of the night in Australia when I sent the email, so I didn't expect a quick response, but she emailed back within a couple minutes. She said she remembered meeting at the conference and mentioned that I said back then I planned to get in touch with her soon. She said it was about time. She would be happy to talk, about her work, or anything else."

"So eager. Sounds like she has a crush on you Perry," I teased him.

"We emailed back and forth a few times and she shared some interesting things."

"I'll bet."

"She said that her research group had been focused on creating a single instance of a human personality AI and they were finally having some success with that. I asked if it could be used to create large numbers of AI personalities and she said, "Maybe"," but the intelligence of each would vary depending on how much computing power you gave it, and the components used in the nested cellular autonomy hive for each."

"So? Impractical for us?"

"But listen. They got some success with various NCA components running on a just a few dozen networked computers and smartphones. They didn't use a big data center."

"Right. And I bet their simulated human was dumb as shit."

"Not necessarily. They tried tying in links to commercial generative AI services as expertise components to make it really smart, but that didn't work well. And they preferred avoiding the big data center computational energy required for those. Aiming for minimalism, you know."

"How is this relevant?" I asked.

"A couple of things: She said that their AI worked pretty well without big data center computing power, and she speculated that if you were doing large numbers of AI entities, they could share NCA components. A lot of the basic components could be essentially the same or shared and the computational energy requirements per unit would be even smaller."

"Okay if that worked it might help with scalability, but it probably doesn't really work. It still seems dum…impractical for our purposes."

"Maybe. But there's more. She said they had considerable flexibility on what components to use for expertise, provided that the communication interfaces between the components supported a positive earned trust mechanism to guarantee that nested cellular autonomous components did not mislead one another as they built up the emergent simulated intelligence."

"Okay it sounds like you are about to get to a point."

"Here's the key point. She said *Positive Earned Trust* or PET was key to assembling a working healthy emergent intelligence. When using the commercial generative AI components, besides being energy wasteful, it was difficult to maintain positive earned trust."

"Okay. I'll bite. What's Positive Earned Trust?" I asked.

"That's what I wanted to know so I called her. Here's a transcript of some of that call." He handed me his iPad showing the transcript.

I thought, do I really have to read a call transcript? Can't he just tell me the main points? I looked at the iPad and quickly read,

Hi. This is Perry Lee. Sorry if its late there.

Hi. Perry. No problem. Nice to talk to you again. It's been ages since that conference. I should get back to the states again one of these days now that Covid is mostly behind us. Maybe I'll get a paper in the next conference at INCA.

Yeah. You should try. I'm calling because I'd like to know more about that positive earned trust mechanism you mentioned in your email. I don't remember that in your presentation last time.

Positive Earned Trust. That is my PET project. Ha ha. It's a twist that's not published yet. Before we added PET, highly complex emergent intelligences tended to degrade or become unhealthy after a short time. They would start to show signs like paranoia, anxiety and

depression and eventually stop functioning. It seems to be working better since we found ways to establish positive earned trust. I do need to finish writing it up. It's still got some minor issues I'm trying to work out first.

I'd love to read more about your PET as soon as you are willing to share more.

You should already know all about it. It's from your own dissertation work. If you invert the equations in the functions for your descriptive hive model to give a generative hive model instead, it's pretty obvious. The coefficients between communicating constituent cells have to be positive, or the generative model won't converge. We figured out that those coefficients map to earned trust. In a sense the interacting cells have to be able to trust the messages from one another, and the trust has to be justified.

Tell me more.

Basically, if cells in a hive intelligence are misleading one another, or if I they are being misled, then their joint actions eventually become self-destructive to the larger emergent being. The bees in a hive or ants in an ant colony trust the messages other bees or ants with the same hive or colony scent, and those messages tend to be authentic so the hive or the colony functions as an emergent unit. In our AI work the analog to the ants are the various NCA component modules for sensory, memory, language, social perception, motor-function, learning, all the various kinds of expertise that coalesce to make up an emergent simulated human AI. You know it's a lot more complicated than that, but you get the idea.

Oh. Yeah. Obvious. I'd love to take credit for that. Of course, I had all that in mind when I wrote those equations. But seriously, send me the writeup you have on that as soon as you can. I'd really like to read it. It sounds amazing.

I stopped reading and asked, "When do you expect the paper?"

"She sent a draft. It does need a lot of work, but I pulled out the relevant parts for you. Check your email."

After we both read it we agreed that Positive Earned Trust might hold promise as a basis for generating a positive emergent intelligence. I suggested that Perry follow up with Dr. Atwood to find out more.

Early 2024

Over the next few months Dr. Geraldine Atwood and Perry corresponded and talked frequently, and Perry became convinced that her work could be useful. Her work was different from other AI technology in the news. At that time ChatGPT and other generative AI engines were producing sophisticated visual, textual, and other products that previously would have required expert human creative efforts. But they generally relied on a huge amount of data processed at large data centers, consuming large amounts of energy, and some of them had issues with hallucinations and questionable reuse of copyrighted work.

The Atwood AI on the other hand, was a simulated human personality, which some of the other AI projects could also do, but hers was based on nested cellular autonomy, it seemed to be much more efficient, and it ought to be able to scale up to handle large numbers of simulated personalities.

The bigger breakthrough for me was in her formulas for explaining how to generate a healthy positive hive intelligence. Her equations for a positive generative hive intelligence based on positive earned trust was new to Perry and me. We suspected that we could leverage those principles to try to create a large-scale positive hive intelligence to counteract the growing negative one. Or maybe, more accurately, to help the existing unhealthy negative one to become positive and healthy. But Perry was also curious to see if the Atwood approach could really work to create artificial human personalities for the simulation. He was intrigued by the possible efficiencies of sharing components and getting large numbers of unique simulated personalities with only a small additional computing investment for each.

I doubted it could really generate even a single realistic simulated human personality without huge computing investments. I questioned the validity of the test conversations that Dr. Atwood showed in her papers. But Perry persuaded me to let him test it out.

The Zynn Foundation increased the funding to the INCA center to allow it to increase support for researchers at other universities. Specifically, they increased funding for Dr. Atwood's research in Australia and arranged for her to make her software available to the project and to spend a few weeks at the INCA center in California explaining it. Perry got permission from the agency to take on a part time position with the INCA center and got a copy of Dr. Atwood's code.

02/17/24, INCA Conference

While Dr. Atwood was in town Perry spent more time at his office at the university. Normally, he split his time between that office, his agency offices in Irvine, his office in the barn above the server ranch, and time at home with Balaji. He also stopped by his official address at his dad's machine shop each week to pick up mail.

That month we were between nannies for 3-year-old Balaji, so we were relying on Sergey. In mid-February I was out of town for a couple days when Sergey was also not available, so Perry arranged with Camilla next door to have her daughter Josephine babysit while he was at the conference. I wasn't keen on having someone outside the family in the house, but afterwards Perry said there were no problems the days that she babysat. Balaji seemed to be okay with her. He was asleep before Perry got home to relieve her both nights.

During Dr. Atwood's visit Perry learned how to use her software and started experimenting with creating simple AIs. He brought the software home so that he could continue working with it and create more example AI personalities using the agency data at the family server ranch.

03/04/2024 A Birthday Surprise

After some experimentation with personality profiles based on random people from the agency's data, he decided to see if he could create a Min Strong AI based on the Min character that I played in the Min Strong stories. It was crude at first, but he was able to switch out nested cellular autonomy components, such as for more complete language skills and better expertise and personality modules that could be trained. He posed questions to the Min AI from those previously posed to the What Would Min Keep website. He compared the answers given by the Min AI with answers that I actually gave and used my answers as training corrections for the AI. After a couple weeks of this, the Min AI started giving answers very close to what Min did herself on new questions.

Perry showed it to me, and I was not happy about it at first. I didn't like this kind of surprise. I felt that he was mocking me by saying a dumb computer program could simulate my Min personality. And I was afraid that he had put something out in public again without my permission, but he assured me that he had not. It was only in our private server ranch which didn't have any connections to the web. Perry showed me how it would answer new questions that came in, and how it would interact conversationally. I was annoyed but impressed.

"It's not me. It's not even Min. But it's similar to Min. And you say it can be trained?"

"I've been training it with your answers to the What Would Min Keep panel."

"Maybe we can train it enough to do some of the work for me in the Min-iverse. There are always more questions coming in than I have time to answer."

"Yeah. If it would help, you could let it generate responses to questions, and then if you need to, you can correct its answers before they are released. Or I've got an interface that will let you watch what it is hearing, doing, and saying in real time, and you can step in and take control whenever you want. It will adjust and learn from anything you tell it to do that is different than it would have done on its own. You can be like a little voice in its head guiding it. You can set a delay to allow you to see its answers before you override them, or you can just take over and drive it real time whenever you want. It learns either way."

"That sounds like it might be fun. I might try that. Min is a cartoon anyway, so maybe it won't hurt her brand too much if she says some off the wall things sometimes."

"You mean even more off the wall?"

"Easy. That may be true, but tread lightly there. Now if only you could make one of these for my Marta responsibilities."

"Sure. Marta should be easy to clone."

"Hey."

"Seriously, if you train it on all your emails and phone calls then routine calls and emails would probably be no problem."

"Maybe some of my Marta work is routine, maybe a lot, but Marta's job setting strategies and making investment decisions for Zzynarji is a lot more complicated than just some boilerplate emails and phone calls."

"Yeah. Video conferences and in-person appearances are a little beyond the technology right now, I think. Maybe if we could add the full generative capabilities of one of the new AI engines, but you wouldn't want one of those AI companies to know you are generating a Marta Zynn live feed with their tools."

"I could probably get a copy of their code. Or Zzynarji could, with the right investments."

"We would need a lot larger data center than our server ranch to hold all the data they use, so it is probably not an option right now."

"Too bad. It would be nice to get out of going to some of those routine events so I could spend more time on the big Zzynarji strategies…and have more family time. Let's think about upgrading the server ranch and getting some other data center buildings. Meanwhile, give me access to the Atwood code and your MinAI. I want to understand how it works before we do anything more with it."

March and April 2024

I studied the code and made some modifications. I was quite impressed with the architecture and expertise components Dr. Atwood from Australia had assembled, and the interfaces Perry had added, but I had a few ideas of my own on how to make it more secure and better at learning from hints given by an observer without the observer having to control it completely. Instead of always typing full answers to questions to replace those from the Min AI, I could type or speak a word to suggest subconsciously to the Min AI the kind of answer I wanted, or have it pause and generate a list of possible choices, and the Min AI would incorporate the selected concept into its answer without additional delay. That would allow a degree of control without full-time driving and without the delays of reviewing and replacing so many answers.

To test out the MinAI we decided to simulate a Min-iverse online conference panel. We took data from profiles of a few dozen people who were known Min fans with a lot of public exposure and data in the agency data set to create some AI's. Then we had them interact with MinAI at a simulated Min-iverse online discussion panel. Simulating fifty personalities only took about twice the resources of generating the first. They were still shallow simulations, but they had conversations similar to a real Min-iverse conference panel. I'm not sure if that said something about the tool or about the kinds of people who attended Min-iverse conferences.

We observed the behavior of the characters and suggested subconscious words to help guide their actions or sometimes took over and drove some of them for a while. It was crude, but it was quite fun to let it run and see what kinds of interactions the characters would have. It was especially fun to make a character do something outrageous and then see how others would react and how the character would learn from its own unexpected actions and adjust its personality and behavior going forward. Sometimes the reaction would be to behave more outrageously from then on, and other times the behavior would become more restrained, introspective, and nervous. We saved the starting point and various intermediate points for the characters so that we could repeat the interactions with different inputs and different results.

I found some speech synthesis software for giving voices to the characters and graphics software for adding faces to the speech. The mouths would move to match the words being spoken. Expressions were not always perfect, but the overall effect was interesting.

05/26/2024, Multiple Interacting AI characters

"Not reliable enough yet to take over my video conferences as Marta, but maybe it could work for simulating an interactive cartoon Min image in a Min-iverse conference."

"Yeah. And with the built-in machine learning both the personalities and the interfaces should get better over time."

After we spent a few hours running and rerunning various interactions with these AI characters we realized that this was an addictive game. We wanted to keep playing but the new nanny was allowed Sundays and holidays off at this point and was going home soon, and Balaji needed our attention. So, we set it aside but put it on a list of things to come back to it later.

07/04/2024, Tony's PATH

It was the Fourth of July, and the Zynn Foundation had a celebration cocktail party with grant recipients whose funding had been renewed or increased. I walked up to one my assistants, Satchel, who was talking with Tony Marks, the head of the moveable tiny home garden village project. I was curious if Perry was right and there was something more to this project than just a collection of mobile home parks for the homeless.

Satchel saw me coming and said to Tony, "Tony, let me introduce Marta Zynn."

"Pleased to meet you Ms. Zynn," said Tony. Satchel stepped back a step and watched me to see if I wanted to talk with him or with Tony.

I said, "Tony, is it?" Satchel backed a couple more steps away.

I continued, "So, Tony, you've got funds now for the next year, to keep your tiny home villages growing, but what's your long-term vision for this project? Keep adding more units for the homeless? More locations? More garden villages? Branch out to more cities? Where do you see this going?"

I could tell Tony saw this as his chance to share his ideas with the rich benefactor. He seemed glad and a little surprised I knew his name. Satchell moved farther away and talked with another guest but kept an eye on me to intervene if I needed.

Tony replied with what sounded like a prepared elevator speech, "All that, but if you're asking about dreams, our dream is in our name. We call ourselves the PATH project: Personal Autonomy through Tiny Homes. I look for the PATH homes to be everywhere and available to everyone who wants one. They will include services to help people on the path to self-sufficiency and personal autonomy. And before long, our tiny home units will also be autonomous vehicles. For personal autonomy, people need more than just a safe place to sleep. They need flexible mobility too.

People will be able to work and play wherever they want without being limited by public transit or the cost of a separate vehicle. And traffic will not be an issue if you don't have to leave your home while commuting. Making them easy to tow between garden villages for access to new jobs is just a first step."

I nodded impassively, looking around the room and said, "I see." Satchel looked for a sign to rescue me, but I didn't give the signal, so he kept his distance. Internally I thought Perry would love Tony's idea, since he was so much into getting rid of human drivers. Autonomous vehicles that people can live in? That seemed like something Perry would like. Just what we need: more people living in their cars I thought. But my face remained blank.

Tony was hoping for more of a reaction, but he continued, "Imagine when everyone can go safely wherever they want and they can keep living their lives: texting, watching or creating videos, playing games, eating, working remotely, sleeping, or interacting with others. And when they step out of their tiny homes into the world, wherever they are, the autonomous tiny home units will remain nearby. People can go wherever they want and always be no more than a few steps away from home. And they're perfect for isolation if another pandemic happens."

As Marta I nodded again impassively, and as Mara I thought, "Yes. Perry will eat up this idea. It's impractical and not likely to work the way Tony describes it, but it's the kind of idea Perry would wish he had thought of. I wonder if Tony has any idea how to make it happen. I should play along and see how much he has thought this through."

I replied to Tony, "Let me get this straight: Mobile Autonomous Tiny Homes For Rescuing Everyone Everywhere you say? Sounds impractical. Have you done the MATH? It won't be FREE."

Tony noticed my acronyms and smiled. He was surprised that I now seemed to be paying attention. It looked like he was mentally kicking himself for not better preparing the next part of his pitch. He probably never thought he would get this far.

He said, "Well it doesn't have to be everyone everywhere, but I have done the MATH and it will be more cost-effective the more universal it becomes. It will take some time to build and set up the infrastructure, but it will more than pay for itself eventually. You could almost say it could be FREE. And self-driving technology is almost ready today. The price is coming down."

"So, you do have a plan? Tell me about it. How much will it cost? Visions are one thing, but I like to see plans, details."

"I don't have all the detailed plans yet. It will take time and money and learning to work out the details. We are going step by step."

"Have you explored venture capital?"

Tony replied, "I don't want it to be all about making money and lose the purpose of my PATH. I want to maintain my minimalism principles."

"Well, money for good things has to come from somewhere. You're going to need venture capital or a partnership with a big company. Money from charities like the Zynn Foundation are a start, but they aren't likely to get you where you want to go."

"I know it will be cost effective and pay for itself when it's fully built."

"Build it and they will come?"

I could tell that Tony was uncomfortable and under-prepared. I found his squirming confidence in his half-baked ideas strangely appealing.

As Marta I was single and available, although aloof and mysterious, and this Tony guy was interesting to me. Maybe I should let Marta act more like Marta. After all, I had been Marta most of my life. Acting like

Marta for once might help protect my hidden identity as Mara. It could be good for Mara.

I thought about inviting Tony to discuss this more in my hotel suite. Then again as Mara I was committed to raising Balaji with Perry and even though we weren't married. In a lot of ways it was like we were married. From my religious school upbringing, being unfaithful to Perry would feel like a sin. Marta, Morta, Mortal Zynn. I decided to keep it business-like with Tony but stay in touch.

"The foundation has funded you for your current year, but we do new rounds of funding from time to time. With the right plan, maybe we could increase your funding, or maybe Zzynarji could invest if you decide to go for profit. Making money doesn't necessarily mean giving up your principles. Send me your boldest plan how you would like to accelerate your progress, and I will look at it. Maybe spell out your wildest dreams and how to get there fast."

"I don't know. My boldest plan to go all the way right away? I've got pretty wild dreams."

"I bet you do. Just lay it on me and let me decide if the foundation or Zzynarji can help you go all the way."

"I know this full PATH dream will be cost effective and self-supporting once it is fully built, and I'm confident that it will happen someday, because it makes so much sense. Trying to get there too fast might waste money, or worse, it might compromise its principles."

"So, your big dreams for tiny mobile home minimalism are both impractical and expensive?"

"Minimalism means simplicity, economy of space, and avoiding clutter, not always less money."

"Is that a saying? I've heard that somewhere before."

"It's a Min-ism. Are you a fan of Min Strong?"

"No. I can't say that I am. But I've heard that name somewhere. Actor or Musician? Mint Song was it? Are you a fan of his?" I asked.

"Of hers. Of course. She's a hero of mine. She's actually my celebrity free pass. My significant other Anne likes her too. She's her celebrity free pass also."

"Wait a minute. Really? TMI. TMI. Tony." I paused to think what he had just said then continued, "Now I think I remember where I heard that name…Min Strong…Isn't she a cartoon?"

"No. No. She's real. She's just in hiding. Some powerful people are out to get her because her ideas challenge how people live and how big businesses run today."

"Big businesses like Zzynarji? Should I be worried? Are you and this Min against capitalism?"

"I don't want to bite the hand that's feeding me, but even Zzynarji as a corporate entity will change or become obsolete someday when enough people adopt Min's ideas."

"Okay. I didn't know that's what you or she were all about Mr. Marx. I thought you were Tony, not Karl. And I thought that Min character was just a decluttering cartoon. Your attitude on all this is unsettling and provocative."

I looked at him, and it seemed like he was being serious.

I continued, "But I will try not to hold that against you. Let me know when you've got your plans for reaching your fondest desires figured out."

"Yes. Ms. Zynn. I'll get on top of that right away."

"You do that, Tony. Tony Marx. And you can call me Marta, Marta Sin" I continued silently, "Marta, Morta, Mortal Sin."

He didn't notice the spelling I used mentally when pronouncing his name and mine, since they sounded the same, but somehow there was a tension of innuendo on the words in the conversation about wildest dreams, fondest desires, provocative and unsettling attitudes, biting the hand, holding something against you, put in, and get on top, go all the way, and people sleeping or interacting with others along the way. Without saying more, we looked at each other briefly with an interest that went beyond the surface of our conversation. I again considered inviting him to my suite. But before I could he looked away.

Tony later told me he wondered how to interpret the looks he got from me. I was a billionaire businesswoman and philanthropist. He had a pretty good relationship with Anne and Marta didn't seem like his type, but he was interested. He had heard Marta was single but didn't know anything about her private life. Some people said she didn't have one. Marta was all business. Working all the time. No one knew of anything she did in her private life.

But a thought occurred to him then. Even though they were completely different, somehow, Marta reminded him of Min Strong. There was a something in some of my facial expressions that seemed like one of the Min Strong cartoon images he looked at many times. "Wouldn't that be funny," he thought, "if this hard-ass uber-capitalist businesswoman was secretly Min Strong, or vice versa. That would be really interesting." He laughed as he walked away towards a colleague from PATH who was trying to get his attention.

"That was Marta Zynn. You talked with Marta Zynn. What does she think about PATH?" asked the colleague. They moved farther away, and I couldn't hear Tony's response.

I had my own conflicting thoughts. As Marta I was supposed to be single and available and should act like I was. As Mara I was a mom and committed to raising Balaji with Perry, although not married. Not married. And as Min, who knows what minimal attachments Min would hold on to. Min was a space cadet.

While I was there that night, I was Marta. I would spend the night in my suite at the hotel. I was planning to fly early tomorrow and land just after 7AM when the morning Orange County airport curfew lifted so I could get home to Balaji and Perry around breakfast time. Getting home to Balaji and Perry tonight was not an option.

I walked away to mingle and talk with other foundation beneficiaries but looked back across the room at Tony from time to time and noticed he was also looking back at me as he talked to others. Satchel noticed the glances and gave me an approving smile.

A little later that night looking out the window from my hotel suite I saw a spectacular fireworks display over the bay. It included a massive grand finale, or two.

July through November 2024

The summer after his second year of college Douglas spent most of his time in the Sierras doing Min Quest hikes and even started guiding others. Sam from next door joined Douglas on one of the hikes, but his sister Josephine didn't join them that time. Sam wanted to test out his new prosthetic leg. Sam came back home after a week, but Douglas stayed away. Douglas seemed to be avoiding the house next door. He went back to school in August.

Josephine, the girl next door had a baby in November. She had turned 18 in February, close to Valentine's Day, and learned she was pregnant a few weeks later. She tried to keep it secret. She had severe morning sickness that eventually led to her missing weeks of her senior year of high school.

Perry found this out from talking with the neighbor mom Camilla during one of their meetings at the curb on trash day or for coffee at her house. Apparently Josephine wouldn't say who was the father, but Camilla was pretty sure it was Sam's college friend Douglas Zynn. Josephine had some other boyfriends, but she had really fallen for the Zynn boy ever since the first time he visited at Thanksgiving a couple years earlier. She missed enough classes in the Spring that she wasn't able to graduate, and she didn't make it up during the summer or the next Fall. Apparently pregnancy and childbirth was difficult for her, and she suffered depression and anxiety.

Camilla didn't like Douglas since she blamed him for Sam losing his leg and for Josephine getting pregnant whether he was the father or not. Josephine had become more argumentative with Camilla since Douglas had come around and seemed to be hanging out with unsavory people. Sam had tried to go back to college in August but dropped out again after a month and moved back home. The pain medication he was taking made it hard for him to get to classes and study. Camilla blamed the Min Quest hike with Douglas for making Sam's leg worse.

After the baby was born in November Josephine had a bad case of postpartum depression and was unable to care for the baby, especially after relying on a mix of prescription and non-prescription drugs. Camilla had been working from home since the pandemic but had to cut back on her hours to take care of Sam, Josephine, and the new baby girl, Isabella. Douglas visited Sam and Josephine shortly after the baby was born but didn't stay long. In my conversations with him as older sister to younger brother he didn't mention those trips south or anything about a baby.

December 2024, Emerging Shape of a Solution

Perry, little Balaji, and I acted like a family when we were together at home. Perry and I never married, although he offered from time to time, with whatever prenup I wanted, and we didn't have much of a romantic relationship, but we were committed to working together to raise our son, and we trusted each other. Three-year-old Balaji called us Mamara and Papa Lee. I didn't run into neighbors much but if one of them referred to me as Mara Lee, I did not correct them. Sergey knew me as Mara Strong, but he didn't mention it to anyone.

We continued to get help from Sergey and a series of nannies, while we did what we had to on our jobs and focused as much attention as we could on finding ways to counter the still-growing emergent negativity in the country and the world.

None of the Zynn Foundation's actions, nor the actions taken by the government agencies so far seemed to stem the negativity tide at all. Misinformation was even more common and more accepted. Division seemed to be growing in America and around the world. Distrust was becoming near universal and expected. The results of the election were disappointing to both of us. I had reluctantly voted for Kamala as the better of two evils.

We felt like a major change would be necessary to change the direction of things, but we were afraid that major change in a wrong direction might be coming soon. Maybe if someone could somehow get people to start using a different kind of social network based on principles that promoted earned trust and allowed a healthy positive emergent intelligence that might make a difference, but it would have to be a big change. Algorithms used by search engines and social networking news feeds were a part of the problem but tweaking those would probably only do a little. And convincing social networking companies to change their algorithms in a way that would reduce their eyeball time and profits was just not going to happen.

We talked more about extrapolating the generative simulated human AI work done by Dr. Atwood in Australia. We had seen that her software could efficiently create a number of functioning AI entities, but we needed to find a way to establish a positive earned trust coefficient between real people on a massive scale in order to create an emergent positive intelligence in the world. The world was becoming more divided into camps of people who had some degree of trust of their political or philosophical bedfellows in the same camp, but which was also based on total distrust of all the other camps, and most camps accepted some things as facts that were demonstrably not true. Some more than others. Politics didn't seem to offer a solution. It seemed to be making things much worse.

Even if some of the camps seemingly had more respect for science and provable facts than others, there was seemingly no path to resolving their differences. It was as if multiple different universes with different basic facts were projected onto the same physical world and were functioning independently. But because these universes shared the same physical world, they collided and generated conflict and contributed to the emergent negativity.

When Perry analyzed the emergent negativity down through its component levels looking for convergence points supporting it, some problems could be traced back to specific troublemakers. Some of those were of interest to the agency as possible terrorists. Others were trying to generate division for personal advantage. But a lot of the negativity was just an emergent feature of the way people got their information and interacted through social media.

The Zynn Foundation kept funding science and education to spread acceptance of provable facts, but the divisions between groups of people were deep and the foundation's efforts were not getting the results we wanted.

We tried to test various scenarios for social changes or new approaches to social media through simulation models. We ran them on our server ranch and some other data centers I built in some underused office buildings around town, disguised as bitcoin mining operations. The simulation models started from the massive snapshots of data Perry had copied. He had been able to update the data from time to time partly from public sources and partly from additional data he brought back from the agency. These simulations relied on a combination of heuristic guesses about how people would react based on their backgrounds and previous actions, and a limited number of simulated-personality AI's based on individual profiles using the AI techniques we got from Dr. Atwood in Australia.

Some of the simulations we ran suggested a possible solution. We hacked the model to assume a new social networking system based on earned trust and provable facts, and the simulation suggested that if we could get a lot of people from various camps to use it, it might eventually change how people interacted with and trusted one another. Two big problems with this hack was that we didn't know how to build such a social networking system, nor how to get people to use it. But if such a system existed and was widely used it would help, apparently.

The hacked simulation suggested that such a system would not eliminate bad behavior of individuals, but it would make it a lot harder to propagate negativity on a large scale. One key for establishing earned trust was being able to clearly distinguish and certify provable facts from falsehoods, opinions, or unknowns and to get people to accept those distinctions. This left us with more questions than answers. Was this theoretical hacked simulation at all accurate? Even if it was, how could such a social network be constructed to sustain earned trust, and even if one could be created, how could it catch on?

Around that time the Personal Autonomy Tiny Homes (PATH) project was coming up for their next round of funding. Tony hadn't sent me a grand proposal ahead of time like I asked, and I had avoided meeting with him. He had reached out to me a number of times by email, since I hadn't given him a private number, asking to meet so we could talk about it, but I was at home with Balaji and Perry when I got each those messages, and as Mara I felt it would not be appropriate to meet privately with Tony, so I made excuses and put him off. On the day of the December Zynn Foundation funding review meeting at the same hotel in the Bay Area as the July meeting, I avoided talking to Tony before the meeting got started. I came into the meeting room at the last minute.

The request Tony brought to the foundation meeting asked for funding for many additional movable tiny homes, additional garden villages, and serious steps towards making a version of the tiny homes that would also be fully autonomous vehicles. Tony's pitch to the foundation committee sounded familiar:

"Imagine. Soon all vehicles will be self-driving, and people will be free to do whatever they want while they are on their way. If they are in their autonomous tiny homes while they are on the road, then commute times won't matter and they can take jobs that fit them best regardless of where they are located. Some people will choose to live exclusively in their mobile autonomous tiny homes. For others it will be like a part of their house that goes with them when they commute. People can feel at home wherever they are. We can give freedom and independence to people who were formerly held back by lack of housing or mobility."

Tony proposed that PATH would seek out alliances with companies doing the sensors, software, and drive motors for autonomous driving rather than trying to develop those themselves, but that his non-profit would do the final assembly of the homes. The incentive for the companies would be the profits they could make selling components when large numbers of these tiny home vehicles were manufactured.

Even though I had thwarted his efforts to meet and talk during the weeks since our last meeting, I had been hoping he would bring a more complete plan for his "wildest dream vision" explaining how it would make financial sense. This proposal had hints towards that dream, but it was not fully fleshed out and even the more detailed written proposal didn't explain the finances. As Tony concluded, the other foundation directors looked to see my reaction and when I seemed disappointed one of them spoke up and said, "Thank you Mr. Marks. I think that is all we need to hear right now. We'll review your proposal more closely and get back with you in 2025."

Tony looked at me expecting me to say something, but I didn't. I avoided contact with Tony after the meeting. I had not shared Tony's elevator pitch with Perry after the previous meeting. I wanted to get the more complete autonomous mobility proposals from Tony before talking to Perry about it. And for some reason I was uncomfortable talking about Tony with Perry. I was hoping for a more complete vision of Tony's wildest dreams for PATH. What I got at the latest meeting seemed vague and incomplete, but at least it gave more of an introduction to Tony's idea of autonomous live-in vehicles.

When I got back home after the meetings I shared the proposal with Perry. Perry loved the idea of being able to keep working in his own space when on the road. He hated driving. A self-driving car would be great, but a self-driving tiny house would be even better. Perry immediately had dozens of ideas for how these units ought to work and features that should be included.

"They should have broad band connectivity with UHD displays on the walls for communication and entertainment. They could even be 3D holo-decks like in Star Trek. They should have standardized portals for accepting deliveries without human contact. Oh. Oh. And that could work with a storage service so they can put things in storage or get them back without human contact through the same delivery portals. They don't need any steering wheel or front seat, or really even any windows. When you take all that away you can fit quite a bit into the volume of a tall cargo van. And you could make them a little bigger and taller than a cargo van to fit even more. They could be configured for individuals, or couples, or very small families, but would probably work best for individuals."

I could tell he was visualizing the 3D space inside of such a vehicle and mentally designing how it might work.

"I want to work on this project," he said.

"I thought it might strike your interest."

"Oh. Oh. And of course, it will need to have a voice interface to an intelligent assistant like on phones. I suppose it could just use any of those existing ones. There could be versions from Apple, Google, Amazon, and others."

"I was thinking maybe they could each have one of those AIs like our Min AI, but with a more helpful personality," I suggested. "It could handle ordering services similar to how those smartphone assistants work, but if it's based on a positive earned trust hive AI, it might help get us to the new kind of positive social media we were trying to figure out."

"Interesting idea. How would that work? Would Dr. Atwood's hive AI's talking to each other generate positive earned trust at the next aggregate level?" Perry asked.

"I'm not sure. We're brainstorming. The whole thing with these live-in mobile pods is a new kind of immersive space where people could spend a lot of time; a new kind of user experience can be created there. Like living inside of your smartphone. Maybe somehow, we can make that experience one that uses a positive earned trust social networking."

I paused, realizing I'd have to think more about how that might work, but I continued, "Earned trust principles would at least be useful for traffic coordination. We could start there. The vehicles will need to cooperate on the road. So maybe if they use positive hive principles to communicate and cooperate peer to peer for navigation instead of relying on a master server that would be a start."

Perry added, "That's right. And communication for coordinating ordering services, delivery and storage could also use that technology."

We thought about it and decided that it was worth considering. We would try to put a version of Jerry's hive AI in each vehicle and let them communicate with one another using the same earned trust hive intelligence principles. That might create an emergent positive hive intelligence over the community of vehicles, at least for traffic coordination and deliveries. That wouldn't necessarily make the humans in the vehicles cooperate, but it could be a start.

Early 2025

With Perry's full endorsement, I had the foundation give PATH more than the funding they were asking for, but with the condition that Tony combine efforts with the INCA project and The Atwood hive AI PET project. At first Tony was hesitant about plugging in someone else's AI inside his PATH homes. Dr. Atwood also objected that her human personality AIs were meant to understand more about people, not to make a new version of Alexa or Siri.

Perry, as a representative of INCA and an expert on Nested Cellular Autonomy, contacted Dr. Atwood in Australia and Tony Marks at PATH and explained how important it was that they combine efforts and look into using Atwood NCA AI principles for coordinating among Tony's autonomous tiny homes. He didn't get into the whole world-wide negativity hive intelligence thing, but he did explain how Nested Cellular Autonomy would allow the collection of autonomous PATH vehicles to create a healthy emergent cooperative intelligence for traffic and delivery management.

Dr. Atwood became an advocate for the idea when she learned that she would be working closely with Perry on the project. Tony came reluctantly on board after a few sessions talking with Perry and Dr. Atwood, and after I, as Marta, told him it seemed like a good idea and his funding depended on it. He still would bring up objections to using elements of Dr. Atwood's version of INCA's AI principles in his tiny homes.

Their separate work in INCA and PATH had been supported by the Zynn Foundation, but I made sure the increased funding would cover combining efforts, expanding, and building on their prior work in a new joint effort that became known as the Autonomy Mobility (AM) project, or sometimes as AM-PATH.

The project grew. More talented people joined the team. Some were paid relatively low salaries as employees of the INCA or PATH non-profits, or as graduate student researchers funded by grants from the Zynn Foundation. Some volunteered time and ideas to the project, while working at other high-tech jobs because they were fascinated by the idea of creating something new and solving big social issues. Between paid staff and volunteers the projects had dozens of people working on designs for the autonomous mobile pods and the infrastructure and software to support them, but most had other job prospects that could make them more money.

Perry and I talked about how best to keep attracting the best minds to work on the projects. He suggested raising their salaries to be competitive with high tech companies. I suggested keeping salaries low and promising them a tiny share in future royalties if the designs they created were eventually licensed for commercial products. I knew we might not ever need to license out the designs if the project was able to scale up for its own production, like Tony proposed, but I figured we didn't need to tell them that. In retrospect maybe I should have been more generous and unambiguous with the profit-sharing terms for the team members.

At that time various companies were perfecting the hardware and software for autonomous vehicles and putting them into service as taxis in various cities. Perry frequently complained about how slow the progress towards wide-spread adoption of fully autonomous vehicles was going. He would bring up a public statement made by the leader of one of the companies back in 2016 that their then current model vehicles needed only a software update to become fully self-driving and yet that promise was only partly fulfilled over eight years later.

Perry suggested that AM-PATH should buy the self-driving technology from one of the commercial self-driving companies and use it as a subconscious component of the vehicle's NCA intelligence but also put some effort into developing the on-board AIs as drivers in case commercial self-driving efforts continued to be delayed. Perry didn't want to spend time on the driving software himself. He thought he should focus first on other aspects of the AM-pods. He suggested I could have Zzynarji donate their autonomous vehicle technology if they ever got it to work. I told him I'd think about it.

Meanwhile the project had many other questions to answer: What size and shapes should the AM-pods have? How would they use PET peer-to-peer networking to communicate with one another? How can they autonomously connect to charging stations without any action from the people inside? How about plumbing? How can they autonomously connect for dumping waste and refilling water tanks? How many charging/dumping stations would be needed and where should they be located? How would the charging and dumping infrastructure be paid for? If people lived in their AM-pods, would they drive to restaurants or take delivery for all their meals, or should the units include small kitchens. How would delivery and trash disposal work? Should they be fully electric or should other types of power be considered? Perry had a lot of ideas for answering these questions and Tony felt like many of them had already been solved by his towable tiny homes.

It became clear that there were a lot of options and design choices to make and not a clear answer as to which choices would be best or how to choose. The team had a lot of strong opinions, especially Perry and Tony, but also a number of others. Of course, some design choices could be individualistic and vary from one vehicle unit to another, but others probably had to be standardized. The project needed to figure out which was which and which ideas were best.

One thing was clear to Perry and me: We needed to move quickly because if the AM-PATH project didn't come up with a great solution soon, some for-profit companies out there might see the same opportunities and dominate the market without the emergent hive positivity. Car companies were already working on standards for car-to-car information sharing based on other principles.

I worked closely with Perry behind the scenes to strategize on how to make this project successful. Perry was in the middle of the project, spending more time than he told his bosses at the agency, figuring that his job at the agency, like most government jobs, could end at any time.

As Marta I didn't publicly say much but provided foundation funding for the strategies that Perry and I chose and eventually had some meetings with Tony to understand his point of view so that Perry could be more prepared to persuade him about various choices. I also generated public interest in the project by having Min Strong mention it and encourage discussion about it in the Min-iverse community: She endorsed AM-PATH for supporting minimalism. Her support seemed to persuade Tony more than Perry's arguments or Marta's threats to cut funding.

MinAI was getting good at answering questions for the What Would Min Keep panel. I set up a process to feed the latest questions from the WWMK site to her in our server ranch once a day and to feed her answers back to WWMK after I reviewed them. I seldom changed her answers except for adding things like mentioning specific projects, like AM-PATH that she didn't previously know about. By this point I also let her do some live events as Min Strong. I closely monitored the first couple but eventually let her participate on her own. Of course, we had to set up roundabout routing for her network connection to the events. She existed only in the server ranch which we didn't want exposed. If anyone tried to trace her connection, it looked like she was connecting from multiple cities on different continents. After each event we would disconnect those network channels so that she was isolated again in our server ranch, and we would scrub the public router and switch records leading back to the ranch. It helped that the Zzynarji Company owned routing networks in several countries and regions including Orange County.

When the AM-PATH team would get stuck between Perry's and Tony's, or sometimes some else's, opinions about certain design choices, I suggested that we use our simulation tools to test them. Repurposing the tools that we had created to analyze charity investments by modelling potential worlds, we created potential worlds where different AM-pod design choices were introduced and tested. The team was already using standard tools, operations research model simulations, as well as focus groups to evaluate design ideas, but people still disagreed about many details, and Perry and I thought more detailed simulation worlds might help.

Tony had committed to delivering thousands of new tiny homes each year and wanted to stay with similar designs as previous years. He couldn't wait to sort out all the details for the fully autonomous models. Each year they introduced some new design ideas and got some feedback from real people using them, but many of the proposed new AM pod ideas depended on the mobility and coordinated autonomy features that were not yet ready.

We created simulated worlds with very large numbers of simulated AM pods to see how well they would work together. I suggested that we let people observe these simulated worlds and give feedback on various proposed features. I also suggested we could create large numbers of simple semi-intelligent simulated people using Atwood AI techniques similar to the MinAI but based on the profiles of real people from the social media data and let those simulated people try out the variations of design choices and see if they liked them. Perry said it seemed worth a try. We worked to have Jerry and Tony both think they had thought of the idea.

Another obstacle we saw coming was the public acceptance of driverless technology. Driverless cars from various companies were in use as robo-taxis in various cities with some degree of public acceptance, and most new cars had at least limited autopilot features, but full acceptance of driverless technology was slow in catching on. Any accident involving a driverless vehicle got attention in the news, even if statistically they were already much safer than cars driven by the average human driver. One of the challenges was how to overcome public misgivings about the safety of driverless technology. I thought simulations might provide more data about the safety of these vehicles.

The designs of the mobile autonomous homes and the simulations to test those designs made a lot of progress over the next year or two. A lot of Perry's initial ideas ended up being included. The effort to include elements of the Atwood AI techniques for coordination among tiny homes was providing some promising results, at least in the simulations. We constructed a method for certifying the truthfulness of messages, at first with regard to commuting and traffic data. This involved a so-called MinStrong encryption, named after and dedicated to the minimalism guru. It was very efficient and virtually unbreakable in a distributed environment. Its author was anonymous, which gave some people cause to believe it was actually written by Min Strong. Which in fact it was, or at least I had a lot to do with its writing.

In the simulations, when virtually all traffic used the same cooperative techniques, the impact on traffic flow, safety, and commuting times was dramatic. Traffic signals were obsolete. Vehicles could flow and merge and navigate seamlessly with almost never stopping for other vehicles and with no noticeable jostling for people within the units. People in the units could feel like they were in a motionless tiny house even if the units were moving on the roads. Collisions also were non-existent. When the simulations included human-driven and driverless vehicles that didn't cooperate with the hive principles, traffic flow and overall safety were significantly worse. The AM pods could still navigate smoothly and safely, but much more slowly.

The project was prototyping homes with AI assistants who would coordinate with AI assistants in other homes using earned trust principles. They couldn't take real units out in the real world in any numbers but could test large numbers of them in the simulations. When simulating a mobile autonomous vehicle capability, each pod's AI would share information with others about their own planned route, as well as perceived road conditions, traffic, and other sensor data and certify that the information provided was a trust-worthy representation of what the sensors observed. Each AI would focus on achieving the objectives of the occupants of its own particular pod but would share knowledge and expertise with AI's in other pods for mutual advantage. I suggested that they could negotiate using microtransactions. Cooperative units that helped other units out more could earn some kind of cooperation points for their occupants that could be spent later. And people in a hurry could spend points to have a faster path.

The project worked out how the pods could communicate securely directly peer to peer without having to go through centralized data service providers. That was efficient for dealing with traffic coordination since most of the communication needed to be with nearby pods anyway. That way also they could reduce the chances for a central authority monitoring or modifying messages or controlling their flow. They could still use data service providers as a channel to legacy services, and as an alternate channel to contact other pods at a longer distance, but near pod to near pod communication seemed to have real advantages.

Proposed possible worlds were designed with different assumptions about the designs of the AM-pods and how universal they were. Other assumptions about each world could be introduced to add narrative interest. The simulation game started to take on a life of its own. The simulation would run using a combination of heuristic predictions for general behavior along with increasing numbers of specific AI characters. It was an interesting game to observe and influence the behavior and interactions of the AI characters.

The nested cellular autonomy computing model that it was built upon made it easy to allow multiple observers using their own computers to run their own story lines around the characters that they selected to observe, and still have the various sub-worlds coordinate into one reasonably consistent whole. Because of this distributed nature of the simulations, the project decided to open them up to allow more people to participate.

People in the AM-PATH organization and in the INCA institute had been able to participate and they reached out to colleagues and friends to give others the opportunity to use the system as well. Miniacs were eager to try out the simulated worlds with the AM pods that Min Strong endorsed. Some people participated as observers with varying degrees of control as "drivers" or influencers of characters. Others helped to create new narrative worlds and story lines or designed more details of physical neighborhoods within the worlds. User interfaces were simple at first, but people joined the project to make the interfaces more realistic. Perry and I also used these new simulations to test possible Zynn Foundation charitable investments by inserting them as narrative features of the game worlds. We could later extract data from the simulations for Perry to analyze for emergent hive negativity or positivity.

The AM-PATH team debated about which user interface to provide with the game. Some wanted to access the game with their phones without any other hardware. Others wanted to use high end 3D VR headsets. An AI company offered photorealistic real-time 3D video renderings for users who wanted to pay for them. Some people even preferred a simple textual version.

We decided there needn't be just one interface. We figured that each observer could run different user interface software for the storyline around their selected characters. Some could be text-based. Some could be cartoons. Some could be realistic high resolution 3-D immersive experiences. Users could choose the point of view as well as the manner and detail of the interface. The view could be from the eyes and mind of a single character at a time, or from a more omniscient narrator observing a scene or a group of people.

The more computing power an observer brought to the simulation and the more they were willing to invest in interface software and hardware, the more realistic their user experience could be. The coordination between storylines in the macro world of the simulation did not depend much on the individual user interfaces. Characters could interact, with one controlled by a user using a text-based interface and another using a high-resolution virtual reality graphics interface and their interactions would still make sense for both of them.

With my advice Perry talked to some game developers about the possibility of adding custom user interface software components that could plug in to give different degrees of realism and compatibility with different display and interaction devices. A few were interested and started adapting their software to work with this simulation. Some interfaces were donated and free to all users and others were add-on options that users could purchase.

I noticed that while the user interface experience of each observer depended on the software and computer power the observer provided, the same was not necessarily true for the complexity of the AI characters that the users observed, drove, or influenced. Some users could take a larger share of the computing power in the distributed game network by utilizing AI components running on other computers. I proposed adding market principles to keep it fair. Add a general concept of game points that could allow micro-credits and debits for providing or using capabilities provided by others. We were already using similar points in negotiating traffic cooperation, and they could be applied to network connectivity, negotiating the use of knowledge, cognitive components, or computing power. Allowing micro-payments of royalties for using specific expertise components suggested a solution for part of the problems the other large generative AI models had with questionable use of copyrighted material.

Background characters that were not being observed by anyone would go about their typical behaviors following heuristics and general modeling principles based on their profiles rather than each exhibiting a full AI personality. When they would interact with more robust AI characters they would get some extra juice from the interaction, borrowing processing power from the characters with which they interacted.

Individual AI characters were primarily controlled from each observer's computer, but each character did not need to run entirely in a single computer. They could use components running on their own or other computers, so even low-powered user interfaces could have sophisticated AI personalities. With a more powerful computer they could also provide processing power for some AI components to be shared with other users. With more users playing the game and providing shared computing power, the AI characters could become more powerful. With the point tracking mechanism that I suggested, a market could be established with benefits for those who provided services used by others, and costs for those who consumed more than they provided.

The game was a distributed multi-personality simulation running as an app on many loosely connected computers, tablets, and smartphones. Someone worked out how to make sure that elements of each AI character and all the components each used could be backed up on multiple computers across the game network, with appropriate point tracking. That way when any one player shut down their computer or phone, their characters, and the components they were running would not simply disappear but could still be there in the game world operating on other computers, possibly at a lower sophistication, until their observer/driver returned. Players who wanted a more powerful character than they could run on their phone could contract with cloud services for extra capacity, but the demand for that diminished as the distributed network of devices running the game became more powerful.

The simulation became a popular game. It was referred to as the AM Pod game or just the AM game. While there was no real reason a game with this kind of distributed multi-personality AI interaction needed to feature AM pods, it was implemented in a way that security modules for the traffic coordination of the AM-pods was reused in the secure communication among Nested Cellular Autonomy component in AI entities. Versions of the game with simulated worlds without AM pods didn't have those security modules and just didn't work as well. Eventually people figured out how to get around this, but for the first few years of the AM game all its working versions featured game worlds with AM pods.

As the AI assistants in the AM pods took on more expertise for giving advice to their occupants Perry suggested the name Abbie, after his mom who was known among her friends as the go to person for personal advice on many subjects. For history buffs, Abby was also the name of an old newspaper advice columnist. When the name Abbie caught on the project started to call the AM pods Abitats.

Spring 2025, Leaving the Agency?

As the AM game evolved and along with it the initial designs for AM pods, or Abitats, Perry wanted to get away from his agency work so that he could spend more time on the designs and the game. In 2025, after over five years with the agency Perry decided he should leave the agency and take a full-time research position again in the INCA institute at the university. His agency position had so far survived the massive DOGE cuts in government jobs, but he still decided he wanted to get out. Most university research labs were also being drastically cut due to loss of government funding, but the Zynn Foundation funded the INCA institute, so it was still well-funded. Taking a job there paid less than the agency job, but money was not really an issue, and he figured he would eventually get rich from royalties from his contributions on the project.

He wanted to be home more, and he wanted to work with people to find real solutions for the negativity trends, instead of contributing to making them worse. Perry's boss Randy had moved to another job in the agency and Perry's new supervisor, George, was a pain and maybe dangerous.

George had recommended that the government take actions against negative convergence points that showed up in Perry's analysis, with little or no additional investigation. Perry explained that they needed confirmation by other methods since they might be just circumstantially connected rather than bad actors themselves. George said taking that time meant missing opportunities to act. Perry was very uncomfortable with that. Innocent people and organizations could be targeted.

But some of the statistics did tend to support George. Whenever Perry's emergent negativity analysis identified potential high-probability, high-value targets in other countries, additional investigation almost always confirmed them as valid targets, even if it didn't spell out what kind of action to take.

Perry wasn't sure if that was because his modelling was just that good, or if the follow-on investigations were biased. The new management at the agency seemed to want to find domestic targets as much as foreign ones and was starting to misidentify domestic positive convergence points as targets. Perry adjusted his models to focus more on the negative convergence points and make the positive ones less visible, but he was still concerned about people who might be targeted without justification and wanted out.

When Perry expressed discomfort, George brought up the fact that Perry himself had said his models should be getting more accurate since he had tuned them with side-analysis he had done offline with large data samples he had been allowed to take back to the west coast. He had specifically upgraded his laptop-attached storage to a uniquely large configuration for that purpose. Perry said that his side analysis was important for tuning the model, but it did not take the place of on-the-ground confirmation. He didn't think it was safe to take actions based on his analysis alone and positive convergence points should always be treated differently from negative points. Maybe if he could have a lot more time with the full agency data sets, he could tune the model better, but even then, it would never be precise enough to justify actions on its own. The models were just models.

George said, "If we take out a few extra questionable characters that's okay if we are getting a lot of the real bad guys too. If they are circumstantially connected, they are still connected." That was very unsettling for Perry and reconfirmed his decision about leaving.

But the fact that George mentioned the data download worried Perry. If he left the agency, they might look into it more and discover that he had copied the data into the server ranch and used some of it in character profiles for AM game worlds. While having a copy of that data in private servers was all for good purposes, it was not approved by the agency, and it violated a number of secrecy and privacy laws. He could go to prison for decades or worse if it was discovered.

Perry decided it was time to leave the agency, but he had a few things to do to reduce the risks before he left.

In case they investigated him after he resigned, he needed to have a plan. One idea was to disappear. Go underground with Mara at the house by the ranch or somewhere new. But disappearing would probably trigger an investigation, and if they wanted to track him down it would be hard to hide. The only addresses that the agency had for him were his dad's Santa Ana machine shop and his former apartment near DC. Those two and his internal agency addresses were the only places he received mail. But there were breadcrumbs that someone at the agency could follow to find where he was really living. Someone could follow him, but they didn't have to. His face and his car's license plate would be on recordings from thousands of public and private surveillance cameras and dashcams everywhere he had been. The agency could access all of those recordings if they wanted to. Having access to analyze almost all the data in the world gave Perry a pretty good idea of what kinds of breadcrumbs were out there if someone wanted to follow them.

He had never given the agency the address of the house next to the farm or of the farm itself and had never told any of his coworkers about them. His name was not on the property titles. They were both owned by shell companies owned by other shell companies that were in turn eventually owned by one trust or another that I controlled. His name was not mentioned anywhere on any of those deeds. He thought his name was on Balaji's birth certificate and his homeschool records but for the most part that was not the case. Still, the agency would be able to track him down if they wanted to. We decided he would be better to hide in plain sight. He would keep the machine shop address, and he would take the INCA job, but he would continue being careful about anything that could connect him to the ranch house or the farm.

He mentioned that the agency had tools to help hide the identities of witnesses, spies, and defectors. Tools that could scan through data systems and mask, change, or remove specific entries. Some tools could scrub specific photos to change someone's face or remove their image from pictures entirely. Other tools could do similar masking to non-photographic data. The agency could collect and read data from sources all over the world and also had the ability to make changes back into most of those data sources. The software he had borrowed years ago to alter images of me for the Min Strong comics and to disguise my voice for Min-iverse sessions were part of a large suite of such tools.

Before telling the agency that he was leaving, he got George's approval for one extra-large analysis run that would tie up most of the computing resources in the agency for a few hours. George wanted to find a lot more domestic deep state bad guys quickly and believed Perry when he told him that a larger and longer analysis run would have a better chance to accomplish that.

With a lot of my help Perry hid code in the analysis package to turn on the image masking and other data masking for Balaji, me, and to a lesser extent, himself. It was also designed to mask evidence of itself running in the agency's systems. We didn't know exactly how well it would work, but we hoped it might reduce the chances they would find the ranch and discover that Perry had copied agency data there, at least for a while. The biggest risk was that this code would be detected and bring down tons of trouble on him, so I put extra effort into making the code hide itself.

We designed the software to remove itself after cleansing the existing data in the agency's control. Any new data the agency imported after the package stopped running would not be masked. We could be more careful going forward to avoid surveillance cameras, but the extremely large existing archives of agency data should have less evidence of his connections to me, Balaji, the ranch, and the servers at the ranch, or Mara's connections to the Zzynarji company. He gave notice to end the lease at his apartment near DC before pushing the button to start the big analysis run. Then he went in to talk with George about resigning and going back to academia.

"George, I need to let you know I'm leaving the agency. I'm going back to the university out west."

George misunderstood what Perry was saying at first and thought he was making another request to work from the Southern California office.

"No need to make a threat about leaving the agency. I'm fine with you moving to the SoCal office full time." He said he wasn't sure why Randy had resisted Perry's requests for so long. Perry was spending most of his time out west anyway. He must have a girlfriend or boyfriend out there although that was none of his business. The conversation went around in circles as Perry was trying to clarify that he really was leaving, and George continued to make concessions.

"I don't want to just do the same work at a different office. I want to get back into academia and work on other kinds of research."

"I know you have made noises about how we use your analysis, but it's working. Your work is important here. It's having an impact. I suppose I could give you some more time to let you do some other work on the side if you really want."

George's immediate career path depended on the analyses that Perry generated, including the big one that was currently running. He believed that the domestic analysis would prove the existence of the deep state and identify its members. This made Perry very nervous.

George said that It didn't matter if Perry worked out west. Improved secure networks allowed full access to the agency's data centers from most agency offices including the west coast office. In fact, he preferred if he didn't have to see Perry so much. Just so long as the analysis kept giving him targets to send for action. George wanted to move up in the agency more quickly than Randy had done, but he needed Perry to keep producing targets.

"George, I'm not sure if I can say this any plainer. I really don't want to be in the agency anymore."

A half hour later when Perry left George's office he was perplexed. Somehow, he had agreed to officially quit, but stay with the agency in a covert role, continuing to build analysis models each month, and checking in directly only with George, while living in Southern California and officially taking a job as a researcher at the university. George said Perry was quite a negotiator. He liked the ideas Perry suggested about working undercover. George realized this could be even better for him as well. Perry could feed George the analysis models and George could claim full credit for them. That could accelerate his career advancement even more. Perry would turn in his agency resignation today, and George would make the back-end arrangements for him to continue covertly.

Later that day when the big analysis run was scheduled to be complete Perry had already turned in his agency credentials and laptop and was back at this apartment packing the last of his personal belonging to take on the plane back to California. For the moment he couldn't check on the analysis run or see what the agency was doing with the data. He was worried about what George and the government would do with the newly identified targets. He hoped they would not be able to find any positive convergence points. And he hoped they didn't notice the data masking changes in the analysis run. He looked over his shoulder many times as he turned in his apartment keys and went to the airport and got on the plane home. He probably kept looking over his shoulder that way ever since.

It was not until years later that I realized that I had made a mistake with the masking software. I made it do too good a job hiding evidence of itself; it was hidden from the cleanup phase at the end of the computer run, and it did not remove itself, but continued to replicate itself and run hidden deep in the background on the agency computer systems, continuing to mask information about us. I probably could have submitted a fix for that with one of the analysis runs that Perry covertly submitted to George after that, but it had been working for years without Perry getting arrested, so I left it alone.

George arranged a secure drop off procedure with which Perry was still feeding analysis models to run about once a month, and George was sending Perry back the results to review for improving the models. George provided Perry with new secure computing equipment and offered to arrange a covert office where he could work. Perry already had an office at the university, as well as desks in his workshops in the barn and his dad's machine shop, so he declined George's offer of new office space, but did get a secure network line installed into his dad's old machine shop in Santa

Ana with access to agency data. The machine shop continued to be Perry's official address.

To free up more of his time Perry started to train a MaxAI based on himself to do some of his work for the agency, but it didn't have as much training material as the MinAI. He could train it to build hive models based on his previous work and his papers on the subject, and on the tweaks he made to each model run. It was soon able to do about as well setting up and running his models as any of his former coworkers at the agency, but that was not good enough. He let MaxAI do the initial set up for each model run and Perry would adjust it and then clean up the results after the run and Max AI would learn from the changes. It was like having an assistant on his agency work. He was able to limit his own agency-related work time for George to no more than a few hours each month. George seemed satisfied with the results he was getting, at least for a while.

Late 2025 to 2031, The Next Few Years

I'd call Douglas or see his updates on social media and occasionally I'd meet him at one of the Zynn family houses. I would encourage Perry to talk with Camilla next door and get more information about Douglas. Apparently, Douglas still kept in touch with Camilla's kids, Sam and Josephine and Josephine's daughter, Isabella. Perry said that Camilla would also invite me and Balaji to visit with him, but we never went. Perry would say I wasn't home or not feeling well when she asked, and Balaji was not willing to go out. Camilla didn't interrogate Perry about never seeing me but told him she was available to talk any time. Perry and I were in our early thirties and Camilla was mid-forties or so then, but she still looked good. I would tease Perry that she was a cougar trying to get him and that I was okay with whatever he chose to do over there.

"I'm never over there for more than 10 minutes."

"You underestimate, but still, 10 minutes?? That's nine minutes to spare."

From his conversations with Camilla, Perry got news about her family and a little about visits from Douglas.

Her son Sam next struggled with drug addiction after taking so many pain meds but managed to go back to school. He barely passed but finished his degree. He didn't find a job after graduating but hung out at home when he wasn't out somewhere with friends or on a backpacking trip with Douglas.

Josephine next door wasn't home much except sometimes to sleep, eat, or ask for money. She didn't pay any attention to her daughter Isabella. Camilla said Josephine was taking classes at the local community college but never completed any degrees or certificates. She was on several meds for her depression and some other medical issues, and Camilla thought she took a lot of other drugs as well. Camilla wasn't sure where Josephine was most of the time but thought she hung out with people who were into drugs. Josephine seemed to have different friends than Sam, but sometimes they went out together.

Camilla continued taking care of Isabella who went to pre-K and kindergarten at the public school nearby, but also got involved in youth sports, playing soccer and swimming. Camilla would drive Isabella to one sporting activity or another just about every day. Isabella and Josephine almost never saw each other since Josephine was seldom home and stayed in bed most of the time when she was.

Camilla mentioned that Douglas visited a few times a year and each time made a point of bringing something for Isabella, often something he had picked up in the mountains on one of his backpacking trips. Isabella called him Daddy, and he didn't object but he didn't offer child support. Camilla didn't try to get any money from Douglas. She was concerned that he might try to take custody someday. She was able to work remotely part time and was okay financially.

Douglas never mentioned Isabella or Josephine in his conversations with me, but occasionally mentioned Sam, his backpacking friend with the prosthetic leg. He eventually finished his bachelor's degree at Cal taking classes between backpacking trips in the Sierras and other mountain ranges around the world. He took the family yacht on some trips along the coast, with a full professional crew, and got another small sailboat for short trips around the San Francisco Bay, but never again did any long sailing trips.

Camilla also talked about a college friend of Sam's who was doing well and who she wished Sam and Josephine had associated with more instead of Douglas. Barack Jackson was his name, but he went by Brock. Apparently she followed him on social media. He worked for a senator in DC for a couple years and got a graduate degree at a university in Orange County before getting into local politics. He seemed to be on his way up. Sam and Josephine no longer kept in touch with him despite Camilla's suggestions. I remembered that Brock had almost sailed with Douglas from Hawaii to Tahiti.

Perry and I were still sharing ideas and working together on AM-PATH and the AM Game as well as other investments by the Zynn Foundation to try to fix the world. The foundation also put more investments into efforts to slow climate change. We figured the climate wouldn't matter if the negativity beast killed us all, but creating a positive hive intelligence across humanity wouldn't matter if everyone died from climate disasters. We had to address both.

Along those lines, Zzynarji worked on small scale nuclear and fusion power plants and got some promising results, but nothing yet on a large commercial scale. They also investigated climate mitigation ideas, such as carbon air scrubbing, space parasols, and non-polluting hydrogen-based fuels. That was in addition to the wind and solar industries they had been involved in for a long time. High speed data networks, space launch, and satellite communications for the government and commercial customers were still a big part of Zzynarji's business.

Perry spent a lot of his time working with the people at INCA. During those years he spent almost as much time at INCA as he did at home. I spent a lot of time as Perry's invisible partner helping with software for PATH and the AM Game, and even more of my time as Marta running the Zzynarji company. It was expanding and very profitable, and I was not giving it away as fast as it was growing. As Marta I found reasons to meet with Tony from PATH now and then.

Min Strong was still popular, and I rarely had to intervene with MinAI other than to check on what she was saying and suggest topics for her to mention. Min AI was becoming quite capable of handling Min Strong's activities. The Max AI was getting smarter too, but still not able to replicate Perry's fine touch on running analysis for the agency, so Perry still spent some hours on agency work each month.

PATH incorporated ideas from the simulations to build newer models of AM pods with some similarities to the Abitats in the AM Game. Some were built with full self-driving, but they needed extra sensors and computers, or remote supervision, so they were too expensive to give away to the homeless in any large numbers and they were not as smooth moving as Abitats in the game. Occupants had to buckle up or hold on while the prototype autonomous AM pods were in motion. To give more mobility to the simpler AM pod trailers, a fleet of autonomous tow trucks provided services, but there were not enough of them to go around, and the charging infrastructure to allow them to recharge without human assistance was limited to areas near to certain garden villages. Most of the AM pods stayed in one location for months or years at a time or longer, like other tiny homes.

A few prototype units with autonomous mobility features were publicized positively on social media and Min-iverse WWMK by their users. They downplayed the costs and limited refreshing capabilities. People watching these testimonials got a biased view of the readiness of the AM pods as fully autonomous and mobile tiny dwellings. This raised interest in the AM pods among Miniacs. The AM Game became popular as a place where people could experience Abitats for themselves and new app versions of the game became widely available.

July 2031, Anxious Little Boy

By the time Balaji turned 11 in 2031 we had long given up getting him to go out of the house to school. When he was a baby COVID was happening and then I stayed nervous about exposing him to COVID, RSV, measles, and other diseases that were going around after the pandemic. So many parents were not vaccinating their kids. He got lessons from us and his nannies, but we wanted him to have some social experience, so after the pandemic died down we tried getting him to go to school.

He strongly resisted going out to an in-person preschool or kindergarten, and at first I thought it was just because he preferred to stay home and play games, but eventually I was convinced that he had a genuine phobia. We tried a number of different public and private schools. He didn't last more than a few hours at any of them. He cried and screamed and fought until we had to take him home.

We tried a combination of private tutoring and remote learning. He didn't like tutors coming into the house but was okay interacting with tutors and other children virtually, although he was often rude. Academically he was ahead of kids his age and he was not shy about telling them. Maybe a little like his mom had been, but worse.

We settled on remote learning for Balaji with a virtual private school. He didn't take many classes with kids his own age. Most he took individually, but some were with older kids. The virtual classrooms meant he had to use a computer for several hours every day. He was okay interacting with a teacher and other students through the computer. It felt like a game to him. Perry set him up with extra-large computer displays on the walls of his bedroom for the virtual classwork. When we were not checking on him, he used them to play games on most of the screen display space while the virtual class was in session in a small window in a corner of one of them. Despite his distractions, he excelled in most of his classes.

His agoraphobia extended to anything out the front door or by car. He was okay going out in our own backyard and even exploring the farm down the path behind so long as no strangers were present. He was okay talking with Sergey in the farm but kept his distance from any of the day workers Sergey hired to help.

I would sometimes watch him on the security cameras when he went outside. One day in the summer of '31 I saw the little girl next door climb over the fence into our backyard when Balaji was there. I turned on the sound.

"Hi. I'm Izzie. Who are you?"

"Balaji. I don't think you're allowed to be here, Izzie. You should go back to your own yard."

"It's okay. My Cam-mah is working. She told me to play outside. You're lucky, Budgie. Good climbing trees." She ran down the slope and started climbing a tree, swinging, and scrambling, quickly getting into branches well above Balaji's head. "See?"

"You shouldn't be doing that," Balaji said. He walked down the slope and stood below her under the tree. "It's not safe."

"It's okay. I'm five. I'm good at climbing trees now. When I was four, I climbed little trees, but now I'm five. Five and a half, actually. Now I can climb big trees. You're a lot older than me. You must be able to climb really tall trees. Climb up."

"No thanks. Please get down."

"Oh. There are some really big trees over there." Isabella pointed through the branches in the direction of the farm.

"Yes. The farm has some big trees. Please get down."

"The farm? Do you know how to go to the farm? Do you climb those big trees?"

"I sometimes go to the farm, but I don't climb trees."

"Let's go." Isabella slid down and swung from branch to branch until she was just above Balaji and dangling in front of him. "Catch me!"

She dropped. He reached but missed her. She landed feet first, and rolled, then stood up, grabbed his hand, and pulled him towards the bushes at the back fence.

"You missed! But I'm okay. Let's go."

He followed her towards the back fence but then showed her the path that led through the bushes and into the farm.

Apparently, she survived the tree-climbing that she did in the farm, because she passed through our back yard many times in the following months.

Balaji was not a tree-climber, but he was a gamer. He started young with game systems. Perry bought a number of game systems and games for those systems. Perry and I disagreed about what kinds of games were acceptable for a young boy and how much time he should be allowed to play. Perry was more permissive and bought him games that I thought he was not ready for. I was away a lot doing my Marta work and I found out that when I was away Perry's little Billy Jay played as much as he could. Perry would play games with him sometimes and encouraged him to play catch or other physical games outside in the back yard or farm or let him help in the machine shop in the barn, but his Billy Jay was not fond of physical activity and afraid of the machines.

Perry was away a lot too. When Perry was away from home, such as at the institute at the university, I would watch Balaji, or we would have a nanny or Sergey check on him. The girl next door was no longer a teenager and no longer available as a babysitter.

Little Balaji would read and sing with me or learn how to solve puzzles or do math problems. I tried to take him to local parks or zoos or kid's museums, but he would resist. If I could get him in the car he would complain nonstop, even from a young age, giving long-winded and well-argued explanations of the reasons it was unwise to go out and all the learning opportunities he was missing by not having access to his computers.

Giving him a handheld game system to distract him in the car would sometimes work. If I drove him to one of those destinations he would refuse to put down his game system and get out of the car and would complain anxiously, cogently, and pathetically until I took him back home. If we had allowed him to decide, he would prefer to be Billy Jay playing games rather than Balaji studying, but he cooperated with both of us in his own way. He understood what we expected but he had his own firm position on limits he would not cross.

When I was home my rules were in force. He would first quickly complete any lesson I asked him to do and then try to play games while pretending he was still working on the lesson. I could usually catch him and make him go on to another lesson. When I was away and Perry was supervising, unlimited play was okay after completing the day's planned lessons, which Billy Jay would complete very quickly, doing the bare minimum.

When both of us were away or busy, and a nanny was in charge, that meant Billy Jay was in charge. Billy Jay would try to take over from Balaji and insist on playing computer games first. Some of the nannies were better than others at enforcing my rules, but none lasted long. Balaji could trick most of them into thinking he was doing schoolwork when he was just playing games. If I didn't fire them for letting him get away with too much game time Balaji/Billy Jay would cause them trouble or invent reasons to complain so much about them that they would just quit.

Perry himself had always had an interest in game systems since he was little. Now he bought more games than I thought was appropriate. I thought most of them were too violent for anyone, and especially for our son. Perry said most of them were for himself, but somehow Billy Jay managed to get his hands on them. Perry worked in his workshop to modify or invent some new user interface devices for Billy Jay to use. Perry got the latest VR visor headsets, but Billy Jay didn't like the feel of them and preferred using large displays on the wall of his room. When Perry played games with Billy Jay or observed him playing, he claimed it was research. He wanted to understand what made a game addictive so that he could help the AM game be more popular. But I think he just wanted something he could share with his son.

09/10/2031, Headset Wanted

Even before he met me, Perry experimented with user interface devices for game play. With the invention of the AM Game he continued to experiment with different user interface devices. He bought and used many different models and also modified and built his own. He gave some to Billy Jay to use with the games that he played at home.

From my briefings as chairman of Zzynarji I became aware of an experimental direct brain interface device being funded by the government, possibly for interrogation. Zzynarji bid on the project and did some prototype work, but another company was ahead and already had a working model that was being evaluated by some government agencies including the one that Perry covertly worked for.

I made the mistake of mentioning it to Perry when he was bragging about the cool VR interfaces he had already connected to the AM Game.

Perry was raving on, "The latest Apple virtual headset is very cool, and it works with the AM Game and most other games now. With the live video AI generated images, you can see and hear everything just like you are actually in the middle of the simulated world. You can see and hear everything. I'm trying to get an INCA version working that doesn't need the commercial AI video."

"You can see and hear everything. That's all?" I asked.

"What do mean, that's all?"

"No taste, smell, or tactile? I just saw a project that's got a working direct brain interface."

"No."

"It's for the government. Not something I'm supposed to talk about, but when has that ever stopped you or me."

"Get me one. I want to try it out."

"Zzynarji's version isn't working yet, but one of our competitors beat us to it and your agency already has a few working prototypes."

"Damn, I might need to talk to good old George again."

"Good old George?"

Perry had to get one and try it out for the AM game simulation. He imagined that observing, driving, and controlling a character in the game could be much more realistic with a direct brain interface, if such a thing really worked. Maybe you could taste, smell, and feel what the character experienced, and your thoughts could guide the action instead of having to speak, type, or gesture. Mainly it was a new kind of toy he wanted to try.

George had changed jobs a couple of times but was still with the agency and still covertly receiving and taking credit for analysis runs from Perry, or usually from Max AI simulating Perry. Perry contacted George at the agency and said that he needed to try the brain interface with the data analysis he was doing for the agency. George said it didn't exist, and Perry reminded him that he was analyzing all the agency's data, so he knew the agency had it. George accepted that even though internal agency data was not supposed to be in the data feeds that Perry worked with. But still George was skeptical about the value in letting Perry use the device.

Perry argued that having a more direct interface to the agency's analysis data he would be able to see even more connections and convergences than without it. He already was much better than others at making sense of the data even without such an interface, but it could only get better with one. Perry's advantage might be related with his abilities for visualizing objects interacting in three dimensions which helped him with designing things to build. He suggested to George that he might be even better at visualizing the multiple dimensions of the data in the models that they ran for the agency if he had this brain interface. Adding this kind of additional human component to the analysis might give additional insights beyond the analysis currently possible. And possibly even more important, if he could get it to work reliably then probably others, including George, might be able to use the same interface to get inside the data and understand the convergence points revealed by the analysis runs. George seemed open to that idea. He'd like to be able to get Perry-level analysis from others or by himself. Perry said, as cover, he could make it look like he was using the equipment as part of the academic research he was doing with INCA at the university. George said no to that. It would have to stay secret. Perry was okay with that.

Perry and I speculated that with George taking credit for Perry's work in recent years he liked the idea that he might be able to do more himself if Perry perfected this tool. Maybe eventually he wouldn't need Perry anymore. We weren't sure if that would be a good thing or a risky thing. George arranged for Perry to get two prototypes of the brain interface devices. At the same time, he shipped Perry some updated computing equipment to host the growing data used for Perry's modeling analysis for the agency.

10/10/2031, Headset Received

When Perry got his hands on the brain-interface equipment at the machine shop he took it home to his workshop in the barn behind the ranch house. He asked me to study the software that came with it. He wanted to understand how it worked before trying it out.

Perry took one of the headsets apart and examined its components, memorizing exactly how they all fit together. Some were unique and custom, but he was able to identify many of the components, either from his own previous experience or by looking them up online. After documenting what he had discovered about the parts and disassembly steps in his own memory he started to reassemble it.

I didn't often go into his workshop but that day I was there to see what Perry was doing with this new toy. I was particularly skeptical about a supposed brain interface headset.

"You really think this thing will be able to read your mind? It looks like some kind of rhinestone-encrusted hat. It's not exactly your fashion style."

"Well, I don't intend to wear it in public, and it looks different when it is all back together."

"It's one thing if it can detect brain activity and interpret some commands from what you are thinking, but if it puts information directly into your brain, who is to say it won't cause damage?"

"I think we can start with just the 'read your mind' part if we are not sure about the 'change your mind' part. But that's why I deconstructed it first. The parts it's made of mostly seem to be things that can be purchased commercially or custom versions of commercial devices. Microsensors, focused magnets, focused antennas. I need to look some of them up still. Parts of it have similarities to the antenna array that I used to access your satellites years ago, but this is a lot more concentrated, smaller scale components and way more of them. It accesses different wavelengths and different kinds of sensors. Have you learned anything from the software yet?"

"Not a lot. I memorized it so that I can study it more later. But I did notice that it seems to want to copy data back to agency servers. I think I can override that and keep all of our data local. We don't want the agency to have access to everything you are thinking about.

It provides a generic programming interface that can take different kinds of data, including sound, visual and 3D models as input or output. It has about a thousand other categories of input and output that I don't understand yet. It works with 3D goggles and audio headphones so not all the input is straight to the brain. It has a baseline brain structure model that gets customized through a learning algorithm to match the wearer during a break-in period. I can keep reverse engineering it, but that doesn't guarantee we will ever understand it. And even if we learn more about how it works, that doesn't make it safe. You know the government wants to be able to use it for interrogations. See what someone is thinking and persuade them to reveal secrets or torture them until they talk. Their safety record in that area is not great."

"I'll be careful. George says it should be safe."

"You trust George now?"

"Not on most things, but I think he doesn't want to do anything that will harm me. As long as he keeps taking credit for the work I do for him."

"Unless he plans to make you expendable."

"Not likely."

"Well. Be careful."

Perry worked on reassembling the unit for a few minutes and then scratched his head and said, "Where did these come from?"

"What?"

"There are two little metal shims left over. Twisty little boogers. I don't remember taking them out and I memorized the image of each disassembly step and followed them in reverse."

He picked up the left-over pieces with tweezers. They were similar mirror-image curved shapes and very small.

"Metal? Looks like some kind of EMF shielding," I said.

He couldn't remember taking them out. He tried to review his mental images of the steps of disassembly and still didn't find where they came from. "That's weird."

I hadn't watched him do the disassembly so I couldn't help him from my memory. "They must have fallen out where you couldn't see them when you took something else apart."

"Maybe, but I'm not sure where they are supposed to go."

"Do you think they were important?"

"Maybe not. They just look like little shims so they may not be important, but spacing in this kind of device is important and if they are EMF shields that might be even more important. I'm going to take it all apart again, but slower and I'm going to take pictures with my phone at each step too, not just with my head, just in case it's my memory that's slipping."

"Remember to use the photo app that saves to our private cloud, not a public one."

"I remember."

"You do seem to forget things sometimes. Should I be worried?"

"No. I just sometimes forget to remember things. I've always been that way. But when I take mental pictures or write myself mental notes, they are good. I bet if I disassemble it again, I'll find where these suckers fit."

"Didn't George send you a second headset? You could compare them."

"Yes, he did, but they are different models, so they might not have all the same parts in the same places."

"Well, be careful. Let me know before you try that thing on."

"Yes, Ma'am."

When he disassembled the unit again and examined each part carefully under magnifications and strong lighting, he did find a spot where the two shims seemed to fit. There were some scratches that matched the shape of the shims between two sets of sensors in similar places on the right and left sides of the headset. He reassembled everything with no extra parts this time.

"I think I've got it now. The shims seemed to shield interference between two kinds of sensors that are close together in matching places on the left and right hemispheres. I'm 99% sure I got them back into the right places."

"I'd prefer you were 100% sure. Is it safe to use?"

"The kinds of sensors and antennas and other instruments all seem like they are probably harmless. The levels of radiation and magnetic force they can produce is not high, although they are very tightly focused. The magnetic signals are orders of magnitude weaker than in a TMS treatment for depression. Like I said before, I will try it in 'read your mind' mode a few times before trying the 'change your mind' mode, so it should be safe."

It bothered me that he would mention the Transcranial Magnetic Stimulation treatments that I sometimes got for my own depression and anxiety. They did seem to help me through some difficult times when medication wasn't enough. At least I was getting treatments, not like my dad. Was he suggesting that I was messing with my own brain more that he was with his? I decided not to go there and just said, "You have to start in read your mind mode anyway, for the initialization. But I don't like this. You should send it back to George and say you changed your mind."

"I'll do that if you tell everyone that Mara, Marta, and Min are all you."

"That's not the same."

And he didn't take my advice. He put on the cap and 3D googles and used the handheld controller that came with it to connect to a single player game on the home computer network. He said, "I'm not turning on the cap. Just seeing how it all feels."

I was sitting in a chair in the room where I could watch him while I studied the code in my mind's eye. The goggles and controller seemed to work because he seemed to get into a game dodging attacks and shooting at opponents. After a few minutes he took off the goggles and said the 3D goggles and controller were not as good as the high-end VR goggles and controllers he liked to use, but passable. The main difference was it felt like he had a heavy and tight hat on his head. A little bit uncomfortable, but okay once he got used to it. He put the goggles back on and resumed his game.

After about 10 minutes more he paused again raising his goggles to his forehead and said, "That's pretty cool."

"What's cool?" I asked.

"I think it's starting to know what I'm about to do before I do it."

"I thought it wasn't turned on or initialized yet. The instructions say it has to map your brain structure before it can start reading your mind. I thought you didn't turn that on."

"Nobody reads instructions but you. I already notice a difference. It's not a huge difference. I'm not able to make it do things just by thinking about them, but it is reacting faster than before." He lowered the googles over his eyes again, held up his controller, and rapidly tapped the controller. "Oh. That was cool."

"What?"

"I got off more shots faster than I ever did before. And more accurate."

"How do you feel? Can you feel anything when you are using it?"

"Inside my head? Nothing so far."

"That sounds normal for you. Nothing in your head."

"Hey."

He continued aiming and gesturing and shooting in the game but making a point of shooting in my direction.

"You should take a break now. The nanny is leaving soon. Your turn to play with Balaji."

"Five more minutes so I can finish this part of the game. I'm getting more points than ever before in this level. Pleeease, Mara." He didn't show any sign of stopping.

"Balaji may be 11, but you are the little kid."

Later while Perry was playing with Balaji, I analyzed the data in the mental map that the headset had generated while Perry was playing. It showed a lot of changes to the baseline brain structure model compared with before he used it. Even though he did not invoke the user initialization mode or explicitly turn on the cap the system was sensing and mapping the activities in his brain while he watched the action and manipulated his game character with the handheld controls.

I talked with Perry about it later.

"Even without doing the normal initialization, it seems to be learning, but I don't know yet how to make sense of the model it is building."

"Well, I guess brains are complicated," he said.

"Really? Even yours? That's a surprise."

"Hey!" He gave me a fake hurt look.

"Okay. Yeah. That is true," I conceded. "I don't know if I can ever reverse engineer this enough to understand exactly what the model is capturing. Whoever built this must either know a lot about brains, or else it has one hell of a learning algorithm. Maybe both."

"And they probably wanted it to be hard to reverse engineer just in case someone from a competing company like Zzynarji got their hands on it," Perry commented. "Maybe we will just have to judge it by what it does."

"Maybe. But let's be careful. I still vote to send it back."

"Not yet. But I'll follow the instructions and do the initialization steps."

10/11/2031, Perry Uses the Headset Again

The next day Perry came into the house from the back yard wearing the headset.

"I finished the first 10 initialization sessions," he said.

"How was it?" I asked. After doing the first couple sessions with me watching, he had started doing them on his own out in his workshop office in the barn.

"Pretty good. I can control actions without moving the controls on the handheld controller. I guess it might also be responding to eye motions in the goggles but I'm starting to get the hang of thinking it to do things."

"Time to take a break?"

"Maybe a little break. That finishes the 'read your mind' initialization. The next fourteen sessions do the 'touch your mind' initialization."

"I don't think you should do it. Why do you need this? I don't like the idea. Who knows what it will do to your brain."

"The system seems to work reliably on the 'mind-reading' part. I'd really like to see how it works on the 'mind-touching' part. That's where it should get really interesting."

"If you insist on trying this, please do it in small doses and only when I'm here to help if something goes wrong."

"Okay. Fair enough. It has 30-minute segments. I'll check with you before I start one. I can even bring it in the house and do it at my gaming chair instead of out in the workshop, if you insist."

The next day Perry sat in his gaming chair with the headset on and started playing a game. Billy Jay saw his dad playing with this new headset and asked if he could use it, and both Perry and I said no but I worried that it was not good for Balaji to see this. I got Balaji to go outside in the back yard to play. I saw the little girl from next door run and tumble across the yard and Balaji followed her like a clumsy puppy. Perry resumed playing his game.

After a few minutes he stopped and took off the goggles and headset. I was sitting in a nearby chair reading a book.

"How is it working? Did you start the next initialization segments?" I asked.

"No. I told you I wouldn't do that without telling you. I played some games and used it a little bit to fly through the hive intelligence data model looking for negative or positive convergence points. Actually, it is pretty cool. I have much finer control than I did with the normal handheld controllers or keyboard interface. I'm able to zero in on points that were hard to see before. It might actually be useful even without the mind-touching part. The story I made up to get George to loan it to me might not be bullshit after all."

"Well, you know my opinions. I'd rather you didn't use this headset at all, and I'd rather you weren't still helping George. But why do you think it works better? Is it reacting faster to your control thoughts?"

"Yes. But I think the headset software might also be seeing what my brain perceives and matching it with the data being presented in the audio and visual output. It may be changing the audio and visual output to tailor it to be perceived better. There must be some kind of feedback loop to improve perceived resolution."

"Really? I can look at the software again to see if it does something like that."

I stared at the wall for a few seconds while I brought up a view of the software code in my memory. I scanned through it to find the code used when viewing 3D images through the goggles.

"You are right. It does have a feedback loop. It's part of fine-tuning the mind-reading module. It looks like that feedback loop is used all over the place in this software. That may be why you got better performance even before you turned on the initialization. The feedback loop seems to do some brain-modeling personalization even when the mind-reading is turned off. That seems like a design flaw."

I planned to spend more time analyzing the code and the brain model. I didn't mention to Perry, but I had some ideas I wanted to test about how to play back visual and sound inputs recorded in the brain model, maybe even including subvocalized thoughts. No reason to let him know about that before I figured out if it really worked. And not that I would look at those.

Perry said, "Well, it's cool the way it works. I think I might play with this some more before doing the rest of the initialization. I wonder if it would work with the AM Game."

"I don't see any reason it wouldn't. But…"

"You don't think I should use it."

Late October 2031, More with the Headset

A few days later Perry had proved that the headset worked well with the AM Game and for agency analysis as well as for a few different commercial games. He also wore it most of the time when he worked on designs for Abitats.

One day he found me and said "I promised to tell you before I do the next initialization steps. I'm going to start today."

I watched while he did the first 30-minute segment. He sat relatively still during the session, not moving the handheld controller. Afterwards he removed the googles and described the experience.

"How was it?"

"I did see and hear things, but they were fuzzy and weak. Like listening through walls and looking through layers of gauze. The system gave audio or visual input with the goggles and headphones or with brain stimulation or with both and it was kind of like an eye test: Which is better A or B? A or B?"

"How do you feel? Do you feel any different?"

"I feel fine. Maybe disappointed. I was hoping for something clearer. But it is the first time. There are 13 more training segments. I'm sure it will get better."

"I'd be fine if you stop right now and send it back." From the look on his face, I could tell he was going to continue. "At least, maybe you should take a break. Take a walk or work on something in your workshop for a while before you do the next step."

"Yeah okay. Take a break. I've got an idea for something we could do together." Without taking off the headset, he stood up and put his arms around me. I wiggled out of his grip. He continued, "Or maybe not. Okay.

I'll be in the workshop." He walked out the back door towards his workshop, still wearing the headset.

A couple hours later when he got back in the house he said to me, "We should ask Sergey to trim the bushes by the steps. It's getting hard to see the opening to the path, especially when it's getting dark."

"You were gone longer than I expected. Did you take a long walk or find something to do in the workshop?" I asked.

"Workshop. And I think I'm getting absent-minded."

"More? What do you mean? You've always been kind of an absent-minded professor. When you focus working on something you lose track of time and everything else."

"This is different. I went to the workshop to make a model for a part of the interior of an Abitat and when I finished it and put it in the cabinet, I found another one like it already there. I must have forgotten that I had already made one. I don't remember when I did it."

"Okay. I don't know if it has anything to do with the headset, but I think you should stop using it just in case."

"Headset? What headset?"

I looked at him with concern.

"Just kidding. My memory's not that bad. Yeah. I'll have to think about it. It does seem like a coincidence. That was today, right?" He smiled, but I think he really was not completely certain that the trial run with the headset was earlier today.

At the time I didn't know what happened while he was out of the house, but it wasn't long before I learned how to play back memories, especially visual and auditory ones. Sometime later, after Perry became non-communicative, I played back more of his memories including what happened that day.

Some of his memories I wish I hadn't seen, and I won't recount those. For his privacy I put some restrictions on retrieval of Perry's memories from the brain map in case Balaji or someone else figures out how to access them someday.

Anyway, here's what Perry did, said, and thought earlier that day.

He went through the back yard and down the steps of the path through the back fence to the farm. He paused to look at the steps. Sergey had used old stones instead of new concrete for the steps and they had an appearance of something that had been in place for decades even though at that point it had only been 11 years.

Perry said or thought, "Has it already been ten years? I guess so. Billy Jay is ten now." Did he really forget that Balaji was eleven?

He left the steps and started towards the workshop barn and paused and turned back. The steps were hidden from view by a ten- or fifteen-foot-tall thick green hedge. The gap in the hedge that led to the steps was hardly noticeable.

Talking or thinking to himself again, he said, "Good thing I know my way. It would be hard to find that path if I didn't know where it was."

When he got to the workshop, he tapped in the passcode and opened the door, and then he stopped and asked himself, "Why did I come out here? Was I looking for something?"

He puzzled over the question and looked around the workshop. Finally, he said, "While I try to remember I'll make something in the workshop."

He pulled up plans on the computer for a miniature prototype of a collapsible bathroom for an Abitat. He sorted through a rack of materials to see what he had to work with, picked out some plastic and aluminum stock, and powered up one of his machines. He sat at the computer and brought up more 3D drawings and went to work.

By later that evening he had assembled a 1/20 scale mockup of a room with a toilet, sink, and shower stall, all with walls and fixtures that could collapse and fold into a space no wider than the toilet bowl and then could extend back out to a roomy bathroom with a spacious shower stall.

"Left some space in the walls. I'll mock up the plumbing and wiring inside the walls next time."

From the brain map memories it wasn't clear if he was saying some of these things out loud or only thinking them.

He put the unit on a shelf in a wall cabinet near his workbench with other finished or near-finished projects. He closed the cabinet doors and headed back towards the house.

Outside, he searched for a minute to find the gap in the bushes. Once he found the path, the steps themselves were hard to see in the dark with the trees and bushes around them. He always liked to go fast when going up stairs to get more exercise benefit, but this time as he took a little leap, he missed a step, slipped, and fell. Twisting to try to land on his butt he fell backward and then bumped the back of his head on a stone of a higher step.

He was startled by his fall and sat on the steps for a couple of minutes looking down towards the hedge and the far beyond.

"Okay. Why am I here?"

The hedge in front of him looked overgrown.

"Maybe I should go to the barn to get some shears and trim it. No. I'll ask Sergey to take care of it."

He stood up and looked around and decided he would go to the workshop and work on his next project like Mara had suggested. As he walked through the hedge, he stopped and rubbed the back of his head. A lump.

"I wonder what that's from."

In the workshop he sorted through a rack of materials to see what he had to work with, picked out some plastic and aluminum stock, and powered up one of his machines. He logged in to a computer which was already in an app to view some 3D drawings for a collapsible bathroom for an Abitat.

"That would be a good one to work on."

When he finished cutting and assembling various pieces, he decided that was enough for tonight and he went to put it into the cabinet and was surprised to find another almost identical, but more complete model already on the shelf.

"That's weird. When did I make that one?"

November 2031, More with the Headset

Over the next few weeks Perry tried out the headset a few more times with different games and applications. He could skip the handheld controller completely. The read-your-mind features seemed to be working for him, and even though he didn't finish all of the touch-your-mind initializations he could see, hear, and feel more details in most of the games each time he played. Sometimes I noticed him sitting still with his eyes closed, wearing the headset, but no goggles or earpieces, and gently rocking or twitching. Apparently, the touch your mind features were working well enough to skip the video and audio inputs.

He thought it gave him finer control on the agency analysis, but he spent more of his own time tweaking his analysis results. Perry wanted to be sure George thought he was getting value from letting him use the headset.

He didn't take the headset with him to the university or show it to the others he worked with at INCA and PATH. The agency wouldn't like it if he was showing it off to people without agency security clearance.

After a while Perry was wearing the headset for hours every day. At first, I could ask him to take it off and he would act like he forgot it was on and take it off, but later he resisted and wanted to keep it on unless I gave him a good reason to take it off. He had to take it off when he went to the INCA or PATH offices at the university, so he started to make excuses not to go there. He also was less open to going next door for coffee with Camilla.

"You really enjoy wearing that thing all the time?" I asked him.

"It's easier to keep it on rather than having to look for it whenever I want to do some work that needs it. I hate it when I waste 15 minutes trying to remember where I left something."

"Keep it in the same place."

"Yeah. Maybe. How about on my head?"

"It's controlling you more than you are using it to control your games and work."

"Don't be silly. It doesn't control me." He put one hand on his head and adjusted the cap.

2031 to 2035

This part is not exactly chronological. I'm capturing in no particular order a number of things that happened during those years. I might come back and rewrite it with more chronological details someday.

During those years, with a little pushing from Perry and me, Balaji kept doing high school and college-level online courses—in between playing games. His only exercise was walking out in the back yard and down the path into the farm. He was more likely to go there when the little girl next door climbed over the fence and was exploring. Balaji followed her around. He said he needed to make sure she was safe, since the farm was a dangerous place for a little kid. He was about 4 years older than her, but she was always more athletic than him.

Perry did reluctantly take off the headset and go next door occasionally and got updates from Camilla about her world. He told her about Billy Jay being anxious about going out of the house and about Isabella climbing over the fence. Perry encouraged Camilla to allow Isabella to continue, since it was good for Billy Jay. When she asked about me and why she never saw me anymore, he made excuses. I was very busy with work and a very private person. Maybe social anxiety ran in the family.

Camilla had been legal guardian for Isabella for some time. She was very proud of her and the athletic accomplishments she was making. She was very coordinated and strong for her age. But Camilla was disappointed with her grown kids and the bad example they were setting for Isabella. Sam and Josephine were always asking for money, and she thought they had been stealing from her to buy drugs. Josephine had been one class away from finishing high school for a few years and always needing money for books or class fees but never finished. She took some crafty art classes, but not ones that led to a diploma. Sam, Josephine, or some of their friends kept having accidents and wrecking the cars Camilla provided them. When she stopped repairing or replacing them, they 'borrowed" her car and wrecked it too, even though it had all the safety features and was supposed to be capable of self-driving.

Finally, Camilla got fed up and kicked them out. She changed her locks and got a restraining order. She got a new security system and changed the locks again after some of her jewelry disappeared when she and Isabella were at soccer practice. She gave the monitoring service instructions to call the police if the security cameras detected them or strangers on her property. She wasn't sure where they were after that, but she thought they were finally staying away. Perry said he saw them sometimes in the farm out back, maybe doing tasks for Sergey. He didn't ask.

Camilla told Perry that Douglas Zynn still visited Isabella a couple times a year and brought some gifts. He never stayed for more than a few minutes. If she asked him about Sam and Josephine, Douglas said he didn't know anything, but Perry said he thought he saw Douglas with them in the farm at least once.

Camilla lamented often to Perry that Sam and Josephine should have turned out more like Sam's old college friend Brock Jackson, who she still followed on social media. He got a master's degree, worked in DC for a while and more recently was working locally for the county government or a congressman. She thought he was probably going to be governor or president someday.

Around the same time, Douglas started asking me questions about how much of the company I was giving away to various charities including the PATH and INCA projects. He was repeating talking points I had heard from Carl Heinz who said he was relaying things said by some other company executives. I wasn't sure if Douglas was influenced by the same executives or if Carl was behind all the complaints. Douglas said we needed to keep more control, and the company needed to keep growing if it was going to be able to have the most positive impact on the world. He even started saying he should have a bigger say since he was a real son of Sandra and Carlos, and I was obviously adopted and wouldn't have the instincts to continue on their path. I had been in charge long enough, he said. It was his turn to run things, he said.

I didn't pay too much attention to his complaints and his racist and misogynist comments since he was not able to think clearly while he was on so many drugs. In some ways, I thought, he was still just being Douglas.

He didn't seem to be aware that the majority of the company was owned by the Strong Trust, and he had no rights to that part. Or maybe he was being told that he had as much right as me to control the company. The company had grown more under our mom Sandra Zynn's leadership than before my birth parents died, so there was an argument. But it had grown even more since I took over. I assured Douglas he could participate in company meetings and get more involved. I designated him as an executive vice president, but he didn't show up for company meetings. He spent most of his time backpacking and partying.

The AM-PATH project continued to receive funding from the Zynn Foundation. Tony Marks was involved with the refinements to the design of Abitats and their charging infrastructure. The project continued building Abitat Villages and in small numbers of Abitats to give away. He wanted significant funding to start building them in much large numbers. As Marta I continued to meet with him frequently to discuss the plans and explore options for securing funding. Tony was no longer with Anne, who had moved to the Midwest, but they had a daughter who lived with Anne. He made frequent trips to visit his daughter.

As the AM-PATH software for navigation and traffic control in Abitats was being refined it was made available for use by car companies if they agreed to certain conditions regarding keeping the integrity of the software. This was an attempt to get them to use the positive earned trust mechanisms for coordination. Some car companies incorporated it into the self-driving navigation features of their cars. One company called itself Autonomous Motors, trying to co-opt the AM Game initials. They planned to eventually build Abitats but started with cars.

Cars using AM-PATH software and networking could navigate cooperatively and some were able to autonomously connect to charging stations that supported the prototype Abitat docking features. At other charging stations the cars' occupants would have to step outside and connect the charger. Many companies continued to release their own proprietary navigation systems that did not coordinate the same way, but there was a trend towards using the Abitat standards, since they were freely available and allowed improved traffic flow. Prototype Abitats were very rare and hard to get, so Perry decided to get one of the cars from the AM company to at least test out the cooperative navigation. After we bought it, Perry said it was my car. He installed a fast-charging station for it in our garage tied in to the solar and battery capacity in the farm. He was so confident about the design of docking stations for Abitats that he also installed the power and plumbing for one on the other side of our garage. He custom-fabricated the connectors for it himself in his machine shop, based on designs from the AM Game, but he left it wrapped in plastic to stay clean until he could get a real Abitat. He had plans for remodeling the garage to give it a taller door to allow full-size Abitats to enter but never got around to making those changes before he got sick.

Meanwhile the AM Game was popular and available on many different computers, phones, gaming systems, and tablet devices. Some devices were being made with hardware specifically supporting the AM PATH MinStrong Peer-to-Peer networking that communicated directly between devices rather than over traditional mobile data, WIFI, or internet service provider networks. Other devices connected over more traditional networking but still used MinStrong encryption.

Many people were spending a lot of time involved with their game world characters, trying out different roles in worlds simulating various futures with widespread uses of Abitats. The distributed and cooperative Nested Cellular Autonomy nature of the AM Game running on millions of devices gave a tremendous boost to the simulations in the game. Characters had richer personalities and more knowledge. World simulations had richer details. The economies of scale and NCA component-sharing allowed each new individual character to use a tiny fraction of the incremental compute and storage resources we had used on the original standalone MinAI simulated personality. Smartphones and other devices also had more powerful processors every year, giving more power for the Game.

We still had some important data and software in the Strong Server Ranch, like MinAI and MaxAI, and even though it had redundant power and battery backups and fire safety systems we were concerned that there were ways it could fail. If a perfect storm of failures occurred, such as a grid outage, extended cloudy weather, and failure in our backup power systems, or flooding or fire, we might lose much of MinAI and MaxAI. We considered backing them up to different private server farms in other buildings, but we would have to find a secure way to transfer data between data centers. When we worked out the best way to keep the data transfers private, we realized that we had another solution.

The most secure way to transfer data was through the same encryption and communication techniques used for the distributed storage in the AM Game. If we used the AM distributed network to transfer data then we didn't need to send them into another server farm. We could let them stay in the distributed network. They would exist holographically distributed across the devices in the AM Game hive network.

With the security of the AM Game network, we felt safe in letting MinAI and MaxAI out of the private server ranch. With elaborate authentication we could access and control them from devices outside our home if we wanted, similar to AM Game characters. MinAI, MaxAI, and some of our other early home-brewed characters were not exactly the same as a typical AM Game character because they had been created before the templates for such characters were refined and they were not embedded in a specific game world, but they had similarities and could be stored in the distributed game infrastructure. They would be safe from anything short of a total collapse of civilization or everyone everywhere simultaneously deciding to remove the AM Game app from all their devices, which probably amounted to the same thing. MinAI and MaxAI became safe from a future power outage, fire, flood, or other event taking down our server ranch. We could even shut down the server ranch if we wanted to.

Perry was still using MaxAI to generate outputs for the agency. I was still letting MinAI do her thing for the Min Strong fans. They both existed in the background of the game cloud, but we could still control them when we wanted to.

The AIs of Min and Max continued to learn and grow, but Perry on the other hand was having memory issues. I started to retrieve "memories" from his brain map to answer some question about what he had been doing earlier that day if he said he could not remember. I didn't tell him I was doing that, but he should have known I could. Sometimes I think he was just hiding things from me, but other times he seemed to not be able to remember.

Eventually he finished the steps for the 'touch your mind' part of the headset initialization, but he probably didn't need to. He had been using the headset without goggles, earphones, and hand controller for months before that. The brain model that the headset built from Perry's use was large and growing. I knew it contained a lot more than just the visual and auditory memories from when he had worn the headset, but I wasn't able to decipher much else.

Similar to our concerns about MinAI and MaxAI, we had concerns about losing his brain map if the server ranch data center failed someday. And similar to MinAI and MaxAI we backed up his brain map to the distributed AM Game NCA hive network. It didn't use the same NCA data structure as Min and MaxAI or AM Game characters, but we were able to wrap it with MinStrong encryption and make it compatible enough.

Perry said that the agency data he was still getting showed views of things people were doing in the AM Game, but only through the views of players who shared their data. The agency didn't seem to have access to the data that was encrypted and distributed in the game network if it wasn't publicly shared. We figured the brain mapping was safe from agency snooping in the AM network.

Around that time Perry noticed that the MaxAI was finally producing analysis models that were good enough to give to George. He still looked at them and made some fine adjustments to make them even better and train MaxAI a little more, but the results were usually acceptable. Perry wondered if maybe some of his brain mapping from the headset was now available to MaxAI after backing both of them up to the game cloud.

I told him that was highly unlikely because the headset brain map and MaxAI had coexisted in our server ranch for many months without MaxAI being able to do the fine tuning on Perry's hive analysis. Also, the headset brain map had a different kind of data structure than all the NCA models for AM Game characters and MaxAI and MinAI.

We asked ourselves, what was different for it to work better now? Time had passed and MaxAI had additional training each month when Perry fine-tuned his analysis for George. Maybe it was coincidence that MaxAI just happened to cross a competence threshold at the same time as we copied it out into the AM Game cloud.

That was possible but seemed unlikely. Another possibility was that even though they had different underlying data structures, encoding and encrypting both MaxAI and the headset brain map to be stored in the distributed AM cloud may have somehow made them more accessible to one another. Even though we didn't understand how that would work it seemed like the more likely explanation. If that was true, what else would MaxAI use from Perry's brain map? Augmented with Perry's headset brain map, was MaxAI becoming a clone of Perry's brain? That was an intriguing idea as Perry's own mind declined, but also a concerning one.

We considered trying to pull Perry's headset brain map back out of the AM Game cloud and keep it just in our server ranch or another server farm. But it was already distributed on thousands or millions of devices playing the AM Game and we didn't know how to remove it, short of shutting down or possibly destroying all of those devices at the same time. I concocted a couple of possible solutions for removing it from the game cloud but didn't dare try either of them out. The surest way was to kill the whole game cloud. Release a poison pill virus to erase all of the data in the distributed game cloud. That would eliminate everything, including all of the characters and game world knowledge distributed throughout. I could write such a virus, but that was not something we wanted to do. The other was less certain to be effective and less clear about impacts. It would be a similar virus specifically targeting the encrypted brain map objects, but because of the holographic nature of the data distribution it would probably remove or change random elements of the cloud with unpredictable impacts. Maybe someday in an apocalypse I could try one of these approaches. In the meantime, we would leave the brain map out there and watch for other side effects, but we both planned to figure out more about how it worked when we had time.

For a while Perry and I were still able to have conversations, but they were getting shorter and more difficult. I suggested that he get medical diagnosis for his mental lapses. He argued that he was fine, but at my insistence he did get an MRI once, which was inconclusive. Later he wouldn't go out or take off the headset so the best I could do was to have a neurologist and a psychiatrist talk to him by phone. Their diagnosis was inconclusive. One suspected some kind of progressive dementia. The other suspected a mental illness such as paranoid schizophrenia. I got Perry to take some of the medications that the doctors prescribed, but he stopped after a few weeks.

Perry spent more of his time at home. Eventually he stopped going out entirely. He didn't want to take off the headset at all. He took it off briefly when he washed his hair and he started shaving his head to minimize that need.

He gradually got worse, rarely holding a coherent conversation with me. He would sit for hours wearing the headset and holding his tablet computer. Looking over his shoulder at his tablet I could see that for a while he was still working on the AM Game and the designs for Abitats, but eventually the tablet display seemed to just show gibberish. Maybe he was still working purely through the brain interface of the headset, but I couldn't tell. He would shout at me if I tried to take off his headset. He even needed reminding to eat or get up and go to the bathroom or the shower.

I made a deal with teenage Balaji. He could spend more time playing games if he helped me take care of his dad. At least remind him to eat and go to the bathroom. I still wanted Balaji to keep learning and eventually find himself a career, and he agreed to keep taking classes, but I needed help. Perry barely spoke with me or Balaji, but sometimes when Balaji helped him to the bathroom he said, "Billy Jay, try the AM Game." Balaji would tell him, "No thanks, Dad. Pretending to ride around all day in autonomous vans with toilets does not sound like fun."

07/13/2036, Balaji's Birthday

Balaji turned 16 and he was still an agoraphobe and still spent too much time playing games. I was proud of him for finishing several online college degrees. By degree count he was ahead of my academic pace, although I wasn't sure these online degrees were equivalent to my Stanford or his dad's UCI education. I suggested he choose a field he liked and go for his PhD like his dad but, like me, he had trouble picking one area, and he said most good universities required some in-person attendance for doctoral work, which he said was impossible. I told him there were ways around that. I didn't want him to spend all of his time playing games. He agreed to keep taking classes in a variety of subjects, while helping his dad and spending most of his time playing games. By this time Perry was needing a lot of help.

If Balaji was 16, then little Isabela next door was probably about 12. One day earlier that year Balaji told me that he had always thought of her as being five like when she first came over the fence. He said, "She's not five anymore." I wondered if my little boy was having a crush on the little girl next door. She was still way too young for him, but four years difference was just a little more than between his father and me. So maybe someday.

Balaji didn't get much of a chance to follow Isabella around that year. For years before she had jingled a windchime in our backyard almost every day to alert him when she was there so that he would know to come outside. On windy days Balaji would be constantly looking in the back yard for her as the wind chime rang in the wind.

Balaji said he didn't see her as much anymore because she had so many sports practices. By that time, she swam an hour or two early every morning and had other sports after school. She probably also hung out with school friends. In the first half of that year she came over the fence about once a week to run laps around the farm, sometimes kicking a soccer ball as she ran, or she would shoot hoops at the old court near Sergey's house. She still liked to climb trees, especially if it was windy. On a given day with strong Santa Ana winds Balaji was likely to get seriously nervous watching her climb high in one of the farm's eucalyptus or other tall trees to ride the swaying branches in the wind.

When they were together, he would half-heartedly try to run after her, shoot a basket, or kick a ball back to her. She liked to talk about sports and Balaji played some sports video games to have something to say. Sometimes she would tell him about what she was learning in school, and he would explain his understanding of the subjects to her. He had more patience for her than he did with students in the virtual classes he attended. He felt they should be able to keep up with him, but since he thought of her as five, and almost family, it was okay if she needed some explanations. Sometimes she listened, but I think she was only giving him something to talk about, since on her preferred topic of sports, even with the sports video games he played, he was dumb and uncoordinated.

One time shortly after his birthday when school was starting again, she brought a friend from school with her into the farm and Balaji almost had a fit. He went quickly back into his room and hyperventilated with anxiety. I'm not sure if it was from being exposed to a stranger or because he realized Isabella had other friends. I'm not sure if he knew which himself.

After that Balaji's visits with Isabella dropped off precipitously. By the end of that year the only time the wind chime sang was in the wind, or when Balaji jingled it himself. If she came over she didn't ring it, and he didn't catch her. I didn't realize it at the time, because I didn't snoop on

Balaji very much, but as Isabella stopped coming around and as his dad got sicker, Balaji started trying out the AM Game. He wasn't the only one.

In 2036 the AM Game was popular and the designs for Abitats were close to ready. I was close to granting 11 billion dollars from the Zynn Foundation to the PATH project to build factories and start manufacturing Abitats and their recharging stations in large volumes. It would mean selling off some parts of the Zzynarji company to free up the cash. We had buyers who were interested in acquiring different parts of the company. The one I was leaning towards was a foreign company owned by distant relatives of my birth mom, Ami Narji. I guess some of the bosses there might have been my third or fourth cousins, but I never tracked that down exactly. Their company name didn't include the name Narji, like Zzynarji did, but I suspected part of their interest was because of the Narji connection. I'm not sure if they had tracked down the Marta Zynn story and suspected that I was biologically related. If so, they probably planned to leverage that connection in negotiations.

There were some regulatory and export issues to overcome for the sale, but they seemed to be achievable with the right government connections. I planned to have an executive meeting between the two companies sometime in 2037 to meet the cousins and sort out the details of the sale and possibly sign an agreement. Hawaii seemed like a good location to meet since the Narji cousin's company had a presence all around the western Pacific and some of the Zzynarji space launch facilities they wanted were in Hawaii.

Douglas was still giving me grief about the way I was running the company, but the things he said never made much sense. Sometimes he would say I should give the whole company to the Zynn Foundation now and other times he would complain that I was giving away too much. He still spent a lot of time in the wilderness. I didn't pay much attention to what he said nor to some similar opinions Carl warned me about from different executives in my company. I did get the impression that maybe Douglas was listening to different executives in the company and getting confused by their differing opinions but the common theme he took was that he should be in charge.

November 2036

Late in 2036 Perry stopped getting pay from his covert job at the agency. Or at least the payments were no longer showing up in the account that he had been using to get them. He hadn't met with George in person in years and I'm not sure if he was still sending analysis packages to George. MaxAI might still be generating them, but Perry didn't seem to be with it enough to review them and do the secret transfer to get them back to George. Maybe he did or maybe MaxAI had learned how to do that too, but probably not, since otherwise why would George stop paying. Then again, maybe George had moved on.

I was still using the MinAI to generate interest in the AM Game and Abitats, but she didn't need much help from me. When I met with Tony Marks to plan the big expansion of the PATH project, he would mention the latest things that Min Strong had said or done and how much it was helping. He liked to tease me that he thought I was Min Strong, and it was me who was doing those statements as Min. I pointed out that I was too busy and most of her virtual appearances were at times when I was with him or in meetings for Zzynarji. I couldn't be in two places at once. He said, "Nothing is impossible for you…or Min."

03/04/2037, Mara's Birthday

The fourth of March of 2037 was Mara Strong's 40th birthday. For the occasion I converted $40,000 into AM Game points attached to my Mara mobile phone to cover immediate expenses at the ranch house and maybe buy a nice meal. Most businesses accepted AMPs by that point. Marta Zynn's 40th birthday was approaching on April 3. I wanted to stay 39, so I thought of myself as Marta between those dates. I planned to give myself a birthday payment of $40 Million as Marta after completing the upcoming business deal in Hawaii.

Perry's 43rd birthday was also coming up on March 30th. I could buy him something from my Mara funds, but he probably wouldn't notice. Maybe just a cake. He didn't seem aware of much of anything, including either of our birthdays. Balaji was also clueless. I should be back from Hawaii before Perry's birthday. When I got back, Marta would still be under 40.

Monday, 03/23/2037, Before Trip to Hawaii

Before the trip to Hawaii, I made sure that Balaji was ready to take care of his dad for a few days. I actually had a little bit of conversation with Perry before I left. I would talk to him every day and usually get silence or grunts and twitches in response. I told him I would be away for a few days and that Balaji would be helping him.

He opened his eyes and looked at me with a glazed look and said, "Care…ful."

That seemed odd, both that he was cogent enough to say anything and that he chose to warn me.

I asked him, "What should I be careful about?"

He just twitched and rocked, closing his eyes again. I wondered if it meant anything and if it had to do with his no longer getting paid by the agency.

"Do I need to be careful about George and the agency looking for you? We've been careful about that."

"Sin," he said.

"Sin? You are worried about my immortal soul?? What I choose to do is my business. We are not married."

"Zynn." That time it sounded more like Zynn than Sin.

"Marta, Morta, Mortal Zynn. You sound like my little brother. What are you trying to say? If you can't speak, try to send me a message. Are you still sending messages to people at PATH and INCA? I'm still helping you hide from George and the agency. I'm still keeping my Marta Zynn life separate from my Mara Strong life. If you are starting to care about sin, then I'm not going to help you there. You've had your share of personal indiscretions. This trip should help make some steps towards fighting the emergent negativity, but that negativity isn't sin. It's a global illness. Just what are you are talking about?"

He rocked and twitched said, "Almost..."

I said, "Yeah. We are almost there. This deal will let us take some big steps. Maybe. Okay. I'll be careful. I don't know what you are saying but we can try to talk more when I get back in a few days. Be kind to Balaji. Try not to shit your pants too many times while I'm gone."

I checked on Balaji before I left and made sure he knew what food and drinks to give his dad at what times and how often to make sure he went to the bathroom.

"I'll be back in four days. Clean up this room before I get back." I looked at the clutter of clothes, dishes, and fast-food trash in his room. "Is four days enough time for that?"

"Just stay out of my room. It just gives you a migraine when you come in here."

"You know what you need to do for your dad?"

"I've got your list. We'll be fine, mom. Go do what you need to do. With Dad sick I know you need to keep working."

"If you need anything, send me a message. I might not be able to answer my phone so send a message and I'll get back with you. You know how to do that, right?"

"Yeah. Yeah. I know how to use the family message app. You nag me there all the time."

"Sergey might be able to help you too. He should be at his house. Okay? I guess I'm off."

I got in my car and tinted the windows. I had it drive out of the neighborhood while I put on more of my Marta look. I checked my Mara phone. No messages from Balaji. No immediate emergencies. He and

Perry should be fine without me for a few days. I turned off that phone and checked my hair and makeup while the car drove to the airport. I got out at the normal spot for picking up my Marta car near the car rental area and let my Mara car go on its own to park in the parking garage. I drove to the beach house to finish changing then turned on my Marta phone. While I was at the beach house, I called Douglas and was surprised when he was already in Hawaii with Carl Heinz and some of the other Zzynarji executives.

He said, "I flew commercial. First class on commercial isn't so bad. You should try it. More than two hundred people can fly commercial for the same amount of fuel as you use on that business jet of yours."

"I'll stick with my plane for now," I said.

"It's a waste and it is destroying the planet. Some day you will have to pay for the damage you're causing. Sooner than you think."

"Frightening. I look forward to seeing you at the meeting, Douglas. I'm glad you'll be there. We can talk more afterwards."

"I'll fight you on selling ZSIG. It's a bad move."

"We'll see. We'll see."

I went to the airport and took the company's converted 737 business jet to San Jose. I was thinking of replacing it with something newer and bigger. Maybe I should look for something more eco-friendly just to appease Douglas.

This trip from OC to SJC, it was just me and the two pilots. I planned one night in San Jose before getting back on the plane early the next morning for the flight to Maui. I took a small overnight bag for the stay in the hotel tonight and left a bigger bag on the plane for the days in Hawaii. My assistant, Satchel, would bring additional bags with appropriate outfits for me for the days of the meetings so I really could skip packing myself, but I liked picking out some of my own outfits even if I usually went with Satchell's recommendations.

Satchell would be on the plane in the morning before I got there. If the other company executives going to the meeting were already in Hawaii, then maybe it would be just Satchell and me on the big plane. Douglas had a point, but I still wasn't going to fly commercial. Too public. And too many germs. I could consider chartering a smaller jet. I had read about a new one that was supposed to be low-polluting, hydrogen-electric, and very fast. Supersonic over the water. Maybe I could surprise Douglas by showing up with that one. Maybe I should check it out for a future company jet. I looked it up and there was one available to charter out of the San Jose airport that week. Something to think about.

In the lobby of the hotel that evening while waiting for Tony Marks I turned on the Mara phone in AM Game network mode to securely check on the family app for any messages from Balaji. Still none. Before Perry got sick Balaji had resisted his dad's entreaties to try out the AM Game, but I managed to get him to at least use the AM Game messaging system. It was supposed to be completely private, and it might get him to try out the game. His dad would have liked it if he did. I sent him a reminder to check on his dad at least every two hours, figuring that then maybe he would check every four, and listing the food to give him for the next couple days.

Tony came into the hotel lobby. I turned off and put away my Mara phone, and we went to my suite where dinner and a bottle of champagne was waiting. We celebrated the imminent sale of Zzynarji Space International Group and the $11 billion in funding for the PATH project to make Tony's wildest dreams come true. I checked that all of my phones were off that evening and didn't turn them back on until the next morning.

A little later in the suite Tony gently grasped my arm from behind and said, "Tell me, really? Are you Min Strong?"

I turned and looked over my shoulder at him. He had a bottle of champagne and a glass in his other hand.

I said, "How could I be Min Strong?"

"I can only stay here overnight if you are Min Strong."

"Well then, I guess I must be Min Strong." I turned around and faced him, taking the bottle and taking a sip.

"I knew it. By the way. I don't understand minimalism. Can you teach me?"

"Teach you? Well, you don't need this." I set down his glass and handed him the bottle.

He drank and asked, "What else?"

I took off his glasses and said, "You don't need these."

"Well sometimes I do, but... okay." He took them from me and set them on the table.

As we drank the champagne, we found other things we could set aside, including my inhibitions.

Tuesday, 03/24/2037, 9:00 AM, Time to Catch a Flight

I wasn't used to drinking more than a sip of champagne and overslept the next morning. As I hurried to get ready to go to the airport, I had trouble remembering some of the details of the previous night. Forgetting was a new experience for me that I kind of liked. It was nice to have some fuzzy spots in my memory which was usually so unrelentingly detailed. On the other hand, I probably would have enjoyed reliving more memories from last night, so that was a shame.

Also, along with my fuzzy memory I had a headache, which was not so nice. Tony declined again my offer to let him come along to the meetings in Hawaii. He had too much to do here getting ready to start building Abitats in large numbers. He left the hotel suite while I drank some coffee and then showered and got dressed. Because of my headache, I took a long shower. I dressed inconspicuously and slipped out of the hotel wearing a surgical mask and carrying my small overnight bag. The rest of my luggage was already on the plane.

Outside, I turned on my Mara phone and checked the family messaging app. There were no messages from Balaji. Not surprising. I considered calling him or leaving him some additional instructions. Should I call or text? A voice call might not be a good idea, since I probably sounded hungover this morning, due to my hangover. But then I thought, he was old enough to handle his dad for a few days. I should leave him alone.

Since the Mara phone was on I used it to hail a robo-taxi to the airport using some of the points I had loaded into my AM Game account. No need to turn on my Marta phone just yet. Most businesses in the Bay Area accepted World One AM Game points as payments.

With my head throbbing, I decided I needed some more coffee. I directed the robo-taxi to drop me off at a good coffee shop I knew close to the airport. I could send Balaji some messages while I got my coffee and then turn on my Marta phone and get another ride the rest of the way to the airport.

Looking at the time on the way to the coffee shop, I realized that I might have to charter another plane after all. I had stressed to Satchell to make sure they got to Hawaii in time to double check the meeting arrangements in person even if it meant I took a different plane. They knew I might be delayed when I stayed at hotels in this area and were good at covering for me. They could make excuses for me, tell people I was on the plane even if I wasn't, and delay things on the other end until I got there. I considered whether there was any chance that Satchell would still be holding the plane for me. Not likely. I was already over an hour late. I decided I would take a different plane regardless. I would take the new faster, cleaner jet and maybe even beat Satchell there.

I started looking online for how to book the faster plane and I saw a news bulletin about a plane crash. A private business jet on the way from San Jose, California, to Kahului, Maui, had gone off the radar a hundred miles or so off the coast over the Pacific.

The robo-taxi announced that I had arrived at the coffee shop. I asked it to wait while I looked for more information about the plane crash still using my Mara phone. There were already reports from the Zzynarji Company executives that the plane was taking Marta Zynn and some of her staff to a meeting in Hawaii and in light of this tragedy the company would be rethinking the controversial plans to sell off the Zzynarji Space International Group. Company executives were meeting with Marta's brother Douglas, the remaining heir to the Zzynarji Company, to determine next steps.

I suddenly didn't need more coffee. I was wide awake. No longer hung over, but feeling sick in other ways. The company statement came out too fast. They must have anticipated the crash. I told the robo-taxi, "Drive around the block a few times." I needed to think.

I stopped at a store and used my AM Game points payment app on my Mara phone to buy ten thousand dollars' worth of pre-loaded debit cards in case I needed to buy a meal or something, and the stores didn't accept AM Points. Then I went to a dollar store and bought a small metal box to store the Marta phone where it wouldn't be accessible to any networks. It was still off, but that might not be safe enough. I wore a mask and avoided touching anything that would leave fingerprints. I also bought a change of clothes and rented a car with my Mara ID and paid with a couple of debit cards for the drive south to Orange County. I was suspicious about the cause of the crash and shocked to think that Douglas might be involved in having me killed. Until I knew more it might be safest if they all thought that they had succeeded.

I didn't turn my Marta phone back on or connect through the AM Game to check on what messages Satchell had sent that morning. I wasn't sure if someone would be able to detect my connection and I wanted to stay invisible until I understood better what was going on. I wondered why no one seemed to know that I wasn't on the plane. Satchell probably lied and told the pilots that I was on board, as part of covering up for my other activities, but I knew Satchell would have sent me several messages with increasing urgency, reminding me about the flight and finally giving me one last chance to hold the flight. Probably four last chances to hold the flight. Surely the company or the government was able to see those messages?

Satchell would also have sent me a message saying the flight was leaving and asking what help I needed with alternate flight arrangements. That would be conclusive evidence about me not being on the flight. Maybe the AM Game messaging privacy we used really worked. I helped design it to be totally private, but I suspected that it might not be.

03/24/2037, 11 PM, Back to OC

When I got back to OC that night after a long drive I dropped the rental car off at the Long Beach airport and had my Mara car meet me there to give me a ride back to the ranch house.

I knocked on the door to Balaji's room.

"Balaji, I'm home," I said through the door.

"Hi, Mom. Don't come in. You're home early," he said through the door. "I was just about to go check on Dad."

"Don't bother. I'm here. I'll check on him."

I went to check on Perry. He was twitching and rocking, reclined in his chair, holding a tablet and wearing the headset cap with his eyes closed. He smelled like he had shit himself, or worse.

"Balaji! When was the last time you helped your dad to the bathroom?" I shouted in the direction of Balaji's room. "And what have you been feeding him?" I knew he probably couldn't hear me with his door closed.

Perry opened his eyes, which seemed bloodshot, like he had been crying and said, "...dead."

"Nope," I said. "But it smells like something died around here. Let's get you cleaned up."

If he knew about the plane crash, it seemed like Perry must somehow still be seeing the news even if he seemed catatonic most of the time. That was interesting. When he warned me to be careful earlier, did he know something was going to happen? How would he know that?

06/20/2037, 11:35 PM, Caught Up

That catches me up for major recent events. I'm not sure if I will add more pages to this in the future. We'll see.

09/21/2037, 11 PM, Thoughts about the Crash

I've added a few pages and then deleted them again a few times now as different stories came out in the news and I went back and forth between certainty that I was assassinated and believing the cause was a mechanical failure. Now that some time has passed I'll try to summarize what seems to be known.

Since the crash in March, I followed the news to see what was happening with the investigation. I needed to decide whether to resurface alive or to let dead Marta remain dead. I came close to resurfacing a couple of times, but for the moment I'm still dead.

Reports about the plane crash seemed to indicate some kind of sudden loss of power including a cutoff in signals from the plane's transponder and radio. That suggested an explosion onboard. Foul play was suspected, but then another explanation came to light.

Most of the plane sank in deep water, but a limited wreckage field was found suggesting that the plane broke up after sinking. Searches of the area found some items from the plane floating on the surface including remains of one passenger. Satchell Gandhi Morris, a valued assistant to Marta Zynn, had apparently had time to put on a life jacket before the plane hit the water. Their partial remains were returned to their family. Additional searches were made over a wider area for signs of anyone else. No remains from the pilots nor Marta Zynn were found. The manifest said that there were four on board: Marta Zynn, Satchell Morris and the two pilots, Mario and Maria Valparaíso. I hadn't known the pilots' names, nor that they were a couple.

Pieces of scorched plastic debris with attached wiring and insulation were recovered indicating signs of fire in the plane's electronics bay. Maintenance records indicated that a battery pack in that compartment was coming due for replacement. Fire from those batteries was the working theory for the cause of the crash. Other planes with similar age and design were briefly grounded for inspection, but others did not have the same battery system, which was a unique Zzynarji design. Definitive answers about causes would require recovering the rest of the plane's parts and the flight recorders from the deep ocean. The Pacific was over a mile deep where the plane went down.

After initially sending out recovery ships with deep sea probes, the company decided to stop the deep-sea recovery efforts. They said that Marta's brother wanted to make that part of the ocean floor a memorial site dedicated to his sister and the others lost on the plane. He did not want her final resting place disturbed by industrial recovery equipment.

Even though it would in no way soften their losses, the company offered to double the accidental death life insurance payments that Zzynarji owed to the families of Satchell, Mario, and Maria, all Zzynarji employees. Marta's accidental death payment would have gone to her only living relative, her brother Douglas, but he declined to receive it. Douglas never spoke or appeared publicly. A company spokesman relayed his sentiments, as he grieved privately.

Even though the public evidence supported an accident, I kept coming back to my initial intuition that Douglas and some of the Zzynarji executives had sabotaged the plane to kill me.

They did a good job of hiding it and blaming it on the battery malfunction. But their initial statement came out too fast and the decision to leave the key wreckage on the deep ocean floor was too convenient. Not to mention my last call with Douglas when he threatened, "you will have to pay…sooner than you think." They must have sabotaged the plane and timed it to occur after the plane was over the deep Pacific.

The electronics bay included Zzynarji satellite communications gear with a separate battery system which had some known problems in the past. Someone must have messed with that system to make it overheat, or explode, or possibly planted a bomb. The battery's location in the electronics bay made it possible for all other electronic controls and communications to be cut off quickly if that unit overheated and caught fire, but the speed of the failure suggested to me a bomb.

I was sad about the possible betrayal and sad about losing Satchell. They must have understood that I appreciated the way they always took care of details for me. I realized I didn't often, if ever, thank them, and I didn't know anything about their private life or the lives of the pilots. I guess I was an inconsiderate boss.

I was angry at Douglas and the executives, but not sure what would be the best way to get back at them. Tony and the PATH project released a statement of profound sadness at the loss of a key supporter, and confidence that the new management of the company would honor the memory of Marta Zynn by completing her commitments to supporting the Abitats Mass-production Project.

Zzynarji's spokespeople said the company is still reconsidering their plans. The additional funding of PATH has not yet gone forward.

01/15/2038, 11 PM, Other Thoughts

It's 2038 now. I never got around to resurfacing. It was nice to not have to travel for work anymore or pretend to be two or three different people. Right after my death I also stopped doing Min Strong. I couldn't completely shut down MinAI, and she kept working on it for a while, but after a few weeks I gave her instructions to cease visible activities. I told her when it comes to minimalism for maximum impact she needed minimal visibility. She could have handled attending Min-iverse conferences and responding to the What Would Min Keep forum without me, but I didn't want to even think about checking on her. For a few months now I've been just Mara, Balaji's mom, and Perry's diaper changer.

Last year at the end of March, soon after I got back and while I was still in shock about the crash, Balaji and I sang Happy Birthday to Perry. Balaji still didn't remember missing my birthday in early March. He didn't know anything about Marta's birthday in April so that day also passed with no celebration. I certainly didn't get the $40 Million 40th birthday present I was planning on giving myself.

Of course, Perry didn't acknowledge either of my birthdays that year. Before he got sick he would make me something and have Balaji give it to me and sing happy birthday on Mara's March birthday. He would privately give me another gift on Marta's April birthday and call it a belated birthday present.

I converted most of the remaining AM Points on my Mara phone AM account back into dollars. I went to 10 different stores that sold debit gift cards and accepted AM Points and bought stacks of cards with $100 to $500 each. I also bought a new pre-paid phone and turned off my Mara phone, even though it still had a balance of points remaining. I wanted to reduce the chances of being tracked.

I would have liked to have Perry's advice about how to handle things. I still talked to him, and I could imagine what he would say. Just tell everyone everything and let the chips fall where they may, like he had said so many times before. But even though I talked with him, Perry didn't speak to me anymore after those few words before I died and after I returned from the dead. He seemed to be lost in his own head and whatever he was connected to with the headset. He would sometimes tolerate me taking off the headset for a minute to wash or shave his head, but he quickly became belligerent with incoherent noises that seemed to threaten violence the longer it was off. I started to just leave it on. Either avoid getting it wet or cover it with a shower cap when bathing. I told Balaji to just leave it on too. We started keeping him in adult diapers rather than taking him to the bathroom every hour.

In the summer of 2037, somewhere around the time he turned 17, Balaji said he was done with school. He had completed the requirements for five online bachelor's degrees and said he didn't want to do any more. I pushed him to find a job. He wouldn't consider anything that required leaving the house. I forwarded him job postings for jobs that could be done 100% virtually. He said feeding, washing, and changing his dad several times a week was a big enough job. I should be satisfied with that, he said.

Late in the year Zzynarji announced that they were honoring the long-term wishes of their founders and of their recently deceased leader, Marta Zynn, with full support of Douglas Zynn. They were turning over full ownership of the company to the Zynn Foundation, renaming it the Zzynarji Foundation, a non-profit. That sounded good at first, but then I found out more details. Douglas and several of the company executives were appointed as directors of the foundation, although Douglas didn't seem to attend any meetings. He seemed to have dropped out of sight.

The Zzynarji non-profit company gave high but legal compensation to their executives and legally questionable subcontracts to businesses owned by some of the executives. They seemed to do a minimal amount of actual charity, primarily with training and research that directly benefitted Zzynarji, or 'public education' that advertised for government policies that would benefit them.

Zzynarji did not sell off its international space group and did not give $11 billion in funding to PATH to build millions of Abitats. The funding to PATH and to INCA was drastically reduced rather than increased. Without the extra funding Tony's Abitat Mass-production was severely hampered. I really wanted to set things right for Tony, but every day that I was dead I felt it harder to explain why I had waited to surface so I continued to wait.

Douglas has been invisible. I'm pretty sure he hasn't visited the little girl, now teenager, next door since before the crash. I can't say for certain because Perry is no longer talking with Camilla, but the last time our street-view security cameras' facial recognition alerted for his face was before the crash.

Maybe Zzynarji killed him too. I could understand if the executives wanted to get rid of him. He was a loose cannon. Maybe good riddance. Or maybe not. He was my brother. I should have spent more time with him. I was his only family, and I only saw him a few hours a year. No wonder he was led astray. Not that talking to me more would have made a difference. Oh well. Nothing I can do for him now that I'm dead, and he is missing and presumed dead.

12/31/2038, 11 PM, Looking Back on 2038

It's the end of 2038 now. I've started writing new pages a few times but deleted them without printing. It's been almost a year since I added any pages to the safe. I'll try again to capture some random thoughts.

Balaji hardly ever goes outside into the back yard and the farm anymore. I don't think he's walked in the farm with Isabella next door in the last year. Maybe a few years now. Records from security cameras in the back yard and around the farm show Isabella still runs around the farm almost once a week, but she no longer shakes the wind chimes when she slips through our back yard. Balaji hardly goes outside anymore. His daily walks became weekly and then less often. Whenever he does go out back, he still taps the wind chimes like he's checking if they still work.

Balaji turned 18 last summer so Isabella must be 14. She is looking more grown up. Still too young for him if you ask me. I considered telling him how to use the security system to get alerted when she was out, but I figured if she wanted to see him, she would shake the wind chimes herself.

Most of the time Balaji stays in his room playing games. I think he actually followed his dad's advice and checked out the AM Game sometime in the last year or two. One time when I told him to get a job he said he has several jobs and is making a lot of money. I think they are all in the game.

Apparently the AM game is popular and different companies have been saying they would start selling their own versions of Abitats. They got held up for a few months when the Zzynarji Company claimed exclusive rights to the intellectual property after funding the work of the INCA and AM PATH projects. Tony Marks was eventually able to show the contracts that stated the IP rights stayed with the projects as long as they were being used for the public good and otherwise became public domain.

Tony's AM PATH project was scaled back but didn't stop. Instead of immediately building billion-dollar factories and going into large scale production to get millions of Abitats on the road, with tens of thousands of Abitat villages and millions of public docking stations, he negotiated with some of the for-profit companies to start building them. His business sense was not great. I kept wanting to give him a call and tell him how to get things moving faster. But I didn't.

Some companies seemed to consider Abitat designs public domain and moved forward without any formal arrangements with Tony's project. They started reverse engineering designs that could be seen in game worlds and hiring engineers and scientists who had worked at INCA and PATH. Autonomous Motors continued to build cars that used licensed Abitat-navigation, and they also started to build their own version of Abitats. I was hoping that licensing would lead to some royalties back to Perry, but not so far.

If Tony's project had gone according to plan the tiny fractional royalty payments that were supposed to flow to the original AM-PATH and INCA employees and volunteers should have turned into a healthy cash flow to Perry, given all the features that he had designed. He had mentioned the bank account that would receive the payments. He joked that it would be a way he could keep contributing if his memory got bad enough that he would have to stop working. But this scaled-down version of Tony's project didn't seem to be generating any royalty payments back to Perry. At least not yet. At least not in any accounts I could access. Maybe there will be some next year if the Abitats start being built in numbers.

I've been burning through the money in my debit cards for groceries for Balaji, Perry, and myself. I even started to do some of my own cooking. I've been lonely and depressed. Balaji is too absorbed in his games to have a conversation. I still talk with Perry, but he doesn't talk back, so that's not much help. I miss spending time with Tony.

I even miss my conversations with Douglas. He must be dead. His social media accounts were suspended, and the Zzynarji Foundation no longer mentions him. He used to visit Isabella next door, but his face hasn't been detected next door by our cameras.

I considered re-engaging as Min Strong with the Min-iverse conventions just to have someone to talk to, but not so far.

The Strong Family Trust still owns a few shell companies that own the farm, the ranch house, and a few other assets worth a few tens of millions of dollars but it no longer has any control of the multi-billion-dollar Zzynarji Company since that has been given to the Zzynarji Foundation and converted into a charity personal slush fund for Carl Heinz. I probably could contest the donation of the company, but I would have to resurface as Marta and probably as Mara too. Maybe Perry was right, and I should just tell everyone everything. No.

I could probably still sell other assets in the Strong Trust, but I'm nervous doing so. If someone challenges me as Mara Strong, I might have to appear in person and then someone would see that I am the same person as Marta Zynn.

As long as I do nothing, the accounting firms and lawyers who handle the Strong Trust assets are still paying themselves from trust income and managing those assets. Taxes and utility bills get paid, and Sergey still gets his salary.

Meanwhile, I rely on the dwindling balance of funds in debit cards. When they run out what can I do? Maybe Perry was right, and I should just tell everyone everything. No.

For a few months my routine was repetitive. I would do household chores taking care of Perry, shopping, cooking, and cleaning, checking on Balaji. I checked for any royalty deposits. Still none.

I also spent time following what was happening with Tony's project and trying to figure out what happened to Perry's brain. Perry isn't speaking any more, but maybe there is a way to reach him through the headset? So far I can't find one. Is he still communicating with people in the INCA and AM-PATH projects? Not that I can see.

I worked to better understand the brain model that had been growing ever since Perry started wearing the headset. I made some progress. Like I said before, I was able to play back some of his visual and auditory memories from the years he had been wearing the headset, but it was hard to find interesting bits. Recent bits just showed the view from his bed when he was awake. I found data structures that I think represent memories from before then, but their encoding is different. Sometimes I think I'm close, but I have not yet cracked it.

I started to make some progress understanding that the model contained sections of data that represented different categories of knowledge or memories. I wasn't able to make sense of the encoding in most of the sections. Certain sections of the data were mapped to autonomic functions. Others to motor skills. The largest parts seemed to represent memories, both short and long term.

Maybe in a way his brain map was something like this notebook locked in an unbreakable safe: a pointless record of memories that no one would be able to access.

But there must be a way to open them up. The government paid to create these headsets to read the minds of bad guys and find out the secrets they were keeping. If I could guess the secrets for unlocking Perry's memories, I could have some of Perry back again. I tried various approaches without success. I found papers by people who worked at the company that made the headsets, looking for clues. Nothing that I tried worked. At least not yet.

I was lonely and bored. I started playing games. I did some exploration inside of AM Game worlds, looking for traces of Perry, but mostly played simple old-fashioned video games that didn't require much thought and didn't involve any blood and gore. Pac Man, Tetris, Candy-Crush, things like that.

January and February 2039, Deleted pages

Apparently the data the headset has been gathering from Perry's brain includes long-term memories. I figured out how to decode some of Perry's memories from before he started wearing the headset. I started a few times to write my reactions to what I found but I keep deleting them before printing, or printing and then burning the pages.

This is a placeholder to remind me to consider what parts of those revelations I want to talk about at some point in the future.

03/04/2039, 11:59 PM, My 42nd Birthday

No one noticed.

03/30/2039, 11:30 PM, Perry's 45th Birthday

I went to the kitchen this morning to get some coffee, but we were out of coffee beans. We still had a few tea bags, so I heated up a mug of water in the microwave to make some tea instead. In the pantry cabinet besides the few tea bags, was a cannister of protein powder and a few cans of beans. I need to buy more food, but I should make this last, since I'm down to my last few debit cards.

Checking the fridge, I found an almost full carton of almond milk, a half dozen eggs, a few old carrots, some cheese, some hummus, and a half a loaf of bread. Looking in the freezer I found we still had a bag of frozen berries and a pizza. I could make berry smoothies with protein powder that would probably keep Perry and me alive for a few days. Balaji might even be willing to drink some. Perry can't really eat pizza anymore, but Balaji could have that for a lunch or dinner. For breakfast I could fry him a couple eggs and make toast, or, better, he could do it himself. Why should I have to do all the work? He can come out of his room and do some work for himself.

While my teabag steeped, I checked on Perry. He was awake and mumbling while holding his tablet, twitching, and rocking side to side on his back in his bed. I wasn't sure if he ever slept. His headset was in place, like always. I adjusted the bed to raise him to a sitting position.

"Happy Birthday," I whispered to him.

He continued twitching and mumbling without any acknowledgement of what I said. Neither he nor Balaji had noticed my birthday earlier that month, so I figured I didn't need to do anything special for Perry on his this year. He wasn't aware of it anyway, so a simple Happy Birthday was all he was going to get from me. Maybe I would change his sheets later.

I looked at him and continued whispering, "Don't expect anything more from me. I shouldn't have to take care of you. It's your own fault. I told you not to use that headset." I wasn't sure his decline was caused by the headset, or an injury or a disease, but I still blamed him for it. I moved away the covers and pulled his legs to the side of the bed.

"Time to get up and pee," I said.

He didn't respond. I helped him scoot out of the bed and kept one arm around him while walking him to the bathroom. I put one of his hands on the grab bar on the wall and helped him back up to the toilet. He still held this tablet in his other hand. I pulled down his pajama pants and adult diaper. It seemed dry. Thank goodness. There had been a time when I would have had some interest in what else was staring me in the face from his crotch, but not lately. I sat him back on the toilet. He seemed to be stable holding his tablet. I went back to the kitchen to get my tea. I could hear him peeing as I left the room.

04/03/2039, Around 11 AM, Marta's 42nd Birthday

When I looked in the kitchen this morning I found one tea bag and a few condiments and spices, but the rest of the food was gone. I could try sharing my last cup of tea with Perry, but after that I wasn't sure what I was going to do. I was pretty sure he wouldn't go for spiced soy sauce water, or mustard with hot sauce.

April 3rd was the day I had celebrated as my birthday growing up, usually with my choice of meals prepared by professional chefs, either at one of our homes or at a restaurant or destination resort. No feast today. It's been a few years since anyone recognized this birthday. My parents are dead. All of my parents are dead. My brother is probably dead. Perry is no longer aware, as good as dead. Is there anyone else who might think of me on this birthday? Maybe one, but probably not. If so, they think I am dead too. Being dead seems to be the theme of my birthday. Being dead would be one way out of this. Hey even Mara may have died as a baby. Maybe I've always been just a ghost. Balaji never knew about this birthday, so I can't blame him for forgetting it. But he forgot the birthday he was supposed to know about last month. He doesn't seem to have much of a life either. These days he stays in his room most of the time, playing games, although if I insist, he might grudgingly come out to help with his dad. He turned 18 last summer and still doesn't show any sign of trying to get a real job or doing anything but play games in his room. He was such a fast learner he could do or be almost anything, but all he does is play games in his room. I haven't seen him take a walk outside in a couple months. Maybe if I leave him no choice, he might start figuring out how to live. But I don't care anymore. I'm alone and unhappy, and I don't care anymore. I have a $38.32 balance left on one last debit card. Apparently, Balaji took and spent a few of the cards. I'm pretty sure we weren't robbed.

I don't know what I can get with $38.32, or why I should bother. Maybe I should go to the store today and do what I can. I opened the safe in my closet and took out the small metal box with the phones that I haven't used in two years. It's been almost exactly two years. It seems like decades. I was 40, or maybe 39, then. and now I feel like ninety-nine. Like my own depleted energy, the batteries in both of the phones were drained over the last two years. Something else dead. I found a charger and set my Mara Strong phone on it and covered it with the metal box lid in case it woke up. Could I bring it back to life? Did I want to? The other phone had all of Marta's contact numbers. Wouldn't some of those people be surprised if I turned it on and Marta started calling them? I left that phone dead in the metal box. "Marta is officially dead," I thought. After a minute I lifted the metal lid from the Mara phone on the charger and verified it was charging but not on, before covering it again. I wasn't sure what I was going to do with it. It should have access to a thousand dollars or more in AM points connected to my Mara personality in the AM Game World One. Most online stores accepted World One AM Points now. That might give us enough to live on for a few days, but it would be risky and what then? I realized I could use that phone to contact the attorneys and accountants for the Strong Trust as Mara Strong and probably get access to enough money to live on for centuries, but that would be even more risky. I realized I could have contacted them at any time through any phone or by computer through the Game network. They might recognize the number from this phone, but otherwise it was no safer or riskier to use this phone. The same reasons not to contact them still applied, although I was having trouble remembering exactly what they were. Okay. I had some choices.

- Wake up Mara's old phone and have money for a week.
- Wake up Mara's trust and have money for years.

- Wake up Marta's phone and cause hell.

Any of those actions risked exposing Perry, Balaji, and myself to possible enemies. What else?

- Lose Mara and wake up Balaji to stand on his own?

If only Perry was still alive. Technically he is still alive, but if he were still getting money from the agency or from the AM PATH royalties he expected, then it wouldn't all depend on me. Where are those royalties, Perry?

I took my tea and went to Perry's room. He smelled like shit. I couldn't remember exactly how long it had been since the last time I took him to the bathroom. Why didn't Balaji check on him? Why is it my job? I should be running a company and saving the world and not changing dirty adult diapers. I'm done. I set out some clean clothes and sheets for Perry. I went to my desk and typed these last few pages. Maybe I'll actually print them and put them in the safe this time.

04/03/2039, 12:30 PM, FAREWELL?

I'm going away. Balaji will just think I'm going to the store. Perry won't even know I'm gone.

Maybe I'll change my mind and come back, and if I do, I'll shred this Farewell page, and maybe rewrite some of the other recent pages, like I've done before a few times. But this time probably not. This time I think I'm really going. I'm even taking the little metal box with the phones this time. Give myself some options. Option A: Mara's phone. Option B: Marta's phone. Option C: Just disappear.

Balaji needs to realize he can stand on his own. He won't do that until he is forced to. He's smart. He will be able to take care of himself and his dad once he realizes that he has to. I faced something similar when my parents died twenty years ago and look how I turned out. I don't know. Maybe I'll just go to the store and get one more meal and decide about options again tomorrow. We'll see.

I started these recollections after Perry started losing his memory. I wanted to have a record in case something similar happened to me. I didn't know if I would ever let anyone else read it. It looks like that's not going to happen, if I really leave today, but at least writing these thoughts down helped me think about things. Even the pages I burned or deleted without ever printing them helped me think about things.

When I put this page in the safe with the others they should stay there. Forcing open this safe without the access code will supposedly destroy its contents. The code for the safe is something that only Perry and I know, and he already doesn't remember anything so this probably will not ever be read by anyone unless, somehow, I end up coming back, from the dead. We'll see.

Appendix A:

Guide to Characters in Mara's Memories

Name	AKA	Role
Ami Narji		Cofounder of Zzynarji; birth mom to Mara; died in 1998 at age 36.
Balaji Lee	Billy Jay Lee	Son of Mara and Perry; agoraphobic; game player
Bella	Izzie, Isabella Muller	Daughter of Josephine, raised by Camilla Muller; childhood friend of Balaji
Ben Strong		Cofounder of Zzynarji; birth father to Mara; died in 1998 at age 36.
Brock	Barack Jackson	College friend of Douglas Zynn and Sam Muller.
Camilla Muller	Izzie's Cam-ma	Neighbor to Perry, Mara, and Balaji; single mom to Sam and Jo-Jo; raising Isabella
Carl Heinz		Executive in Zzynarji; possibly behind crash of Marta Zynn's plane.
Carmen Kovich	née Carmen Lee	Estranged sister of Perry; daughter of Wilson Lee and Abigail Serrano Lee
Carlos Zynn	née Carlos Anderson	Cofounder of Zzynarji; dad to Douglas; adopted Marta; died in 2019 at age 57
Douglas	Douglas Zynn	Heir to part of Zzynarji fortune after death of his parents Sandra and Carlos Zynn; step brother to Marta Zynn; MinQuest guide in the Sierras; presumed father of Isabella.

Name	AKA	Role
Fletcher	Fletcher Muller	Missing father of Sam and Jo-Jo; moved away when Jo-Jo was a baby.
George		Perry's ambitious supervisor in the agency; arranged for him to continue working covertly.
Dr. Geraldine Atwood		Worked with Perry on game and Abitats; inventor of AI personalities based on Nested Cellular Autonomy.
Jo-Jo	Josephine Muller	Negligent mom of Isabella; sister of Sam; daughter of Camilla; into drugs; kicked out by Camilla.
Mara Strong	Marta Zynn, Mara Lee, Min Strong	Mom to Balaji with Perry Lee; heir to majority of Zzynarji fortune after deaths of parents Ami Narji and Ben Strong.
Marta Zynn	Mara Strong, Mara Lee	Adopted by Sandra and Carlos Zynn; heir to part of Zzynarji fortune after their deaths.
Max AI		Early AI personality created by Perry to perform some of Perry's tasks for the agency; not in a particular game world.
Min AI	Min Strong	Early AI personality created by Perry and Mara to perform Min Strong tasks; not in a particular game world.
Min Strong		Animated guru of minimalism revered by many; originated the "MinQuest"; invented by Perry based on Mara's actions; expanded and controlled by Mara.
Perry Lee	Perry Wilson Lee	Dad to Billy Jay; data scientist and inventor; son of Wilson Lee and Abigail Serrano Lee.
Randy		Perry's initial supervisor in the agency.
Sam	Sam Muller	Brother of Jo-Jo; college friend of Douglas Zynn; into drugs; kicked out by Camilla.

Name	AKA	Role
Sandra Zynn		Cofounder of Zzynarji; mom to Douglas; adopted mom to Marta; died in 2019 at age 57
Satchell	Satchell Gandhi Morris	Personal assistant to Marta Zynn; died in plane crash in 2037
Sergey	Sergio Carlos Hernandez	Groundskeeper of Rancho del Fuerte farm adjacent to the childhood homes of Billy Jay and Bella.
Tony	Tony Marks	Leader of PATH; trying to solve homelessness with mobile tiny homes; friend of Marta Zynn.

Guide to terms:

Name	AKA	Role
Abbie	Uncommonly, can be renamed	Intelligent assistant based in an Abitat and dedicated to the well-being of its inabitant; unable to intentionally deceive.
Abitat	Various names	Autonomous tiny home vehicle
AM Game	The game	Simulated worlds with autonomous characters that can be observed and influenced by players; typically, where Abitats are commonplace.
Amps	AM Points, Points	Currency used in the AM Game and in the worlds that have adopted it.
DBI	Direct Brain Interface	Technology for direct transfer of sensory experience and knowledge or motor control to and from the brain by way of a headset.
NCA	Nested Cellular Autonomy	A technique for recognizing (or generating) emergent intelligence from a hive of interacting components; field of PhD topics of Perry Lee and Geraldine Atwood among others.

Acknowledgements

Plots and characters have their own autonomy, discovered by authors as we write. Readers, like *players* in the AM Game, also participate in influencing the behavior of characters and the unfolding of the worlds of these stories, not only in their personal interpretations as they read, but also by sharing their reactions and participating in discussions with others that lead to a community of interpretation.

I acknowledge the valuable contributions of early readers who commented on these stories. Some drove the story with specific suggestions and words, and others with more subtle influences, questions, and reactions. All helped shape the story as it is today.

Most of all I appreciate my wife, Diane, who has been my partner for many years in raising our family and completing many adventures together. In her career as an art teacher she influenced the characters of hundreds of students as they discovered their own autonomy and talents under her guidance, and she has been the most important influence on my own character in the game world of our lives together.

This story depicts fictional characters dealing with various personal challenges. I take full responsibility for any shortcomings in my depictions of those struggles.

Questions and suggestions to feedback@auto-no-mo-us.com may influence future versions or expansions of these stories.

Books in the AutoNoMoUs Series
by Christopher L Truxaw

AutoNoMoUs

Part One

Friday, May 26, 2056

Struggles with memories, identity, and
connection in an allegedly post-homelessness
and post-disinformation world.

Part Two

Saturday, May 27, 2056

Life and death challenges.
Surprising choices and discoveries.

Part Three

Origins: Mara's Memories

Back story of the world of AutoNoMoUs.
Two bright young minds set out to fight
negativity and disinformation.

www.ingramcontent.com/pod-product-compliance
Lightning Source LLC
Chambersburg PA
CBHW020359110726
47899CB00006B/1786